Praise for Nico Rosso's
Black Ops: Automatik series

"The palpable chemistry between April and James was absolutely something to see. It was real and raw and, at times, heartbreaking."
—*The Romance Reviews*, Top Pick, on *Seconds to Sunrise*

"High stakes and sexual tension will keep readers eagerly turning the pages."
—*Publishers Weekly*, starred review, on *Countdown to Zero Hour*

"Rosso's talent for incorporating romance in the midst of a gang war and military mission earns *Countdown to Zero Hour* a spot on every bookshelf. It's an enticing, scorching-hot read!"
—*RT Book Reviews*, Top Pick, 4.5 Stars

"THIS is how romantic suspense should be done!"
—*The Romance Reviews*, Top Pick, on *Countdown to Zero Hour*

"The sexual tension and chemistry are done really well. Highly recommend this one."
—*Smexy Books* on *One Minute to Midnight*

"Mr. Rosso has quickly become one of my must-read authors, and I will recommend his books to anyone who craves INCREDIBLE romantic suspense!"
—*The Romance Reviews*, Top Pick, on *One Minute to Midnight*

**Also available from Nico Rosso
and Carina Press**

The Last Night
Heavy Metal Heart
Slam Dance with the Devil
Ménage with the Muse
Countdown to Zero Hour
One Minute to Midnight

SECONDS TO SUNRISE

NICO ROSSO

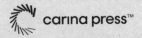

carina press™

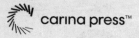 carina press™

ISBN-13: 978-1-335-47400-1

Seconds to Sunrise

Copyright © 2017 by Zachary N. DiPego

Recycling programs
for this product may
not exist in your area.

www.CarinaPress.com

Printed in U.S.A.

Dear Reader,

Thank you for picking up the third book in my Black Ops: Automatik series. There's plenty of action in *Seconds to Sunrise*, just like the others, but some of the biggest battles James and April fight are within themselves, created by their pasts. I hope you go along for the ride as they journey to defeat the bad guys while their romance helps them find relief from their darkness and gives them hope for the future.

All the best,

Nico

SECONDS TO SUNRISE

CHAPTER ONE

APRIL BANKS WAS being attacked. The world around her seemed ordinary. Fully stocked shelves in the El Paso, Texas, supermarket. No holes in the high ceiling from artillery fire. The woman behind the register wasn't taking cover from flying bullets. But in the murky distance, featureless men worked to steal from April and the people who had trusted her.

Still, she had to eat and shop for food and do all the normal things people did. The brightly colored packages promised countless flavors and nutrition benefits, but she couldn't find any hunger. She was empty. Nothing seemed like it would ever solve that. *Dammit.* She'd hoped she'd never know that hollowness again. Four years ago it had felt like it could've killed her. After months of searching she'd found a way to crawl out. But she was right back down again.

"The pantry must've been bare if you're buying cans of sardines." The woman behind the register, Theresa, waggled the tin in the air after scanning it, then sent it down the conveyor to the teenaged bagger.

April didn't remember putting them in her shopping cart. "I can make a quick pasta sauce with them."

Theresa wrinkled her nose. "Too briny for me. And I couldn't get them past the kids." Her pace at the scanner slowed. "Edgar would've loved it, though." The words trailed off with an echo deep in her chest.

April understood. The loss never went away. "Make it for your kids sometime. Tell them about him. Even if they hate the food, they'll know more about their dad."

Theresa brightened. "Good idea. I'll do that." She rang up more of April's food. "See, that's what I miss with your site being down. We're not talking and sharing ideas. I miss that."

April had created foundafter.com as a project to pull herself out of the cold darkness and had wound up helping a lot of other women. They'd all been married to military men. They were all widows. April's site gave them a forum to talk and rant and cry and laugh. Anonymously or with their own names, the women joined from all over the U.S. and even other countries. As the community had grown, April had built in funding capabilities, so the women could support each other when the needs arose. The credit card and financial information of thousands of women was too much of a temptation for the hacker to pass up.

"I miss it, too." Part of her was lost without the voices of that community. "The cyber attack really did a number on the site. I'm doing what I can."

"I'm sure you are." Theresa reached across the register and gave April a light touch on the forearm. "I wish I could help. We all do."

The contact only highlighted how far away the normal world had become. "Hopefully it won't be too long." But April had no idea when the site would be safe. If ever. The security had been compromised and data stolen. Her encryption made that data useless, for now. It was just a matter of time until the hacker broke through her security. The sensitive details of the women she'd tried to help with the site would be exposed and sold to dangerous strangers.

She went through the motions of paying. The transactions were so common, but so precarious. Her credit card information was being sent out into the world for criminals with enough knowledge and bad intent to find. The rest of her identity was in her purse. Her license plate outside told more about her. No piece of information was personal anymore. Nothing was safe and secure. She thanked the bagger and said goodbye to Theresa.

The checker shook her head with a warm smile. "I still can't believe I was the one trying to tell you about your website."

The woman brought it up nearly every time they met. April had just been reemerging into society and had been able to admit she was a widow without breaking down. She and Theresa had bonded over their common loss, in this same spot, with a bag of salad between them. Then Theresa's face had lit up when she'd described April's own site back to her, and the incredible community of women who supported each other through the toughest of times. When April had told her she was the one who'd created and ran foundafter.com, Theresa brightened even further, then teared up with gratitude.

The same sheen of emotion showed in Theresa's eyes now. "You'll get it sorted out. If anyone can, it's you."

But it seemed impossible. The expectation that she should be able to solve this only dragged her deeper into the hollow pit in the center of her chest. "Thanks, Theresa."

April pushed her cart into the cold West Texas

morning. Bursts of white clouds punched through a shocking blue sky. Thunderstorms muscled together on the eastern horizon. Winter wind pushed dry leaves across the parking lot. They collected and shivered against curbs and the wheels of her car.

She was pulling her keys from her purse when a man's voice called out to her with a country twang. "Excuse me, ma'am." A white man in his twenties with short blond hair strode toward her, the tall cuffs on his jeans nearly black with dirt. Despite the cold, he only wore a hoodie.

She straightened her posture and squared her shoulders. All business. No bullshit. But he kept coming toward her.

"Ma'am." Was he really this polite, or was he just faking it? "You dropped something. Out of your purse. Is that your wallet?" He pointed to the ground behind her.

She was compelled to look, but instinct made her swing her shopping cart between her and the man before glancing back. There was nothing on the ground. His footsteps rushed faster toward her. She looked up to see him slam his hands on the front of her cart. It crashed into her hips and pushed her against her car. Pain flashed from the impact, but was overcome by the fear and anger that made her legs burn to run and her heart pound.

The man was close enough for her to see the red rimming his eyes and the ragged stubble around his grim frown. He tried to yank the cart away, but she gripped the side to maintain the smallest cushion of safety. The man growled and swiped a hand at her. It grazed across the top of her chest. Her muscles clenched tight to her, trying to never be touched by him again.

"Dougie!" the man yelled with breath that stank of cigarettes.

More footsteps approached. Her pulse thundered and fear stole her breath. She had to run before she found out what the hell these men wanted with her. Shoving as hard as she could, April jammed the cart into the man's legs.

He winced in pain. "Fuck!"

She kept pushing until he backed up one step. She took the opening and sprinted.

Right toward the next rushing man. Dougie wore a heavier coat and a thick beard. He balled a fist and swung it toward her as he ran. She clenched her jaw and threw her hands up to guard her face.

The blow never came. Another man, dressed all in black, lunged out from between two parked cars and tackled the bearded attacker to the ground. Whoever this new guy was, he was well accustomed to fighting. While he rolled on the ground, he used his long limbs to gain leverage and rain down vicious elbows on the bearded man's face.

Another man, this one with red hair, sped past her in the direction of the first guy who attacked her. She wasn't interested in staying to see the outcome. They were all violent, and the best place to be was as far away as possible.

She ran, wondering if she'd gotten in the middle of a gang war or drug deal gone bad. If the man in black had been a cop, he'd have identified himself. But he'd been silent with brutal intensity. Dark eyes and a scowling mouth.

The fight had blocked her route back to the store, forcing her to speed along the sparsely populated parking lot toward a stand of storefronts that had been empty for months. Ragged shrubs kept her from a city street and the safety of other people. An alley between two buildings offered her only escape. She ducked into it, wishing her legs could move faster.

"You don't need to run." A man's voice pursued her. He was amazingly calm. Maybe it was the British accent that made him seem matter-of-fact. But he didn't have the polish of the upper crust. A rough edge sharpened his words. Accent or not, she had no plan to comply.

The alley narrowed with debris. She slipped in a greasy puddle and scraped her shoulder against the cinderblock wall. Her jacket took the brunt of the blow, but the impact buzzed through her and forced her to take a quick gasp to steady herself. Every second she lost, the man came closer.

Adrenaline burned through her veins. She built her momentum up again to race down the alley, then skidded to a dead stop. The man wasn't behind her anymore. He was in front of her, blocking the exit. His hands were raised, palms out. His chest moved from the breath of his run. It looked like he could go another dozen miles.

"I'm here to help you." Serious dark eyes. A tight beard framed his dusky face. His hair was cropped short. The man appeared to be of East Indian descent. Military?

She still had her keys in her hand and shifted her grip so they stuck out from between her fingers when she made a fist. He smiled. Not as a threat, but with a glimmer of respect in his eye.

"You're a right fighter." He lowered his hands but didn't step closer.

"You don't want to find out." She expected one of the other men to come up behind her any second.

"I don't." He nodded. "If I had my way, there'd be no fighting and you wouldn't even know I was here."

Her first response choked in her throat. Since the hack, nothing had felt safe. Was it because he'd been lurking nearby? He was taller than her. And faster and stronger. Her phone was too deep in her purse to call for help. "Just let me go."

"I'm not stopping you." He took a step forward.

She retreated a step and glanced at her exit. It was clear for now.

"But," he continued, "it's safer with me." Black jeans, black T-shirt, black leather jacket. He didn't look safe.

"I'm leaving now." She continued to back away.

He moved with her, one step for every two of hers. "Me and my teammate, my team, we're protecting you."

"I never hired anybody." Her path out remained open.

"You didn't have to." Shadows flickered in his look. "We're not for hire."

"Well, thanks for your help today. I'm going home." She was only a dozen steps from the exit of the alley.

"Those blokes who came after you *are* for hire," he explained. "And there will be more of them, April."

Her name from him slammed into her gut. The raw

fear, which had been subsiding, thundered back. Her legs wanted to run again, but she couldn't.

He must've seen her tensing, and took a step back and raised his hands again. "April Banks." His voice was even, as if he could calm the storm that raged in her. "My name is James Sant, former Corporal, Squadron D, British SAS."

She'd been right, he was military. *Former* military.

James glanced up and down the alley and lowered his words to a near whisper. "I work for an organization that's been tracking the hackers who attacked your site."

No one cared enough about her and the other women on the site to put in this much effort. Even the web hosting service told her to scrap the site and start over with new data.

"We're all retired special forces. We owe you a debt for that website." He took a long breath. "We owe your husband a debt." Was the emotion in his eyes real, or was he as good at putting on an act as he was with his elbow into the side of the man's head in the parking lot?

"Let me go." Invoking Mark just then, with her emotions peaking in all directions, threatened to tear her apart.

"I told you, I'm not holding you." James took a symbolic step to the side, clearing space for her. Not that she'd risk walking within striking distance of him. Though the way he moved, it seemed like he was always in range.

But she still didn't move. Could it really be safer with him in this alley? She'd seen the cruel eyes of the man who'd first attacked her. James seemed to have way more life and honesty in his face.

He shifted his awareness around them, even checking the stripe of sky above the alley. "Your website was hacked on nine December. We'd been aware of your work before that. We run parallel operations in a way. Helping people. Your outage was noted. We knew you'd have it back up in a few days, and when you didn't, understood it must be significant. Our cyber team jumped on the trail."

He was right about the date. All his details had lined up. "A lot of effort for my tiny site."

"Small but important." He had an answer for everything.

"You're not the cyber team." His combat boots and leather jacket showed wear. His sharp eyes didn't spend a lot of time staring at a computer.

"When we started seeing the sophistication, the established network, we thought it best to keep a security detail on you." He flexed a fist. "In case they got threatened and retaliated."

A chill ran up her back. "How long have you been watching me?"

"A bit over a week." He didn't even look sorry. "And it's a good thing—"

"No." She still held the keys like spikes. "Even if this is real, if those men in the parking lot are who you say they are, it doesn't justify you fucking spying on me without letting me know."

"April." He pursed his lips and seemed to search for words.

"That's not protection." She wanted to shake him but couldn't get that close. "That's an invasion."

"Understood." He nodded. "It was to protect you from them. And from knowledge of us."

Was she crazy for believing what he was telling her? But the attack in the parking lot had really happened. And she hated to think of what might've happened if James hadn't shown up. "What's the name of your organization?"

He stared at her, piercing. Reading her. His potential danger grew with his stillness. He didn't blink. "Automatik."

"I've never heard of them."

"You wouldn't." A little smirk curled the side of his mouth.

"I've heard a lot." Through the extensive network of her website forum, from Mark's service, from her father's service.

"We're quiet," he whispered.

"How can I trust you?" Part of her still wanted to run, despite what felt like the truth coming from him.

"I don't expect you to trust me." He stepped forward, dead serious. "Just believe me that it's safer at my side than out there alone." His momentum carried him closer. She raised her fist with the keys, and he barely glanced at it as he passed her. He continued talking with his back to her, walking out of the alley the way she'd entered. "You can come or not. It's your choice."

"If I don't go with you, you'll still be watching." Did that make her feel safe, or did it reinforce that she was falling deeper into dangerous territory?

He stopped and nodded, face still turned away. "Until the end."

"Of what?" She knew about endings. They never felt good.

"Until the end of the bastards who stole from you." He resumed walking and slipped out of the alley. She could follow, or she could exit the other way, placing her out on her own. But still under his watch.

An ally in the parking lot fight was an obvious advantage. The hackers had made this a very real, flesh-and-blood battle. She seethed, wanting to punish them. James had mentioned a cyber team. That kind of support could change the whole game. She'd been sifting through internet hash for weeks, trying to track the hackers. More processing power could shut those sons of bitches down.

She turned and walked out of the alley in James's direction.

He waited for her, leaning against a parking lot lamppost. His body seemed relaxed, but she could see the way his broad shoulders were squared under his European-style motorcycle jacket that he was still poised and ready. He stepped away from the lamppost and walked to meet her. Beyond him, her car and cart full of groceries were undisturbed. The two attackers were gone, as was the red-haired man.

"We mop up fast." James joined her, the two of them moving closer to the car.

"Like it didn't happen." Fear needled into her again. The attack was terrible, but how different was the world she was in now, where things like that can be erased?

"But we know it did." He stopped near her car and looked down. Blood dotted the asphalt. It was where he'd tackled the man. "The ginger cowboy with me should have everything under control, clearing our exit—"

"April?" Theresa stepped out from the front of the supermarket. "We thought we heard yelling, but…" She sighed relief when she saw April standing unharmed, but still held a worried hand over her chest.

April stammered. What story should she tell? The truth? But there was no proof anymore, besides the traces of blood. That would only raise more questions. James and his organization definitely didn't like questions.

A surprisingly charming smile spread across James's face as he addressed Theresa. "There was no trouble. Just some kids having a laugh and wanting to ram shopping carts into cars. We scared them off."

Theresa looked to April for conformation. James had sounded so natural. How did he come up with that so quickly? April did her best to laugh it off. "They won't try it again. James scared them good."

Theresa's glance moved between April and James. "You know him?"

El Paso was a big city, but in the smaller corners like this one, almost everyone recognized each other. April scrambled to find an answer. "Web host," she blurted. Then she calmed into the lie. "He's with the security team from my web host. We're trying to resolve that hack."

James casually lifted one of her grocery bags from the cart. "Most often, we work from our desks, but this job is particularly complex."

The keys were still in her hand and she unlocked the trunk. He loaded all her groceries while Theresa watched him, then gazed back at April with marked appreciation. He was a good-looking man. Tall and fit. Angular, bold features. And that accent. If April could've just seen him from across a room, rather than first thinking he was there to attack her, she might think he was sexy.

Theresa gave April another light touch on the arm and it grounded her, slowed her heart rate a little. April placed her hand over Theresa's and gave it a squeeze.

"I'll see you online." Theresa parted with a smile and a wave and returned to the supermarket.

With her gone, some of the charm drained out of James. He closed the trunk and held out his hand. "I'll drive."

She gripped her keys. "We drive on the right over here."

A smile glimmered in his eyes. "On the wrong side, you mean." Then he became more serious. "If they have another go, I need to be behind the wheel."

How much control was she handing over? The life she'd constructed over the last few years in order to recreate herself had already been shattered by unknown forces. Nothing seemed like it was hers anymore. She struggled to find something private. And safe.

She gave him the keys. "You already know where I live."

He nodded. "I do."

"And where I sleep." Her heavy coat wasn't enough to make her feel covered. He must've seen everything and she'd had no idea.

"And where you shop." He slid into the driver's seat and she got in on the passenger side. She'd never ridden in that position in her own car before. Everything was scrambled. James continued, "Which was how I was able to help you today. And I'm going to go on helping."

He put the car in gear and drove out of the parking lot. Was James her new stability? One man and a

shadow organization somewhere behind him? Until a
few weeks ago, she'd controlled everything. Now she
was a passenger in her own car and didn't know where
she was going.

CHAPTER TWO

PAIN SPREAD FROM James's elbow where he'd smashed it into the attacker's skull. The sensation would dull to an ache soon, but this detail wasn't going to get any simpler. In a split second, a simple protection assignment had escalated to the point of spilling blood.

April sat in the passenger seat, looking focused and not completely torn apart by the assault.

"You handled yourself well back there," he told her.

She rubbed her knuckles. "You're lucky you didn't get the business end of my keys."

He stood about a foot taller than her, yet she'd still filled that alley with her presence. "With those other blokes, I mean. They were the real problem, and you didn't back down." Automatik had given him this operation because they knew how valuable the stolen website assets were. But the damn cyber intelligence wing couldn't track the hacker down fast enough to avoid this upturn in violence.

James navigated the El Paso streets he'd memorized from maps when he'd first been assigned to April's security. He'd read her dossier, watched her from a distance. Her smarts and determination were evident in the website she'd created. Her heart showed in its purpose.

"My dad was army. Showed me some moves when I was in junior high and high school." Her hand trembled slightly as she smoothed her sleek black bob haircut. "I looked Korean enough for the bullies."

Her file had indicated that her father was American and her mother Korean, married when he was stationed there. But there was no mention of what fighting skills April might have. "We're dealing with a class of bastard above what you'll find on a school yard."

"I could see that." Her mouth thinned to a line. "What were they really there for?"

There were a few possibilities for what those men would've done with April if he and Raker hadn't intervened. None of them were good. "The goons might've been hired to intimidate you away from trying to track the hackers."

"Or?" Her jaw was set. Dark brown eyes cut into him, seeking.

Did she really want to know? She'd already agreed to go with him. There was no use in scaring her further. "Or they might've been there to eliminate you." But he couldn't lie to her.

Her eyes unfocused and gazed out past the car, past the landscape. "In broad daylight."

"These jokers weren't skilled." The fight still pulsed through him. Though the adrenaline of conflict waned, an undercurrent of anger remained. If she hadn't run when she had, he might've stayed on the unconscious assailant, pummeling him. He steered the car off the busy streets and into a neighborhood. Simple houses and shade trees. "The next batch will be."

She took a ragged breath.

"But you'll be safe," he reassured. His phone buzzed in his jacket. He threaded an earbud out of the pocket and clicked on the cord to listen.

Raker twanged, "Didn't take much to crack these yokels. Especially after you dropped the hammer on the one guy. A windowless van ride to an abandoned warehouse got them."

"They sang?" James felt April watching him, wanting the answers.

"Couple of locals. Outstanding warrants. Taking jobs for drug money." Road noise on Raker's end told James that he was already on the move. "The gig was set off by a text and money wired to a check cashing place."

"What were their orders?" He gripped the steering wheel with one hand, hating to think of her coming to harm. She was his assignment, a good person who didn't deserve to be in the crosshairs. Were the hackers scared enough to have her killed?

"Just to send a message," Raker answered. "Rough her up. Get her scared, and to let her know worse was coming if she kept pushing."

"Understood." He had to remain sharp. The hackers would play another card. April raised her eyebrows in a question, wanting his information. He held up a finger to delay her. "They're out of circulation?"

Raker chuckled. "Local PD has them. Anonymous tip had them breaking and entering the warehouse. They'll stick to that story, unless they want to implicate themselves and add today's charges."

"Thanks, partner." He and the former Green Beret had been teamed up since James had joined Automatik two years ago. They could work in the field without words and shared what stories they felt fit to tell over pints after the shooting was over. Their trust was proven, yet there were still black chapters from James's past that he'd never told his friend. "See you at the safe house."

"Just keep your hands off the glazed raised and we'll be okay." Raker hung up, and James disconnected the call. The donut shop that served as their local front was less than a mile away. In a few minutes, April would be out of danger, and he could breathe easy.

"Safe house?" She shook her head, color rising to her cheeks. "I can't hide."

A weight seemed to compress his shoulders. The job just got harder again. "It's not hiding," he explained. "It's laying low until our cyber security team can root these guys out." She looked to be about his age, mid-thirties, and should have a realistic enough view of the world to understand the value of staying where the bullets couldn't find her.

"Not an option." She tilted her chin up, defiant.

"You do remember what happened in the parking lot today?" How much convincing would he have to do? He couldn't force her anywhere, but if she insisted on running around out in the open, he couldn't completely guarantee her safety. "They started with fists. They'll go to razors, then guns, then gasoline."

She blinked at him and recoiled. He wanted to back away from himself. His past had risen too close to the surface as he'd recounted the details of the situation.

He kicked his old self back down into the murk. "It'll be secure and comfortable. And it won't be for long. We have crack computer people, and they'll locate the hackers in no time. Then we erase their hard drives and they can't touch you again." She didn't look convinced. He remembered some of the cyber team talking about the security measures of her site slowing the hackers. "Whoever created your data encryption did a great job and will keep the bastards on the hook long enough for us to find them."

"I did it." Her defiance returned.

"What?"

"The encryption. It's mine." Anger burned in her voice. "And they're using it against me. Hiding behind it." She ran her fingers through her hair with frustration. "The web host was no problem for them, but they haven't gotten through mine yet."

"That's good." He made another turn, more than halfway to the safe house.

"Not good enough." Emotion glossed her eyes. The pain was personal. "They're going to get the identities. The women, all of them who trusted me. Personal information. Financial information. And then the hackers can link that to their dead husbands. Thousands of identities served up for anyone who'll pay for them. It could ruin their lives..." She choked on the last words.

"We won't let that happen." James had read about her husband's army service and the IED attack that had killed him in Afghanistan. But now he felt that history emanating out of her. The pain and loss and subterranean sadness.

"*I* won't let that happen." She seemed ready to open the door and leap out of the car.

He slowed to a stop at a curb and turned toward her. "We're here to help you, you don't have to do this alone."

"I do have to." She was unbending. "They're hiding behind my own tech. If I log in, they'll follow my lead and find the way through. But from their servers, local, I can shut it all down and give them nothing."

He'd glimpsed her determination in the alley. She still looked like she'd fight rather than back down. Heat blushed her cheeks and she spoke through clenched teeth. "I have to be there."

His mind spun through different strategies. The least appealing was having the woman he was assigned to protect wearing tactical gear and throwing herself in harm's way. "Can't you just explain your encryption to our team and have them do it on site?"

She scoffed. "You said you're former SAS?"

"That's right." His posture straightened.

"So can you explain to me the best way to assault a hostage situation on an airplane, then expect me to execute it perfectly?"

"No," he admitted. "But we can secure the room, secure the server, then fly you in to wrap it all up."

She crossed her arms over her chest. "Not possible."

An exasperated laugh burst from him. "I knew you were going to say that."

"Your cyber team wouldn't wait that long, and neither can I." She uncrossed her arms and gestured with fine fingers. "Do you know how many automated tasks can be assigned in a computer? Every second I don't have my hands on that server could mean a breach and a failure."

This assignment was slipping way out of the parameters. "No bullshit?" His question was her last chance to change her mind and go to the safe house.

"None." Fear flickered in her eyes. Maybe she was realizing how dangerous what she wanted was. "I'm not reckless."

"But you are stubborn." He swung out of the car and walked to the curbside while pulling out his phone. The cold air bit at his neck and hands. No clouds threatened weather, so he welcomed the relief from the heat that rose in him each time this assignment became more complicated. He dialed a secure connection to an Automatik hub and waited.

She remained in the car, watching him. Deep eyes. They'd seen pain, her own and others'. How far into him did she see?

"Central," a voice answered on the other end of the line.

"Sant."

"Raker updated us."

"A new wrinkle." James explained April's position as clearly as possible until the Automatik officer cut him off.

"Let me route in cyber."

More waiting, with only a random click on the line to let him know he was still connected. Automatik was much more streamlined than the military, with less brass and red tape, but there were still necessary delays as everyone involved was given all necessary information.

Inside the car, April stared at him with an impatient look on her face. She'd built the website and created encryption the top hackers couldn't crack on her own. Clearly she wasn't used to answering to anybody. She swung open the door and stepped out. A tall boot reached to below her knee, then jeans covered her thighs. He looked away when he caught the curve of her hips and waist beneath her open jacket. Leering at the woman he was there to protect was not good form. A charge still ran through him. He hadn't felt it while watching her earlier in the detail. But that was before he'd seen her steel and determination.

"What's the word?" She brought his attention back to her face. The edge of fear remained in her eyes.

"Still waiting."

Her long breath hitched with nerves.

Finally the line connected. "Central and cyber on the line."

James explained the situation while April listened, ready to jump in with any missed details. But he knew the whole story and related it without interruption. Silence on the line.

Then the answer, "Makes sense here. Is it doable for you?"

He stepped off the map. "I can make it work." They disconnected, and he put his phone away.

A 9mm automatic, with a full mag. Two spares on the other side of his shoulder holster. A knife in his pocket and one across the small of his back. His phone was charged, with an extra battery. A multi-tool and a lighter in his jacket.

And April, a live wire he couldn't predict.

"You're on the team," he told her, walking around to the driver's side.

She remained motionless. Maybe the reality of it finally struck her. Good. She needed to be scared and aware. Her shaky hand reached out and steadied herself on the open passenger door.

He drew her attention. "I'm not going to leave your side."

She blinked, then took a breath. Her eyes met his, and he saw her resolve shimmering beneath the dread. "Albuquerque."

He tilted his head for more.

She got into the car before him, her impatience already rising. When he joined her, she explained, "I got an IP hit there from an early probe they'd sent at my site, phishing." Her eyes flicked to the key in the ignition, wanting to move. "I kept waiting for something else to reinforce it. But nothing came. And I didn't feel safe going alone. It's the only lead I've got."

"Then that's where we begin." He turned the engine over and pulled onto the street. "But first…" The hackers' attack had set this off. If Automatik could've resolved it within a week, April never would've known about his existence. But blood had been spilled, her life was threatened and now she had to open all the doors of her world to a man like him. "We have to go to your house."

DREAD CRAWLED OVER her skin as James drove April to her house. She was a passenger in her own car and didn't have to give him any directions. Her privacy had been invaded by the hackers, and now it seemed like there was nothing she could claim as her own.

She chewed her lower lip as jolts of anxiety shot up and down her legs. James was completely steady as he drove, focused and serious. At times she'd seen a little light of a smile in his face, but that had all gone away as soon as she'd insisted to be part of the hunt.

"Do you know all my secrets?" Small talk with someone who already knew where you lived was uncanny.

"Those are yours." He didn't even glance at her. "Mine are mine."

Not that she imagined her interrogation skills were

good enough to pry personal information out of him. "How much did you see when you were watching me?"

His gaze remained on the road and his voice was flat. "Nothing personal. My attention was on potential threats to you, not your intimates."

The word pushed a blush across her chest and up her neck. She rubbed the back of her hand across her cheek, hoping to hide the telltale flush she was prone to. This stranger had silently moved past some of her defenses. He already knew her. She hadn't given anybody that kind of access in years.

He pulled into her driveway, putting the car in the same spot she always did, and killed the engine. She only sat three feet away from where she normally did and the house looked foreign. The brown edges of the low bushes next to the door were more evident. A loose shingle cast a shadow she'd never seen before.

James brought her back to the moment. "Do you have a go bag?"

"Never thought I'd need one." She got out of the car on shaky legs.

He stood from the car and spoke with care. "We'll pack you one."

She automatically started walking up the short brick path to the house, then discovered she didn't have her keys. James was at the trunk of her car, collecting the groceries. He caught up to her and gave her the keys so she could unlock the door.

It felt like she was breaking into someone else's house. She had to learn the furniture and hallways as if she'd never been there, though it had been her home for eight years. James knew it better. He went immediately to the kitchen and stuffed the groceries into the refrigerator, bags and all.

He returned to her, motor running high, but not rushed. "Duffel, backpack?"

"Carry-on?" She pointed at a hall closet where the luggage was stored.

"That'll do." He opened the door and tipped his head toward the back of her house. "I'll meet you in the bedroom."

The hallway seemed to tilt under her feet. She ran her hand along the wall to steady herself. Maybe she'd reach her bedroom and find herself sitting in the comfortable chair by the French doors to the backyard. Dozing. Dreaming. Because this was feeling less and less real.

But the room was empty, just as she'd left it. Bed unmade, yesterday's clothes piled on top of a low dresser. She opened the drawers and stared at the contents. How many days should she pack for? Where would this take her? How would it end?

James entered her bedroom and placed her rolling carry-on bag on the bed. "Six days."

She wanted to start grabbing clothes, but the thought of him that close to the space in the sheets where her body had been slowed her. The calm of sleep, the intimacy of a quiet morning, were laid out for him to see. Her privacy burst like a glass bubble.

He moved to her and slowed his pace. "Six days ought to do it." His voice soothed, and returned her to her task.

She might be part of the team, but at least he wasn't shouting at her like a drill sergeant. That might've made it easier, though, when she had to grab a couple of handfuls of panties and shove them in her bag. No man had seen her bedroom or her underpants since Mark. Loss shuddered through her. The new contact made her nerves prickle. She threw more and more clothes into the bag until she had six days of functional outfits.

James stepped into the adjoining bathroom and opened the medicine cabinet. "Any medications you need to have with you?"

"Caffeine." She slid past him into the bathroom and the nerves that had tingled woke up to a full lightning storm. When she'd first seen him tackle the man in the parking lot, she'd been so caught up in the danger that she hadn't understood he was one of the good guys. But learning he'd fought to protect her gave her a new appreciation for his quick, strong body. Moving this close to him forced her to feel his thrumming energy. Knowing he was on her side changed the landscape. Part of her cooled with relief. She'd been searching on her own for the hackers, and having an ally like him was a welcome boost. But it also meant her normal isolation had been replaced by this very potent man.

He backed out of the bathroom to give her space. "We can stop for coffee on the way out of town."

"Not tea?" Without any personal details on him, she had to hook into his accent.

"If you can find me a decent chai in El Paso, I'll pay you in gold." He crossed his arms, highlighting his broad chest.

She collected her glasses and contact lens solution from the medicine cabinet and returned to the bedroom. James hovered by the bedside table next to where the blankets were bent back.

"Do you have a gun?"

Her jaw clenched and her shoulders tightened behind her. If he opened the drawer he was reaching for, he'd find her e-reader and vibrator. She loosened herself enough to explain, "Mark had one, but I got rid of it." She'd traded the pistol in to the police department for minor league baseball tickets. Never went to the game.

Still, without a gun, violence found her. It was present all around. Even in James.

He stepped away from the table with a disappointed sigh.

"I have a big flashlight."

He nodded and held her bag, ready to close it. "Bring it."

She dove next to the bed and grabbed the heavy flashlight and tossed it in the bag. It was coated in dust and kicked off a piece of lint as it landed. "Sorry my place isn't tidy."

"No worries." He zipped up her bag and headed back toward the front of her house.

She followed, her home already feeling empty, as if she'd been on vacation for months. "Do you guys clean houses or just crime scenes?"

"My mum was a house cleaner." He paused and his eyes grew a little less focused. Like he was peering past the present. Then he snapped to again and started toward the front door.

She, too, reeled with his personal revelation. Was it better to know more about him, or to just think of him as a soldier with a job? She couldn't follow just yet. "I don't have a gun, but I do have a weapon."

The office was dark, the way she always kept it.

She collected her laptop and accessories into a case and joined James at the front door.

They exited and she locked up, feeling like she was shutting her former self inside forever. Who would she be now? She walked toward her car, but James diverged from her path toward a compact SUV parked at the curb. He tilted his head for her to follow, and she did.

Once she was close enough, he spoke in a low voice. "We'll leave your car so we can't be tracked." He opened the back door and tossed her bag in.

She barely kept her voice to a whisper. "You're stealing this car?"

"It was dropped off for us." The keys were in the ignition.

The block was silent. No sign of whoever left the car in the impossibly short time they'd been in the house. "Holy shit."

"Automatik," was his only explanation. He opened the passenger door for her.

She clutched her laptop bag to her chest and hesitated. "Was Mark part of… Automatik?" Just saying the word dragged her into the shadows.

"No." He looked at her with sympathy. A knowledge of pain. She sat in the passenger seat, and he closed the door. He got into the driver's seat, started the engine and turned to her. "But you are now."

CHAPTER THREE

"How BLOODY BIG is this country?" In the two years James had lived in the United States, his longest road trip had been from Los Angeles to Las Vegas. That epic trek through the desert had convinced him that flying was the best way to cover the vast distances between cities. On his last op, he and Raker had jetted into St. Louis, then driven two and a half long hours to Morris Flats, Illinois. "We'd be through four countries in Europe by now."

"This is still El Paso." April focused on the road ahead. "Highway 10 is going to merge onto 25 north." Her nerves had waned for a few minutes, but clearly jumped again as the car sped out of the city.

"Have you left town in a while? Traveled?" The mission was odd enough with a noncombatant as a teammate, but how much management was the day-to-day going to take?

"Four years." She stared out the side window. He couldn't see her expression. "We moved here for Fort Bliss."

"Spend your time in that office, working on the site?" The unlit space had seemed very safe and far away.

She turned to him, blinking away light tears in her eyes. "If I want sunlight, there's the breakfast nook or the back of the bedroom or the yard." Her stubbornness kicked in with steel in her voice. "I'm not a shut-in."

"You're a field agent." The highway interchange took their attention. She navigated while he changed lanes through traffic until they were speeding north where they needed to be. A shopping complex with a supermarket rushed past the highway. He tried to cover all contingencies in this changing op. "Feminine supplies?"

"Gah… Well…" She stammered, glancing at him, then her hands. He kicked himself for being so straightforward. He could've danced around that a little better for her sake. But she surprised him, gathered herself, straightened her back and took out her phone. After checking a calendar app, she declared, "I should be good for another couple of weeks."

"Roger that." Now he kicked himself for not giving her enough credit. "Just let me know if any kind of need comes up."

She grew bolder. "And your teammate will drop off cold brownies and an iced mocha like he did this car?"

He chuckled with the thought of Raker delivering the sweets on a silver platter. "He's hovering in support, but not that close." His partner could be reached on the phone, but was miles away. "We're moving fast and light so we can't be followed and we can adapt quickly." He shifted in his seat and felt the press of his sheath knife along the small of his back. "Nimble." But he was feeling undersupplied and didn't have a change of clothes. "Then, when the time comes, we call in the hammer."

She turned her phone over in her hands. "I'm assuming I can't tell my parents where I am, where I'm going."

He gave her a sympathetic look. "No contact." There was a lot his parents didn't know since he'd left the SAS. Automatik kept a subterranean profile. And his jobs before joining them were nothing he was proud of.

She nodded and put her phone away. They fell silent, surrounded only by road noise. She reached for the radio, then pulled her hand back. "I need a detail," she told him.

Briefing her on the Automatik end of the search for the hackers could make this whole process go faster. "Tell me what you need."

"From you," she explained. "You know where I live, where I sleep. You know where I am on my cycle. I need a detail from you."

Refusing would only add an uncomfortable cold edge to their time spent together. But how deep did she expect him to dig? Beneath the skin, he was either classified or unspeakable. "I already told you my mum was a house cleaner."

"Unprompted." She drew a line through the air with the tip of her finger. "Doesn't count."

His mind flipped through the files of his existence. "I live alone in an apartment. I've broken my left arm twice. I don't like chewing gum."

She tipped her head back and forth, absorbing. "Sisters?"

"Only child." He gave more than he'd expected. "Why that question?"

"You asked about feminine supplies. You've got some knowledge."

"I'm not new, you know. I've been paying attention to the world around me for quite a while."

A small smile crossed her face, sly. "You gave me more than one detail."

"Now you don't have to ask me for a while." The unexpected trek into his past made him brusquer than he wanted to be.

She receded and turned away to look out the side window. "You can just give me your file to read."

"It's all redacted." He laid on more throttle as if he could rush the assignment and return to the basics of what his life had become. As if he could outrun the past.

Silence descended again like a cloud of smoke neither wanted to breathe. She reached out and turned the radio on. AM news mumbled out. She punched buttons until an old hip-hop song set a grooving pace.

The mood lightened slightly. He acquiesced, "Glad you know the stations out here."

"I hope classic hip-hop works for you." She patted the armrest to the beat.

"I can pop and lock." The old neighborhood hadn't crossed his mind in years.

She brightened and looked him up and down with slow assessment. "That's the kind of detail I wanted." The attention brought his own awareness to his body. Not as an operator who had to be ready for combat, but as a man riding in a car with a woman. He was tempted to show off a little, shake his shoulders to the music. Grind his hips. But that would've been way outside the operational parameters of the mission.

It took a breath to get the heat rising through him to recede again. What would she look like dancing?

Free, not holding herself back with the thoughts that fired constantly behind her eyes.

Another song came on, this one from somewhere in the early 2000s, taking him straight back to the apartment block. "Bloody hell."

She nodded to it. "Classic."

"I can almost feel the lager can in my hand and the damp London night on the back of my neck." Shouting and laughing with his mates. Trying to get the girls to stop and talk to them.

"Leesville, Louisiana. When my dad was at Fort Polk."

"That when you were brawling on the school yard?"

She kept her body swinging to the music while making fists and bringing her guard up. "I got the point across, and they stopped bothering me."

"Yeah." He made his own fist. "We scrapped plenty with any of the neighborhood bastards who didn't like a group of desis having a good time."

"Bet they'd be scared to death now, knowing you're SAS." Her head bobbed to the beat.

"Former," he corrected. "But yeah, that'd be a kick in their bollocks."

"For all I know, those girls were on my website." She grew more pensive.

"What you made with that site is amazing." That gap that had been closing between them widened again. "You don't know them and you're helping them."

The music continued, but she was still. "You did the same for me."

He wanted to take her words in like medicine. But some wounds were too deep to reach. "You deserve it."

This quiet was thicker. Her smallest movements

pressed against the quiet and into him, as if they were sitting shoulder to shoulder. But that connection was impossible.

He spotted a shopping complex near an upcoming exit and swerved into the off-ramp lane. "Detour."

She jerked around to look behind them. "Someone following us?"

Not now, but it was a possibility. "I need spare bloomers." The ramp curved near the large stores, including a hunting and outdoor supply. "And bullets."

The highway dumped them directly into the shopping center, and he drove to the store he wanted. It was a two-story affair faced with fake rough-hewn timbers. A mountain lodge in the middle of the desert.

April stared at him the whole way into the parking spot. "Bullets for what?"

He turned off the car and made a show of stretching. His jacket opened enough to reveal the handle of his pistol. She sucked a quick breath and leaned back. Her lips moved around words she didn't say.

"I didn't need it against those blokes in the parking lot." He rearranged himself so the gun was hidden. "I might need it against whoever's coming next. And the last thing I want to do is run out of bullets." Sitting and thinking about their situation, or talking and talking about it, wasn't going to change anything. So he got out of the car and waited for her to follow. She was quick to rebound and strode toward the store with barely a wrinkle of concern on her brow.

It was his turn to catch up to her. "For a civilian, you wear a good mask."

She smiled at him brightly. "This is my going-out-in-public face. I learned it to keep people from asking me, 'Are you doing alright?'"

"It's fucking brilliant."

"Thank you," she chirped.

He lowered his voice to a private tone. "Your secret identity is safe with me."

She lost the smile and looked at him with quiet gravity. "Thank you."

They entered the store, he grabbed a basket and headed toward the smell of blued steel and gun oil. A few other shoppers milled about the space, but none of them looked up as they passed. The employees in matching camp shirts all seemed too absorbed in tasks to bother with someone who seemed to know where he was headed. On the way to the back wall of the store, he tossed a rain shell his size in the basket.

"Did you pack rain gear?" He hovered close to the women's clothing.

"I didn't think of it."

"Grab one."

After hers joined his in the basket, they moved on. He found a pair of functional cargo pants, T-shirt and socks. Still no suspicion in the store. No threats came in the doors. For the people around them, everything was normal. But his mission continued, including April, a brand-new field agent. She watched as he tossed a couple of packages of briefs in the basket. Her eyes skipped from the underpants to his hips, then to his face. She blushed.

He shrugged. "I like it snug." And she liked simple, sporty panties with bright colors, from what he'd seen when she was packing. He had to start walking again to keep a rush of blood from getting to his head. Sharing intimate details had tricked his body into preparing for physical contact. That couldn't happen with her. But that didn't keep him from secretly wanting. Just a brush of her hip against his. The back of her hand against his knuckles.

As he strode to the back of the store, he made sure there was always space between them. She'd already been thrown into a new and dangerous world this day. The last thing he wanted to do was involve her in his futile search for a little humanity.

The sight of rifles and shotguns displayed on wooden racks brought him back to his familiar world. The glass case of the gun counter held pistols of all varieties and their accessories. The man behind it all was a little older than the other employees and walked over toward James and April with casual authority. His nametag read "Greg."

"What can I help you with?" He spread his hands out on the top of the counter like a conjurer. Several soft pads, emblazoned with gun maker logos, protected the glass and stood ready to exhibit the weapons.

James aped Raker's twang, something he'd learned to do while the two of them were out drinking. "Don't tempt me with a new .44 magnum revolver. Today I just need two boxes of 9mm rounds."

Momentary surprise flashed over April's face, but she suppressed it quickly. She busied herself by looking at the handguns, occasionally peeking at James. Was she looking for the model he wore?

Greg clicked his tongue with friendly disappointment. "Too bad about that .44. I could sell you a package: revolver and lever action, both chambered for it."

James groaned like he'd been punched in the gut

and made a broad glance to April. "The lady'd give me hell."

"Gotta keep them happy." Greg nodded, then leaned closer. "Come back when it's your birthday."

James tapped the counter with the side of his fist. "Will do."

Greg walked to a long cabinet along the wall. "Match grade, silver tip, what're you looking for?"

He wanted the best but couldn't arouse too much suspicion. "Well, we're taking her to the range today, gonna teach her some basics, so how about one box of steel case, 115 grain." Not ideal for tactical purposes, but would work as a backup. "And a box of the +P for me." Those would be first into his magazines as he reloaded.

Greg returned with the boxes. "Best to keep her away from the +P."

April joined them. "I'm a little nervous to shoot."

"I'm sure you'll do fine," Greg reassured her. "This fella will take care of you."

James gave her a comforting pat on her back. "You know I will." The touch was necessary for the act. The touch was a mistake. She leaned into it slightly, accepting the support he offered. He wouldn't allow himself to take anything from her. As much as he wanted to feel the quiet solace. She didn't know him, not all of him, and if she did, she wouldn't stand this close.

He wrapped up his transaction with Greg, exchanged the necessary pleasantries and returned to the general shopping of the store. He and April didn't talk as they went upstairs to the camping supplies, where he found metal cups and multi-purpose flatware in case they had to cobble a meal together on the fly.

Checkout at the front counter only took a minute. He maintained the put-on drawl for continuity. April stayed at his side with a distance conveying familiarity. If Greg had seen them, the cover story would be intact. James maintained an outward calm while acutely aware of how close April was at all times. She bumped into him on the way out of the store. Heat flashed up his spine and across his shoulders. He busied himself with an assessment of the parking lot for threats and egress as his body sorted itself again. They weren't in any danger. Still, the heat didn't completely disappear.

They got back into the car and found the highway north again. Her demeanor returned to the thoughtful and aware woman he'd gotten to know. "You don't have to teach me to shoot," she declared.

"I was just setting the stage for Greg."

"Learned from my dad." She crossed her arms over her chest. "I went to the range with Mark."

"Have you ever shot at a moving target?" The last thing he wanted was for this op to fall apart so far that she needed to handle a gun to defend herself.

"Like a man?" She leveled her gaze on him.

"Yes," he answered, just as even. "Like a man."

She shook her head in response. "Is that what Automatik does? Shoot at men?"

"Only when we have to." He didn't count kills anymore. The SAS had as a point of duty and service. In Automatik, killing was never something done lightly. And in his years between the two, when he'd lived on the margins with Hathaway, tallying kills had been financial. "When people are hurting others and won't stop, we step in."

"Sounds vague enough to give you free rein." She wasn't letting him off the hook.

"We have internal checks and balances." And every member of Automatik had a voice if there were any concerns. "You won't see us in the news, but we're no friends to the Russian mob, drug cookers, gunrunners..."

"Hackers," she conceded.

"Exactly."

Her hand flexed, gripping the armrest between them. "I don't want you to teach me how to shoot at a man."

"I don't want you or I to shoot at anyone." Best-case scenario: she located the hackers, he gave them a hard look and they handed over their servers to her.

That seemed to satisfy her, and she settled back in her seat. The road north stretched for miles and miles, their destination way beyond the horizon. Static crackled through the hip-hop as the signal weakened, then April surfed the stations for anything decent to listen to. They drove for over an hour until the need for lunch forced them off the highway and into a drive-through.

She squinted at the menu out the window and took a moment before deciding on a burger combo she told him. He committed her preference to memory, adding it to her file in case he needed to know some time later in the operation. But it was also another personal detail. Something learned. Just like she learned he opted for the chicken sandwich meal.

Once back on the road, she dove into her burger and explained between bites, "I got my run in this morning. It's a hungry day."

"You mean when you were running away from me?" His food was bland, but at least it was hot.

"That was just a sprint." Her laugh was brief. The impact of all that had happened remained. "Got my three miles in before that."

"I know." As soon as he said it, the mood steered further into murky territory.

"Son of a bitch," she muttered. "You were trailing me."

He nodded.

She took a breath, sipped her cola and pulled them both out of the gloom. "At least we set our circadian rhythms. Sunlight gets to the pineal, aligns us to the day."

"They didn't cover that when I studied field medicine, so I'll take your word for it."

"Smart man." She gave him a small thumbs-up.

"Smart woman." He saluted her with proper regimental form.

They resumed their lunches and sped north. The mileage toward Albuquerque marked on the passing signs became more realistic. James itched to get out of the car and pump blood through the mission. He knew this stop was just a link in the chain, but he needed some idea as to how this was all going to play out with April as his partner.

She wrapped up the remains of their lunch and stowed it in the backseat before pulling out her phone. "Don't worry," she said when she saw him watching her screen. "I'm not contacting anyone, even my anonymous online friends."

"Some of them might not be your friends."

The color drained from her face. She muttered, "Sons of bitches."

"We'll stop them." This mission was at the core of

why he'd joined Automatik. "They won't be able to touch anyone else's lives."

"I'll break their fingers before they can." She typed on her phone, shaking her head and growling under her breath.

"Let me do all the breaking." He held out his hand to reveal the scars on his knuckles. "You're there to fix things."

She looked up from her phone and studied his hand. Her gaze moved to his face and deepened, as if she'd learned another piece of him. "I'm trying."

"You're here," he reassured her. "That's more than most people would do."

She returned to her phone without acknowledging what he'd said. "The IP hit I got gave me an Albuquerque address. I mapped it. We're going to a CPA office."

He scoffed. "In that case, I'll let you do all the fighting."

She continued, absorbed, "Second floor of a two-level building with other offices and catwalks outside."

He constructed the building in his mind and began a list of tactical necessities. "Stairways?"

"I see two. And an elevator."

"No elevators if we can help it."

"Parking lot behind the building."

"Ingress, egress?"

She kept up well. "It's all in a line. In one side and out the other."

"We'll put the car by the exit if we can." What kind of opposition might they meet on this recon? "If we're lucky enough to locate the hackers at this stop, we'll collect what intel we can and I'll call in the strike team."

She poked at her phone, rotating the overhead view of the location. "How long will that take?"

"One or two days. I plan the assault, we hit it, you get the computers."

"An office like this probably has internal servers. The hackers might be side drilling so they can piggy-back unnoticed on them." She continued to spin and move the map. "Hard-wired from next door? From downstairs?"

"They can do that?" Half of what she was saying went over his head, but he held on the general ideas.

"If they snuck an Ethernet cable in." She tilted her head side to side, considering. "Maybe?"

"You give me something real to follow, I'll track it to the bitter end." He shifted in his seat in an effort to bring life back to the numb areas on his ass. "As soon as this infernal car ride is over."

She laughed and lightened the air in the car. "Not for road trips?"

"I'll leap out of an airplane. Swim under a sub-marine." He rubbed his thigh for blood flow. "Trek through the desert. But don't make me sit for long."

"A man of action." Another quick and easy laugh helped his circulation move faster.

"You've seen me." And he damned himself for shading the mood again with his violence.

She receded, but not completely. "That's why I run. Can't just sit in front of the computer all day. If the weather's right, I'll do yoga in the backyard."

"Yoga?" He acted like he didn't know.

"You know, stretching and…" She trailed off and looked at him sheepishly. "Ah, sorry."

"I invented yoga, luv." He laughed to let her off the hook. "Just wish I got a royalty."

Her nervous giggle let out some tension. "Did you... Did you immigrate to England?"

He poked his thumb into his chest. "Born in London. The parents came from Mumbai."

"My mother was from Seoul. She met my dad when he was stationed..." Again, her words dispersed into the road noise. She looked at him with piercing eyes. "You knew that."

For someone who spent her time at a computer, she deciphered faces well. He didn't want to lie. "I read a file on you."

Her mouth turned down. "So Automatik is full of good guys, but they keep files on normal civilians."

It grated him to backpedal. "We don't keep files, we amassed it when we knew you were in trouble."

"I feel so much safer." Her sarcasm cut like a knife.

The sun swung down toward the western horizon, stretching shadows across the highway. The orange-and-yellow desert stones burned hotter, but he could feel that the air outside was cold. The atmosphere inside the car chilled as well. He and April didn't talk as she dialed through the radio stations, finally settling on classic rock. Neither of them drummed to the beat or hummed the melodies.

Mercifully, Albuquerque broke through the seemingly endless desert. Conversation started again as April tracked their progress on her phone and gave directions to the CPA office. The wood-and-stucco building wasn't too far off from the mental picture James had constructed. He pulled into the parking lot and stopped the car in the last space before the exit.

It was bloody good to move his legs again. He and April walked from the parking lot to the front of the building, where the staircases stretched up to the second floor. Some of the office doors on both levels didn't have any names on them. Dead quiet. April hung at his side, following his lead but keeping her eyes alert. He saw her tracing different elements of the building, especially where the electrical conduit snaked over and into walls.

"Anything?" he asked under his breath.

She searched. "I... I... Nothing definitive."

The paint on the building was old, but he couldn't find any areas that were unusually worn or chipped away. And there were no recent repairs to spots that might indicate retrofitted wiring. Everything seemed tight so far.

He paused at the bottom of the stairs and stood next to her as he continued to scan the building. "Breathe like yoga."

She drew a long breath through her nose and released it through her mouth. Her body settled after she did it again.

He looked in her eyes, then glanced up to the second floor. She nodded, and the two of them headed up. They headed right at the landing and stopped at the door to the CPA office. Chipped gold letters were painted across the steel: *Ashford, Bell & Jones.*

Before reaching for the handle, he indicated he wanted April to stand on the other side of the doorway. If someone fired from inside, the bullets would most likely fly in his direction, and he had more experience getting shot at. The anxiety wound her up again. Her shoulders climbed toward her ears. He took a breath as an example. She nodded and followed, loosening up a little.

He grabbed the handle with his left hand, keeping his right free to draw his pistol. It was only recon, but he couldn't take chances with April so close. She chewed her lower lip. He calmed the buzzing nerves that were growing and tried the handle.

It was locked.

April let out a disappointed sigh and checked her phone. "It's not even four. I guess they don't get a lot of walk-in business."

He checked up and down the catwalk and patted his front breast pocket. "I have picks. We could get in now." The whole building seemed to have gone home early.

She put a hand on his forearm and spoke under her breath. "We're not even sure this is the goldmine. What would we say if someone catches us?"

His urge for action had clouded his judgment. She was right. He let the tension drain from his legs and shoulders and promised himself that he wouldn't be hasty at any point forward on this mission. "You're right. Thanks." He moved his arm out from under her hand and patted her on the shoulder. "We'll get them in the morning."

She stilled. Had she not thought about what the timeframe he'd laid out really meant?

"That's right." Even when they weren't directly tracking the hackers, this op was bloody complicated. "We're spending the night."

CHAPTER FOUR

MAYBE SHE SHOULD'VE gone to the safe house. All her reasons for needing to be personally on the hunt for the hackers were real. Pride and stubbornness and the need for revenge hadn't clouded her judgment. But she hadn't considered spending a night at a hotel with James. When he'd talked about the mission taking more than one day, she'd vaguely imagined having a cot at a barracks or another impersonal space. Nothing like the richly appointed Valdez Hotel.

James did the talking at the broad, marble-topped front desk. Ornately carved dark wood accented the space, in contrast to the modern adobe look to the lobby. Lively conversation poured out of the bar/restaurant in one corner and echoed against the tile floors of the new hotel.

"Simon Pandya." James spelled the last name for the woman behind the desk, then handed a credit card over. "Two queen beds, if you have." His accent smoothed out, higher class.

"Let's see what we have." The woman typed and watched her computer screen. April had wanted to book a room via the internet and not have to deal with any face to face, but James didn't trust any online security. It was a good point. And her concerns of human contact making them easier to track were calmed when James took on this Simon persona to check them in.

Nothing else in her was calm. She kept reminding herself to breathe slow, but the nerves always came back like steady ocean waves. She was in over her head. James was an SAS spy guy with a gun and lock picks, and she was just stumbling her way forward, trying to fix something that might be broken beyond repair.

The woman looked up from her computer and glanced between "Simon" and April, who remained quiet. She imagined this woman had seen it all in the hotel business. April smiled back at her. *Nothing shocking going on here. Just a webmaster and a special forces soldier who met at a parking lot fight this morning and are now chasing the hackers who sent the hit men and may or may not even be in the country.*

"We do have a room." The woman fixed her polite gaze on James. "How many nights?"

"One." His deep voice spread the word out like satin sheets under a full moon. Rare, excited tingling ran up her legs. Or maybe she was imagining his long hands up her bare skin. Her knees weakened and she leaned as casually as she could against the front desk for support.

Her nerves were fried from running so hot and cold with James. He was there to protect her, but that meant he'd been watching her without her knowledge. His care was never in doubt, and he didn't talk down to her. They almost felt like partners on the hunt. The power balance was in his favor, though. He was armed, capable of violence. That was his world. Separate from hers.

She gathered her legs when the woman handed James the room key. He held his shopping bag of clothes and rolled April's bag, and she carried her computer case to the elevator where they waited. The polished brass doors reflected them back. Him tall and lean, rugged in his jacket and close beard. She was shorter, her body undefined in her coat. At least her boots looked cool. She tried to detect any signs of his gun or other weapons, but he was perfectly stealth.

The elevator was taking a long time for five floors. "It's like we're having an affair, Simon."

He turned to her, but she kept her eyes on the reflection. "Simon's a perfect gentleman."

"But you're not Simon."

He looked back at the doors. "James is a…" No definition.

"At least you took me someplace nice."

The elevator finally arrived, and they went to their room on the third floor. James put their bags down and immediately went to the window. The sun had set. The lights of the city blinked in the cold night until he blocked them out with the curtains. He stood at the edge and peered down, his stance ready.

She closed herself in the bathroom, took care of her needs and splashed cold water on her face. Hunger for dinner started to gnaw into her. What had her plan been for tonight? A simple fish dish and vegetables. TV, then tracking whatever leads she could find on the computer. All that was behind the locked front door of her house, hundreds of miles away. Plans and routines were gone, and with them safety and comfort. She already didn't recognize herself in the mirror.

Her eyes had to adjust to darkness after exiting the bathroom. Nervous fear swept along her limbs. She was alone with James in the shadows. Had he seen her secret thoughts about him? Was this his move?

But when she was able to see, she spotted him sitting in an armchair near the window, face focused on his phone as he typed.

Relief grounded her. And an edge of disappointment lingered, where her body was still curious about how he might feel next to her, arm wrapped around her, mouth on the side of her neck. But no. Not at all. That wasn't him, and that wasn't her. Not after all this time. Not after Mark.

She cleared her throat. "I thought we weren't supposed to contact anyone."

He didn't look up. "This is a secure connection to my people. I'm updating them."

"How secure?" She navigated around the shadowy furniture toward him.

His eyes glittered in the dim light. "I'm sure I couldn't explain it well enough for you. But the tech people know their business." He returned to his phone. "Besides, I'm not the one the bad guys know about."

"That's reassuring." She sat on the foot of the bed farthest from him. "My friends online, they're going to be worried about me. We look out for each other." Her phone was in her purse, close by.

He completed his task and put his phone down. "In a few days, you'll show back up and tell them all you got swept off to an exotic locale by a mysterious Brit, Simon."

"They won't believe it." Neither did she. "They know me too well."

He stood. "Would they believe you were here now?"

"Not at all."

"But you are." There it was again, that low, seductive voice. Warmth tumbled up and over her shoulders. Like he was draping a fur coat on her back. Was he doing it on purpose? Or was it his attempt to comfort her?

"I feel like the wheels will come off if I think about it too long." Her determination waned, and she considered having him take her back to the safe house.

"Then keep moving forward." He strode toward the door. "To dinner."

The wake of his energy caught her up, and she followed him out of the room. The elevator arrived quickly this time. She took advantage of the last bit of privacy they'd have before they hit the lobby. "You're getting the room, I'll pay for dinner."

He brushed her comment away with his hand. "Simon's taking care of everything." His accent returned to the usual lower British. "And you're not leaving a trace."

It wasn't worth arguing against that point. "So what does Simon do for a living?" She jumped in before he could answer. "I'll guess, antiquities dealer."

His chuckle sounded like pouring whiskey. "Custom stereos and infotainment systems for the discerning motorist."

"High-end."

He adjusted his jacket crisply. "Very."

"And I am?" She didn't know anymore.

"What do you want to be?"

The elevator arrived on the ground floor, forcing her to think fast. "Reclusive and mysterious modern artist."

"So you're slumming." The doors opened, and he held his arm out for her. She curled a hand around it and felt how incredibly strong he was, even in this calm moment. He took her with him out of the eleva-

tor and into the lobby. They navigated toward the social sounds coming from the hotel restaurant. "I hope
you don't mind eating local." His gaze swept over the
space and he whispered, "It allows us to control the
environment."

"The food smells good to me." The aromas of bright
spices and charred meats drew her closer.

They reached the hostess, and James held up two
fingers. The woman immediately swept them into the
restaurant, past the busy bar and to a secluded table in
a corner. Two large potted palms added to the privacy.
Perfect for a liaison.

Which this definitely wasn't. She took a deep
breath to erase the thought from her mind and scatter the growing heat on her neck and down between
her breasts. But seeing James standing by his chair in
the moody light only pushed the flush higher onto her
cheeks. He waited to sit before settling in across from
her. The hostess handed them menus and drifted away.

The shadows seemed to gather like a shell around
them. The dark wood and light adobe details of the restaurant beyond their table faded. Golden Edison bulbs
dripped small pools of light. One was close enough to
illuminate James's diligent eyes, assessing the space,
watching any person who walked by.

She distracted herself with the southwestern food
on the menu and became so engrossed that James had
to repeat what the waiter had asked. "Would you like
something to drink?"

It took a moment to come back to reality; even then,
she didn't know which one was currently in operation.
"I... Um... What're you having?"

He answered patiently, "Sparkling water."

"I'll have the same." The waiter almost left, but she held up a hand. "With lime?"

He nodded and departed. She tried to gather herself. "What else did I miss?"

James peered past her. "Couple of blokes are two pints past any good decisions. A woman with another group is taking pictures of them and posting to social media. No trouble for us."

The sounds from the bar confirmed what he said, allowing her to picture it all without turning around. "The food looks good."

He flipped through his menu. "It does. I'm still learning what all this means. My business partner's from Texas, so I've got a good instructor."

"The man with red hair." The only detail she remembered from the parking lot. Which, unbelievably, was that morning.

"Raker." He nodded.

She locked the name in her memory, along with Corporal James Sant, SAS. All the other Automatik details were meager. But James became more and more complete before her eyes. "I imagine you don't cook much with a job like yours."

He sat up straighter. "High-end automotive info-tainment?"

She winced inwardly and reminded herself not to get too comfortable in their corner of the restaurant. "Those clients must be very demanding."

"They are." He smiled at her with their secret.

It hit her in the chest, a tight ache around her heart. The sensation was almost painful, like dead nerves coming back to life. Her body wanted so much for this to be real, but she knew the intimacy was a trick of being thrown together with James in the crucible of this crazy mission. Guilt thickened through her and crushed the storm in her chest. She wouldn't allow herself to entertain any of these thoughts, even as a private thrill.

"Do you cook?" he asked, still peering at her. "Or is it only takeaway when you're working on your sculptures of gigantic bird feet?"

The waiter returned with their water and poured for them before taking their orders. After he left, she picked up on the conversation. "It's always very simple now. I used to be more…experimental." The guilt hardened to concrete as she remembered trying different recipes she'd found online with Mark when he'd been home from deployment. He was always game and never complained if they didn't turn out exactly the way they looked in the pictures.

James studied her and frowned. "I bolloxed that. I'm sorry if I…"

"I know you didn't mean to…" Neither could put words to her past.

They stewed in awkward silence until he lifted his glass of water. "Cheers, then."

"Cheers." She clinked against him and drank. The cool water and bright bubbles lifted some of her gloom.

"If you're ever in San Diego, I have friends who run a Russian/Mexican restaurant." He placed his glass down noiselessly. "I haven't been there, but I hear it's excellent."

"I'll put it on my list." For a long time after Mark's death, planning ahead had been impossible. She'd lived moment to moment, getting by. Creating the website and meeting the women on the forum had changed that. But now, with all she'd built in doubt, it was hard to look into any future.

James didn't let her sink too deep into her thoughts. "Where else is on the list?"

"I'd like to see more of California. I hear the coast up north is dramatic." She dug deeper into the quiet hopes and inspirations she'd kept hidden. "Florence. Barcelona. Marrakech."

"Been to all three." But he didn't light up with the memories.

"How was the food?" Always the best way to dive into a new culture.

"Don't remember." His long fingers scratched absently along his jaw through his beard. "I was working."

"So a client doesn't always bring their car to you." She imagined him blending in to any environment he walked into. "You go to them."

"At this level of service, I'll go just about anywhere." He smiled, but it was only on the surface. Was he hiding something, or just weary from running around the world, protecting the innocent?

"If you ever want to give up some of your frequent flyer miles, I'll take them." The bottom dropped out of her stomach with the thought of getting on a plane. Leaving El Paso in a car today had been difficult enough.

"I'm sure you'd put them to good use." His smile grew warmer. "Find inspiration for your sculptures."

"So far," she improvised, "all the giant bird feet have been white. I want to experiment with color."

"I can't wait to see your next evolution." Was that genuine warmth in his eyes as he looked at her? He was too skilled at this game of masks. She didn't want to let herself bask in the admiration, yet her pulse kicked a beat faster.

Their food arrived, making her realize just how hungry she was. James began eating, but she hesitated, the fork awkward in her hand. She switched to a different grip, but that didn't feel natural either. The normal process of feeding herself seemed very foreign. Was it the robust spices wafting up from the plate, stronger than the seasonings she used for herself? Or was it the fact that it wasn't just her at the table? James, a man, sat opposite her, outlined in amber light and dark where the shadows gathered.

"Is the food alright?" He leaned away from the table, ready to flag down the waiter.

"It looks great." She relearned how to use a fork and gathered roasted corn salad onto it. "I'm used to eating alone." She whispered it and wondered if he'd even heard.

Of course he had. Nothing got past James. He stilled. "Would you rather I left?"

"No." And she ate her forkful as proof.

"Alright." He focused back on his food. "But I might be more comfortable on my feet with a plate in my hands. Can't think of the last time I sat across from a pretty woman in a fine restaurant."

She forgot how to use the fork again. If the flattery was meant to put her at ease, it wasn't working. "I doubt that." A man with James's looks, wit and physicality wouldn't need to eat solo often.

"You'd understand if you saw my calendar." He took a drink and his hand blocked his eyes so she couldn't see if the hint of sadness in his voice was mirrored there. When his face was revealed again, he wore a neutral, unreadable expression.

"There's no Mrs. Simon?" She hadn't seen his file as he had hers, but reading him hadn't indicated any wife.

"I wouldn't want to disappoint anyone." Only a glint of the wit shined through. He was serious.

She probed deeper. "Or a standing date with the woman who runs your accounting department? Pencil skirt and a crisp blouse."

He smiled sadly. "I do my own accounting."

As did she.

They resumed eating. She tried to let the bold flavors wake her up, but they couldn't shake her out of her solitude. Her thoughts continued to churn. She couldn't just let go and enjoy the moment. The dinner was fake, a date between two fabricated people. It called into question the little connections she and James had established. All part of the act? He was much more experienced with these scenarios and could just be doing his job while she was being tossed about on a stormy sea.

There were no more distractions after their food was finished and the plates cleared. James stayed still, one hand on the table, one under it, eyes always scanning the surroundings. Any second, commandos could come swinging in the windows, and she knew he'd be ready. Exhaustion and energy tumbled through her. The day had been so long, so full of terror and confusion and anger and motion. But she had to be alert. She had no idea what was next.

"We have to get you to bed." James's voice was free of seduction, yet a wave of nervous anticipation rushed through her. The waiter arrived with dessert options, which they declined, and James requested the check.

Once they were alone again, she asked, "You sure there aren't any more surprises today?"

"One never knows." He spread out his hands. "But that doesn't mean we tighten up and wait for disaster." His credit card was ready when the check arrived so there'd be no waiting. "Good meal, good sleep, good day tomorrow."

His deep voice was almost hypnotizing. The fatigue dragged deeper into her. "It's not always that simple." Even when she kept her own life ordered and contained, the hail of emotions from the past, or worries about the future, would still arrive unexpected.

He adjusted his jacket. The weapons weren't visible, but she knew they were there. Just like the deeper secrets she saw him carrying.

Simon disappeared for a moment as James looked at her. "We know that."

The check came back, he signed off and tipped his head to ask if she was ready. Would her tired legs be able to get her walking once again? Somehow she stood and walked in a straight line out of the restaurant. James remained at her side, careful and protective. Emotions wore raw under her fatigue. She held back tears as they crossed the lobby toward the elevator. Who had stood by her like this? All of her support had been from online friends, her family in the distance. To have someone this close and ready with her revealed how long it had been.

If James saw how she was reacting, he didn't say anything. The intimacy of the dinner table disappeared in the more public space. He was back on the alert. She collected herself and took in their surroundings as well. Two of the women from the bar sat in the lobby, talking

privately on a small couch. The man behind the front
desk glanced at them, the front doors, then down at his
computer. Otherwise, all was quiet.

The wait was short at the elevator, giving her just
enough time to see how tired she looked in her reflection. James showed no signs of wear throughout their
ascent. He walked briskly down their hall and unlocked
the door for her. It closed, heavy, and it rattled her.
They were alone again.

He picked up the chair from the desk and lodged it
under the door handle. "Habit," he explained when he
saw her watching. "I don't think we're in any danger."

But for her, everything was dangerous.

"I'll take the bed closer to the door." He unclipped
a sheathed knife from his belt at the small of his back
and tossed it to the pillows. "Bathroom's yours first."

There was no sense in arguing or negotiating. She
was ready to get out of her contacts and go horizontal
for a while. She dug through her suitcase, found her
toiletries and closed herself in the bathroom. Contacts
out, glasses on. She spent as little time in the uncom-
promising lighting as possible.

Back in the room, she realized she hadn't thought
to pack anything specific to sleep in. Her usual mental lists to account for anything she might need broke
down when it came to overnights with British special
forces operatives. A T-shirt and yoga pants would have
to do. She didn't change until James took his turn in
the bathroom. Water ran, and she imagined him washing his face and hands, perfectly awake and refreshed.

By the time he emerged, she was under her covers
and sinking into the mattress. He flicked off the bathroom light and darkened the entire room. Her eyes ad-

justed and gathered what city light came through the perimeter of the curtains to see him remove his jacket and boots and lay them next to the bed. Hard plastic rasped against rigid fabric, chilling her. He'd pulled his pistol from the shoulder holster. It tapped lightly when he set it on his bedside table, like a scorpion walking across a tiled floor.

"Habit again?" she asked, keeping her voice even.

"I don't anticipate trouble." He stretched himself out on his bed, still wearing his shirt and jeans. "But I hate surprises."

"Then you know how I've felt all day." If she thought about it too much, the fight-or-flight would kick back in again, and she wouldn't get any sleep.

"It was eye-opening for me, too." He chuckled, raspy. "Get your rest."

"Shifts?" He had a gun on the table and a knife under his pillow. She had a…flashlight.

He dismissed her gently. "Not necessary." He took a long breath that ushered her further into her fatigue. "I'm a light sleeper."

"A professional," she slurred.

"That I am," he whispered.

She wasn't. He'd had an answer for every twist and turn, and she was still trying to catch up. She was so inexperienced that she'd let her unexpected attraction to him get into her bloodstream, while he remained as cool as stainless steel. Sleep continued to drag her into the mattress. Tomorrow, she'd wake up with more control over herself and the situation. He was a soldier, and she was critical to the mission. That was all. She was a fool to think of anything else. But it had been so damn long since she'd been foolish.

CHAPTER FIVE

THE NIGHT HAD passed without interruption, and James woke fully before the dawn. April continued to sleep, head on one pillow, arms clutching another. Her legs twitched periodically. Was she chasing someone or running away? He wasn't going to wake her and find out. She needed all her rest and strength. Yesterday had taken it out of her. He'd watched the weariness drag her down at the end of the night. But he gave her credit for keeping the motor running until then. She'd been mostly alert through dinner and had run with the ridiculous scenario he'd set up on the fly as their cover.

He leaned over the bed and retrieved his phone from his jacket. No new messages from Automatik. He'd hoped the cyber team was going to locate the hackers as he and April slept, giving them a strong target to follow in the morning. Instead, they were back to chasing thin leads at the CPA firm.

And he'd be back in her perceptive gaze. Through dinner, she'd drawn him out more than he'd expected. But she didn't know it was like digging at the edges of a buried landmine. Territory she shouldn't be in. He'd seen her past pain during the meal and how the isolation had dug into her. The woman deserved to be happy, chasing whatever food and sights she could collect in those countries across the globe.

He rose and took his pistol and bag of clothes into

the bathroom. A fan turned on with the light, both grating. Better than the mood lighting in the restaurant. Her face had glowed beautifully, and her dark eyes had glittered whenever she'd pierced into him. He'd been stupid enough to wish for an impossible blank slate. As if they could both start over just that moment. No pain. No past.

But he knew there was no future. Nothing could be undone. All he could do was to find the hackers, finish their hold on April and set her free. Then he'd be on to the next mission, then the next. None of them powerful enough to erase his debt. Just as the shower didn't have enough pressure to clean the blood he still felt on his skin.

He showered and changed and stepped quietly into the main room. The sun had risen, leaking light all around the curtains. April was awake and dressed, sitting on the edge of the bed with her packed bag at her feet.

"I need coffee." She raked her fingers through her hair and arranged her bangs.

He took his boots to the club chair in the corner and sat. "I'll be ready by the time you're out of the bathroom."

She shuffled in and closed the door behind her. While she brushed her teeth and did whatever else she needed in there, he got his boots on, reattached his knife to his belt and organized his other belongings. The pistol settled into its usual spot under his arm, then his jacket covered all the weapons.

April reemerged as he was calling the front desk to check out. She'd replaced her glasses with contact lenses and gazed at him with those dark eyes. His body responded with the urge to go to her, pull her against his chest and ask her if what she saw was a complete man. What if they didn't have to leave? What if they could hide in the room all day and he could learn her, show her that life didn't have to hurt all the time? And she could show him that he wasn't what his past had made him anymore.

The front desk picked up, and he checked out.

"Let's get you caffeinated." He lifted his kit and left the room. If April was tired, she didn't show it as she followed him, rolling her bag down the hallway. "You slept through the night."

"I was motivated." Her voice was raspy with morning. "You?"

"Aces." The normal noises of a hotel woke him at intervals, but nothing had him reaching for his pistol.

The hotel lobby was quiet. April grunted when she walked into the cold outside with him. If someone had been waiting for them in the parking lot, the clouds of their breath would've given them away. But the egress was trouble-free, except for the car struggling to warm up after turning over.

April cranked the heat and adjusted the vents. "We're too early for the CPA."

"Part of the rhythm of a job like this." He drove them to their target neighborhood and parked them about a block away from the offices, at a chain coffee shop on a corner. "Stalking our prey."

The morning rush was in full swing at the coffee shop. James and April waited in a long line of shuffling people, some of them dazed, conserving their minds and bodies for the workday ahead. Others were already on their phones. The most energy came from the men and women behind the counter, who coordinated like an artillery team to take the orders and get them out.

He scanned the people in line and didn't detect any firearms on them. None of their briefcases and backpacks seemed exceptionally heavy. A couple of the blue-collar workers had knives clipped in their front pockets, but nothing out of the ordinary. He noticed April watching the populace as well. She maintained a casual external attitude, but those sharp eyes of hers didn't rest, and each new person who walked into the shop was checked out. She wasn't a Green Beret like Raker, but she was more of a partner than he'd expected.

They were close enough to the front counter to hear the specifics of the transactions. He pulled a bottle of juice from a cooler and caught April staring at him with a realization that turned her mouth down.

A charge of danger sparked in him, and his muscles readied to move. He leaned close to her. "What's up?"

She spoke just loud enough for him to hear. "You know what I order, don't you?"

Lying would've only set up more distrust. She was a woman of habits and easy to learn when he was shadowing her. "Large soy vanilla latte. Three shots."

Her face remained stony. "A table just opened. I'll grab it. You order for me." She left the line and sat at a small table, her back to the wall. Her wary eyes landed on him as well during her sweep of the room. He felt her judgment. Normal people didn't secretly follow other people. But he hadn't been ordinary in a long time. Starting with the army, then the SAS. Then... after. If she could really see all the things he'd done, she wouldn't even want to be in the same room with him. Automatik didn't judge him. They'd still reached out when he'd been freelancing with Hathaway. They'd given him a chance to make right where he'd gone wrong. April was another one of those chances.

He reached the register, placed their orders, then waited at the other end of the counter with the rest of the people. Someone there could be one of the CPAs, or one of the hackers. He knew how easy it was to hide.

The hot drinks and warm food finally arrived, and he took them over to April. She stood and switched seats, letting him put his back to the wall.

"Cheers," he thanked her, while spreading out their breakfast on the table.

She'd been alert since early that morning, but became awake as she drank and ate. She tipped her head toward his hot drink. "What's your usual?"

"Green tea, two bags." He toasted her with it and drank the welcome heat.

"Not what I'd expect from a Brit." She maintained a private voice.

He finished her thought, "With Indian blood."

"If I'd been following you for a week, I'd already know your habits." She shot him a look over the lid of her coffee.

"This chai's bollocks." He looked over the thin shoes of the men in line. "And I don't drink Earl Grey like some Square Mile wanker."

"Just when I thought I'd figured you out, Simon." She'd picked up on the name he'd also given the coffee makers for their order.

"Don't try." Any truth she found besides what he'd told her wouldn't be pretty.

She quieted, but didn't shrink. The population in the

coffee shop turned over twice as they completed their meal. April appeared more cautious with him, and he was glad for it. She shouldn't trust him completely. All she needed to know was that he'd complete this mission no matter what. Anything else, anything deeper in him, wasn't going to help them.

He checked his watch. "We know they close early. Hopefully they open on time."

They cleared out of the coffee shop and back into the day. The sun had done little to warm the air, and the cold stung his lungs. Back in the car, back on the road for a block. The parking lot for the business building had more cars. None seemed out of place. He found a spot near the exit and they retraced their steps from yesterday to the second floor.

Before they reached the office door, he asked under his breath, "What do you need to see in there?"

"Their servers. From the type and size, I can see if this is the mother ship." The nerves collected in her again and serrated her breath.

"Yoga," he reminded her.

She calmed and centered herself. "Do you have a plan?"

"We're getting a divorce."

ALL THE COFFEE in the world wasn't going to get her ready for this. James opened the office door and swept in ahead of her. The only updates to the 1980s waiting room were the magazines piled on a table next to the slumping leather couch. The black laminated counter under the window to the receptionist was peeling up, and a fluorescent light buzzed overhead. The dull brass handle of the door to the offices was worn to a shine in one spot.

But the Latina receptionist appeared unaffected by her surroundings. "How can I help you?" she chirped. The woman belonged in a much finer establishment, probably in a corner office of her own.

James used his high-class accent. "We'd like to talk to an accountant about the financial repercussions that would result from a divorce." With the last word, he shot April a look. He certainly sold it. Was he venting his true feelings about having her on this mission with him?

The receptionist remained neutral. "I'll see who has some availability right now." She clicked across her keyboard.

April shouldered past James to play her part and stand up to him. "I'd prefer to see a woman accountant."

"Of course." The receptionist couldn't hold back a split-second sympathetic glance at April. "I see that Ms. Bell has an availability in about fifteen minutes."

From the way the receptionist was typing, April knew she was currently in a text chat with the accountant. Probably telling her about the shit storm that was about to walk into her office.

"Fifteen minutes?" James made a big show of checking his watch.

April rubbed her temples and asked the receptionist, "Is there a restroom I could use?"

"Outside, all the way to the left." The woman pointed with her immaculate manicure. "Here's the key." When she turned to retrieve it from a table along the side of her small alcove, April scanned further into the room and spotted where the Ethernet cables snaked along the floor and around a doorway in the main hallway of the offices. That must be where the servers were. Without even a lock guarding them. The woman came back with the key and handed it through the window.

April swanned out of the small waiting room and made a pointed glance between James and where she suspected the server room to be.

He maintained his smug, irritated expression. "Try not to spend any money on the way."

She fired back, "Try not to lose any bets on how long it'll take me."

The receptionist cleared her throat to suppress a laugh. The cold outside did little to relieve April's rising nerves. The fake argument with James still had barbs, and she didn't like interacting with anyone that way. He and she had had their differences and hurdles since meeting, but they'd never been mean with each other. From the way he talked about it, nothing was going according to plan, but he hadn't taken it out on her at any point. Not that he'd been a teddy bear either. The man hid something. Whenever she came close, his steel gates would close.

She found the bathroom she didn't really need, took advantage of a few moments of privacy, washed up and prepared herself for more of the act. When she returned, James sat on the loveseat, flipping aggressively through a tennis magazine. He didn't move his legs for her to pass on the way to finding her own magazine. She selected a heavy fashion rag and forced her way on to the small sofa. He grumbled as he had to take up less space. She used the thick spine of the magazine to edge into him further. It clunked on the pistol under his jacket. James didn't react, but she immediately looked to see if the receptionist had noticed. The other woman worked her computer, surely trying to duck the bad vibes coming from the couple in her lobby.

After a couple of minutes, the woman left her desk and walked somewhere deeper in the offices. James kept flipping through the magazine and asked, "Did you make the server?"

"Separate room." She considered diving through the reception window so she could check it out.

He nodded and kept his voice low. "Once we get in to an office, storm out."

She had to muster energy just to be herself in public; now he asked her to do more acting. But the servers were close, and if that meant getting her life out of the hands of the hackers, she'd completely reinvent herself. Fuck, she already had.

"What is it?" James didn't turn toward her, but concern thickened his voice.

"What?" Her worry rose.

"You said 'fuck,' like something's wrong." His body tensed, ready, next to her.

"I did?" Had she spoken?

"Most definitely." They were still alone in the lobby. He turned and looked into her eyes. "You alright?"

"Yeah." Her long breath vented out some nerves. "I'm doing it."

"You certainly are." His look softened. They were close on the couch. Barely more than twenty-four hours had thrown them together. He'd taken her on as a partner and treated her as such. Never disrespected her or questioned her abilities. He'd been fighting a battle for her before that, and she hadn't known. And was there something beneath that? In the silence, when he looked at her like he understood her. Did he know all of what she was? The desire she fought. The guilt. The need to find out who she was when she quieted the voices in her mind. His gaze on her revealed keen insight. He saw past the first layers she'd constructed against the world. Being this intimate with him on the couch, shoulder to shoulder, was a test of their connection. Kissing him would tell her so much.

April shattered the web of thoughts and urges that built in her and moved her focus back to her magazine when the receptionist returned to the window. James let out a long, frustrated sigh. Was it because of the broken possibility between them? Or just part of the act? Hell, she didn't know if he'd even been on the same planet as her just then. What if she'd done something idiotic like try and kiss this soldier while he was on a mission? It was her mission, too. She wouldn't ruin the chances of catching those bastard hackers.

She stood and walked off the tension in her legs, pacing across the cramped lobby. No more fantasies. She was a soldier now, too. Like her father. Like Mark. She'd seen how Mark had compartmentalized his life. There was deployment, and home. She wasn't at home anymore.

The receptionist stood from her desk. "Ms. Bell can talk to you now. But she has another client coming in for a scheduled appointment, so she only has a few minutes." A buffer the receptionist built in so the accountant wouldn't have to be trapped in an office too long with the terrible couple. "I'll let you in, right around here." The woman disappeared, then the door to the offices opened.

The hallway was equally dated. Worn carpeting. Fading desert photography on the walls. The receptionist motioned April and James to the left, away from where April thought the server room might be. They passed one closed office door. A few steps farther, and a woman in her sixties poked her head out into the hallway.

"Hello." She greeted them cautiously. "I'm Gwen Bell. I hope I can help you today." The receptionist dropped April and James off with the blonde in the rose-colored suit and retreated back to her alcove. Gwen took a step back, giving passage to James and April.

Hot tears welled in April's eyes. Part of the act. Part of her past. The heavy oak furniture in Gwen's office was the same as the bereavement counselors April had met. Just like the smell of stacks of old papers, complete lives transformed into data for easy filing. The unexpected jump through time couldn't be stopped once it started. She didn't want to visit that pain, but was already thrown back in that point of her life. Heart ripped out. Lost, without direction.

Gwen closed the heavy door behind them and clasped her hands together. "So what is it you'd like to discuss?" She motioned April and James toward the guest chairs.

Neither sat. James straightened his back and announced, "We need to discuss what happens to our money when we get divorced."

"I see." Gwen walked to her side of the desk. "Let's start with some basic information."

April let the tears flow. It was easy. Since the hack, she'd been wound tight. The fear and frustration of the last day had nearly pushed her over the edge. Now, being in this office, thrown back into the past, with James using such final words, the emotion took over.

"Son of a bitch." She spoke between quick sobs.

Gwen flinched at the language.

April continued, wiping at her eyes. "I can't. I need a minute. I need a fucking minute." She hadn't planned on swearing that much, or crying that much, but the locks had been broken and she needed the release.

James placed a hand on her arm. It seemed like it was to comfort her, which only made the emotions run higher. She couldn't take solace from him, as much as she wanted. He was just a soldier assigned to protect her. She pulled from his arm, opened the office door and hurried into the hall.

She really did want escape and fought the urge to slam out of the lobby and into the day. But real freedom meant stopping the hackers. That was when she got her life back, so she stalked up the hall toward where she hoped the servers were, crying, arms wrapped around her chest.

James and Gwen spoke quickly in the office behind her, then their voices came out into the hall. The receptionist turned in her chair to follow the activity. April was almost at the doorway she wanted.

"Wait. Wait." James spoke in more careful tones to Gwen. "Give us a minute, will you?"

April took the last few steps up the hall and looked into the computer room. A box fan sat on the floor, blowing on a rudimentary and out-of-date server setup. She tried to see what kinds of cables were leading into the two beige boxes, but James arrived and blocked the view.

Pain drew his eyebrows together as he gazed at her. More acting? He put his hands on her shoulders. "You cry and it breaks me, my little jaguar." He pulled her into an embrace, which allowed her to fully inspect the room while clutched to his chest.

She wanted to cry harder from frustration. The servers weren't right for the hackers. They were too small and there were no Ethernet cables out of place and nothing additional had been done to modify the setup.

"We can't keep doing this." James squeezed her arm and leaned slightly in the direction of the server room.

She understood his question and shook her head. "No. We can't. It isn't right."

"Can we go?" He still held her close.

She nodded, and only then really felt him against her. The lean strength of his body was solid as a rock. Even through his leather jacket, the muscles of his arms were hard and defined. Her pulse responded with quick kicks. Visceral. Carnal. They'd been close on the couch and now they were wrapped up together. Hot blood rushed up her legs and into her chest, stealing her breath.

"Dry your tears." James shifted them so he had an arm around her shoulder. "We're leaving now and we'll make this work."

She steadied her legs and walked with him back up the hall, sensing his potency next to her and trying to tamp down her body's reaction. The hard bump of his hidden weapons against her shoulder and hip helped chill her back to reality.

The receptionist and Gwen stood and watched from

opposite sides of the hallway as James and April exited into the lobby, then left the offices. April wanted to laugh and cry in release, but knew she couldn't break character yet. Still locked to James's hip, she walked down the exterior stairs to the first level, then toward the parking lot.

But James veered them off to a shaded and secluded part of the building. Had he been affected as she was by their proximity? Was this part of the act? She'd have to tell him no. She couldn't let herself go as far as even kissing him, despite her heart pounding for it.

James released his hold on her when they approached an unmarked steel door. He dropped his high-class accent. "The servers were a bust?"

The shock of hot to cold could shatter her. She cursed at herself for letting the physical fantasy take too much of her attention. She wanted to kick herself. What if she'd told him she couldn't kiss him while he was only thinking about the operation? She tried to tamp down her embarrassment and focused on what she'd learned in the offices upstairs. "Nothing out of place. The hackers must've gotten in via the internet and are just using them as a mirror site to bounce content and throw off anyone trying to follow them."

James pulled a small wallet from the front pocket of his leather jacket. "Watch my six."

She turned her back to him, catching a glimpse of lock-picking tools in his hands, before scanning the building paths and walkways for any trouble. "What are we doing?"

Metal scraped against metal, barely louder than her rushing breath. Then the door opened. James's voice echoed into the room. "Electrical panel for the building. I hope everyone's backed up their data." Heavy switches flipped, and the usual hum of city life died to absolute silence. James closed the door and gave her a quick pat on the back to get them moving again. They hurried to the car and he didn't speak again until they were rolling out of the exit. "Now the hackers can't use those servers for a bit. Might make them slip up as they scramble."

"Nice." Any opportunity to reach out and fuck with the anonymous men was welcome.

Albuquerque streets sped by. April imagined Gwen and the receptionist gawking at each other about James and April's behavior right until the lights went out. The highs and lows of the experience still slammed through her. She might cry again, but instead laughed. "Jaguar?"

"Seemed appropriate." He glanced at her with a gleam in his eye as he drove. "They're fierce loners."

Her laugh deepened with welcome release. "How do you do this, the truth and the lies, and stay sane?"

"Who said I was sane, luv?" He winked at her and returned his attention to the road. His hidden shadows flashed across his face. "One trick is to keep the truth and the lies close. That way, the false front feels real to anyone looking."

She stared at the passing city and tried to justify her impulses to bring herself closer to him as part of the mission's lies.

"You've already done it, I think," he continued. "When you were crying in the office." He chose his words carefully. "That was real, wasn't it?"

She wiped at her eyes. "I was thinking about Mark."

"I'm sorry." His voice carried real emotion. "You did well. Mission was a success."

"We didn't find them." Victory seemed very far off. Or impossible.

"That's how recon goes." His energy continued. "We're hunting leads, collecting intel." He pulled an earbud from inside his jacket and hooked himself up. "One sec." He clicked a button on the cord and listened.

His face grew grim, lip curled. The car sped faster. He changed lanes quickly to head toward a wider street. Her stomach flipped with nerves, knowing something was wrong. She held the handle above the door for a trace of stability. But they were heading toward something bad. Or trouble was about to catch up to them.

He pulled out his earbud. "Get us to the highway."

She retrieved her phone and brought up a map. "What's going on?"

"We can't go back to El Paso." He glanced at her, eyes deadly serious. "We have to get out of Albuquerque."

The map finally updated on her phone. "Right turn at the next light. That'll take us to the highway."

His gaze didn't rest on the street. She checked the rearview mirror instinctually but didn't see anything out of the ordinary there. Finally, James explained, "The two men who attacked you were released on bail this morning. An hour later, they were found dead."

CHAPTER SIX

BLOOD WAS SPILLED. Once death started, it would come again. James had to keep April alive. She rode in the passenger seat, face white, yet still navigating on the phone she held in shaking hands.

"One more block. Then the on-ramp." Her voice was small.

"I see the signs now." He wanted to floor the accelerator but couldn't risk drawing unwanted attention. "Keep an eye out for police. We don't know if the blokes in the parking lot said anything about us, or your friend from the market."

"Theresa?" She put her phone down, closed her eyes and furrowed her brow. "I don't think she'd say anything bad."

"But she saw me with you and if the police start asking her questions, she'll remember that detail and give them whatever she has to help you." The on-ramp was thankfully close and after less than a minute they were off the streets and heading east.

April continued to process. "We haven't done anything wrong, have we?"

He considered the events of the past day and a half. "The worst was breaking into the utility room and killing the power in the building, but I didn't leave a trace and they don't have any physical evidence to tie us to that."

"So if they stop us…"

"We lose time, and we show up on the hackers' radar." He drove through deep shadows where storm clouds blocked the sun. "We have to do this on our terms."

"How?" Her frustration drew color into her cheeks. "We had one lead, we followed it to a dead end and now we know these guys don't just want to rough me up, they're willing to kill."

"I won't let them touch you." Be it with bullets, knives or his hands.

She stared at him, stared into him. A struggle crossed her face, like she was searching. Finally, she said, "I don't know what to do next."

He fell back on tactics. "They made their move, showed their hand about how important this is to them. We broke their mirror. Now we lay low and see how good they are at keeping their heads." He tapped the phone on her thigh. "Find us a small motel in a small town."

She didn't hesitate and started searching. Her resilience shouldn't have surprised him anymore, but every time she bounced back from all these blows life was laying on her, he was newly amazed.

Without looking up, she asked, "Who killed them?"

"Professionals." Like he'd been.

"The next wave? The escalation?"

"Exactly. The men in the parking lot were just day labor." He catalogued his meager load out of weapons. Would it be enough? Raker had told him on the phone that the men had been taken out execution style. A single bullet each. "There are killers on the hunt now."

She watched the landscape transition from city to desert. "Too late for the safe house."

"Backtracking will only make us more visible."

A long, ragged breath didn't settle her much. "About an hour east of this mountain range is a cluster of motels where we intersect a small highway."

"Perfect." At least they wouldn't be in the car too long. "I'm still using Simon's credit card." He shifted her focus away from the deadly danger lurking out there. "We haven't picked your name."

She loosened up enough to crack a smile. "Something worthy of a giant bird foot sculptor…" Her hands came alive, tapping on her legs as she thought. "My parents had a hard time deciding on a name. I could've been Ji-eun or Elizabeth."

He recalled a detail from her file. "So they compromised and went with your birth month."

Her little sardonic laugh didn't brighten her eyes. "Of course you know my birthday." She faced him. "What's yours?"

Instinct told him to lie. Reveal nothing during an interrogation. Reveal nothing of himself to anyone who could reach inside. "Six November." The truth.

"And how did your folks settle on James?" she pressed.

"They wanted the most British name so I wouldn't catch flack for being dark." His turn to hiss sarcastically. "But somehow everyone knew I wasn't a blue blood."

"Shocking." Her look softened. "In the army?"

"Some of the blokes thought I wasn't tough because I wasn't made of Sheffield steel." He'd learned early how to defend himself and retaliate without drawing the brass's attention. "Proved them wrong. All the way to the SAS." And after that, she didn't need to know.

"Yvonne," she declared.

He stared at her too long before having to look back at the road. But she seemed so pleased. A new confidence leveled her shoulders and tipped her chin up. "Yvonne?"

Her poise strengthened. "An artist's name. The kind of woman who uses a long cigarette holder and has bookshelves in the kitchen and a bathtub in the dining room."

"I'm coming to your dinner parties."

"You have to bring bread and cheese." She considered. "And a towel."

"I can manage that." A simple dinner party held a lot of appeal. A different world. He'd heard about some of the Automatik operators meeting up and eating at Hayley and Art's restaurant in San Diego, but he'd never joined up. The people who recruited him into the organization had assured him that none of his new teammates knew about his freelance years, but he always felt they'd find out and hold him off. So he kept himself away.

"Beer or wine?" April asked, breaking him out of his thoughts.

"Beer," he answered. "But I don't drink much anymore."

"Wine." She settled in her seat and looked out at the endless desert. "But not often. Not when I'm alone."

If she wanted solitude, that was her choice. But if she didn't, if four years a widow was too long, April deserved a partner. A lover. She'd helped heal hundreds, maybe thousands of lives with her website. Someone should be helping her.

"Yeah, that can be rough business." He'd drunk alone after jobs with Hathaway. Ashamed to show his face to the world, he'd hidden in his London flat and numbed the memories until the phone rang for the next gig. Automatik had changed that. But had he changed?

April brought her attention to her phone. "About forty miles."

Though it was a chaos, the mission gave him clear directives to focus on. "We'll secure our location first, then take care of food. Work for you?"

"Sure." Though she seemed uncertain.

"Caffeine wearing off?"

"I'm burning through every reserve in my body." She held up her trembling hand. She made a fist and released it, somewhat stilling the motion. "I don't know how you do this without digesting all your muscles."

"As a soldier, you learn how to rest while staying alert." How much had her husband told her about the life? "Which parts of the mind and body you can shut down, and keep the others fired up. You get used to it, but you can't sustain it forever."

She watched the scenery out the side window, hiding her face. "Mark always had to decompress when he came home for leave."

"It's a big transition."

Her gaze came back around to him. "But for you, it's everywhere?"

Those two years of freelance with Hathaway, there wasn't a night he hadn't slept with a gun in his hand, whether or not he was on the clock. He was a bad man in a world of bad men. It was business. Other people's lives. His own life. Commerce. "I was having a pretty good holiday in El Paso until you got jumped in the parking lot."

She darkened. "Now they're dead, and we're running."

He held up a finger to correct her. "We're establishing a new base of operations from which to strike when we have the opportunity."

"Good spin," she conceded.

He clipped out like an old-fashioned officer, "Stay downwind. High morale. Keep the buggers in your sights."

Her laugh lightened the atmosphere. They drove out of the sun and under rain clouds that washed the desert dust from the car. Fat drops of water splashed like a brawl. For a few minutes, the world was closed off beyond the wall of weather. Just James and April in their small bubble of safety. High winds battered the car and sped the clouds on. Crisp sunlight broke back onto the landscape and glittered off the remnants of the rain on the hard earth.

He could spin their circumstances all he wanted, but the reality was deadly. A new enemy stalked the field, willing to kill. He knew how that worked. Part of the money up front, the rest when the job was completed. If he and April and Automatik could find and dismantle the hackers, then there'd be no payment on completion for the hitters. The contract would be called off. It was a race to see who could find whom first.

"You're going over eighty." April stared at the speedometer.

He eased off the throttle. A cluster of buildings appeared in the flat distance. They were getting closer, but the tension that spread up his back wouldn't be relieved until he and April were dug into a good, defensible position.

She swiped through her phone and stared down the highway. "There's a row of motels on a frontage road. Take the first exit."

"Roger that." Closer to habitation meant that there might be police about, and he had to remind himself not to drive too fast to their destination.

It seemed like they were on an endless scroll of desert landscape, but James was able to mark progress by the town ahead getting larger. No other cars exited with them, they weren't being followed. April directed them to the second motel on the row, with better reviews and free Wi-Fi.

The two-story affair was well kept but not luxurious. He parked and noted that he could watch the lot from the front office, and she agreed to wait in the car. A brisk wind rippled the insanely blue water of the small pool. Way too cold for anyone to take a dip. He checked in as Simon at the office and shared a knowing smile with Rohit, the desi man who ran the motel.

April pulled their kit from the car as he returned, then the two of them proceeded to the second-floor room. It smelled of industrial cleaner and aging particleboard furniture. James closed them in, locked the door and wedged a chair under the handle. He closed the curtains after noting the window's view of the exterior catwalk, parking lot below, town streets and highway beyond them. A good vantage for covering approaches.

"There's another window in the bathroom." April stood on the other side of the queen-sized bed that nearly took up the entire room. She switched places with him when he walked to the bathroom, both of them brushing against each other at the foot of the bed.

He tried to ignore the close contact, but his body soaked in the brush of her shoulder against his chest. It should just be business. She was holding up her end as partner and assessing their location. The touch made his breath hitch. She trusted him.

But she wouldn't if she knew him.

The bathroom window was high in the shower/tub surround. He had to stand on the edge of the tub to see anything other than sky and power lines. The limited view revealed the second floor of the next motel in the row.

"Anything?" April set her laptop up on the small table by the front door.

"If someone's going to stake us out, it would be from there." He stepped out of the bathroom and closed the door. "We keep this shut and maintain light discipline so they can't clock us."

"Okay." Her hands hovered over the keys on her computer. "I'm going to grab their Wi-Fi, but I'm in clean mode. Anonymous." She looked at him, waiting.

He gave her a thumbs-up. "You know what you're doing."

She typed like a distant machine gun. "No personal information anywhere in this partition. I can't be traced or touched."

"Stealth." Could she find and erase any mentions of his past? "Perfect for surfing porn." He said it before thinking and wished he could suck all the air out of the room so she never heard it.

Her typing stopped. She didn't move and didn't look at him.

He'd crossed a very personal bridge and felt it crumbing beneath him. More talk didn't help. "Not that there's a problem with that, right? We're all…" His voice dried as he wondered what particular erotic content got her off. He kicked himself. It was damn rude to pry like that.

She nervously cleared her throat, and he laughed, embarrassed. Neither made eye contact. He busied himself with rearranging his clothes and kit. She returned to typing on her computer.

Once he had nothing left to do, he broke the awkward silence. "Lunch from the vending machine?"

"Sounds fine." She looked everywhere but at him.

Aces. He left the room and walked down the catwalk, wondering what kind of porn she now imagined was his particular kink. He shouldn't be embarrassed. It was natural. And it wasn't like he had a steady fling set up with anyone. The time between brief hookups was long, and he took care of himself when he could. Did she?

There he went again, thinking into territory he didn't belong. Another man, with a cleaner record, belonged in that intimate space. If she wanted one. He'd known too many people who'd lost someone to the recent conflicts. Some of them never sought out another.

He collected candy bars, trail mix and other snacks from the vending machines, along with enough drinks for the rest of the day and into the night. Rohit watched from his lobby office, a small smile on his face. James acknowledged him with a smirk of his own and a tip of the head. But when he returned to the room, it wasn't for a liaison.

"The CPA firm is back online." April worked her computer. James distributed the food across the available space on the table. She drank water and munched on thin pretzels. "I got in as an admin to see if I can root around their emails for something."

"How'd you manage that?" He took off his jacket and stretched his arms and back.

She watched for a moment before her gaze locked on the computer again. "I phished an email to Gwen, telling her to reset her password. When she did, I copied it."

"Bloody hell, Yvonne. I'm glad you're on my side." He adjusted his shoulder holster to let his skin breathe.

"Just don't cross me." She smiled. The wicked gleam in her eye sent a charge through him. It was the freest he'd seen her. That glimpse of quick inhibition revealed so much more life beneath her usual reserve.

"Wouldn't dream of it." But he was tempted to tease out more of that sharp spark he'd just witnessed. *Not today. Not ever.* He ate trail mix and paced the small floor plan of the room while memorizing the layout. After two laps, he did it with his eyes closed. "I'm sorry the accommodations aren't as posh as yesterday." They still hadn't discussed the issue of the bed.

She typed, focused on the screen. "I always knew Simon was a little sleazy." Her demeanor changed at the computer. Confidence high. And more free with that smile.

He took a seat on the edge of the bed near her to watch her hands on the keyboard and the flow of information he didn't understand on the screen. "You're in the groove."

She nodded and used the trackpad to select a body of text. "This is what saved me." Fleet fingers manipulated the content. "I already knew some web design from community college classes. I'd taken them while Mark was deployed and I was thinking about stepping up from my admin job at an orthopedics office. When Mark…" She trailed off, and her activity on the computer stopped. A stab of pain lanced through James's chest. She hurt and she didn't deserve to. Would human contact from him help, or was that solace for someone else to give?

He reached forward and placed his hand on her shoulder. She exhaled, long and slow. His body calmed, too, with the connection. She turned and looked at him with a thank-you in her sad eyes. His hand fell from her.

Her voice started rough. "I couldn't work anymore." She stared at the computer, but her hands still didn't move. "My family was there for me. Friends. But there was only so much they could do." She took another breath. "I had to dig myself out." Her fingers hit the keyboard again. "So I dove in. I studied more code. I found online private support groups for widows, but nothing really focused on what I needed, so I made my website. When I added the funding aspect, I got into encryption to protect it. Books, classes, I used resources available to learn." She struck a couple of keys and sat back to gaze at the laptop screen. "The site grew into what it is."

"And what saved you helped a lot of other people." He'd seen war and death, up close and in his hands.

Countless soldiers and combatants. He'd trained and fought and survived. And he was in awe of her strength.

"Until the hack." Emotion roughened her voice again.

"We'll stop them." If only those bastards were on the other side of a door he could kick down. "We'll get all of this back for you."

"Maybe in Phoenix." She pointed at her screen.

"Arizona?" A vague map popped into his head. He followed her finger to a street address written among lines and lines of computer code.

"I picked up this IP address from an email to the CPA firm." She grinned. "I think they'd phished her just like I had. That's how they got in." Her fingers flew over the computer. A new browser tab appeared with a bird's-eye view of a city map. A red marker indicated the address.

His hope for a quick strike solution sank. "A high school."

"They'll definitely have the kinds of servers necessary for the hack." She zoomed closer to the image of the buildings, and he immediately started to plot the best angles for attack and which exits would need to be blocked to bottleneck a fleeing enemy.

"Or it could be another mirror." Assaulting a high school, even if the bad guys were somewhere inside, was out of the question.

"Could be." Her enthusiasm waned. "But it's a lead."

"Absolutely. We'll track it to the bitter end." He had to ask but didn't want to entertain the idea. "Could we be dealing with high school students?"

"I guess." She closed her eyes and rested her head in her hands, as if doing deep calculations. "They'd have to be pretty sophisticated, but if someone's had a computer in their hands their whole life, it could happen."

"But is a kid sophisticated enough to know how to hire a hitter?" Whoever had made that call had gone too far. And would pay.

She looked up at him, the fear again in her eyes. People were dead.

He tapped her computer to focus her on what she could control. "Can you phish your way into this server?"

She switched back to the tab full of code. "I can try, but I feel like it's a more savvy environment." Pieces of text were highlighted as she typed, and a new window with an email appeared.

He returned to sit on the edge of the bed. "Even if you can't get in, we'll go there." He pulled out his phone and brought up the Automatik communication app. "Tomorrow. We can't string ourselves out, knowing the hunters are in the field."

Her pace slowed again.

He tried to bring her back. "I've dealt with this kind of thing before." From both sides of the gun. "You're going to be okay," he vowed.

Her gaze locked on his. She'd steadied herself. "Thank you."

He almost replied, "Just doing my job," but it didn't feel like a job anymore. "You deserve better than all this."

"But life doesn't work like that." It wasn't self-pity. The woman had lived through so much.

"I already told you I invented yoga. Karma was my idea, too." He smiled and got a small one back from her. "It's going to be good things for you. And bad things for them."

"You're the expert." She returned to her work on the computer. "I'll have to take your word for it."

"Do that." He entered all the new details for Automatik, including the Phoenix address to be tracked down. A confirmation came quickly, along with any updated intel from their end.

She hit a key and sat back from the computer, finished. "It's away. We'll see if the assistant dean of students takes the bait."

He completed his communication with Automatik and tossed his phone on the bed. "Still no information on the hitters."

"How does that work?" She turned her chair away from the table and faced him. The curtains glowed behind her, dropping her face to shadows. "How do you hire a contract killer?"

"You used to do it through an intermediary, or pay phones or face to face. Internet made things much easier." The door had been opened to his past. He didn't know far he'd descend. "A lot of the communication happens in chat rooms. It looks like everyone's talking about television cartoon shows, or the latest coupon deals, but there are hookups connecting. Deals being made."

He couldn't see her expression. His was in full light. Did she see into him, his memories? The rush he'd gotten when a new job came in. Planning all the angles. Traveling light and fast. Feeding off the danger, even better when no one else knew what was happening around them. Hathaway distributing the cash.

"But they couldn't put all the details out there. Even

in a private chat, someone could find it." She was processing what he told her and attacking the angles.

"Disposable email addresses," he explained. "Burner
phones." He'd dropped cell phones into the Seine, the
Danube, the Thames. Part of him had sunk with them
and would remain cold under the water forever.

"It's that easy," she mused.

"It's too easy." Strung-out junkies were easy to find
and hire for an intimidation gig. But whoever had killed
those men were professional enough to erase their trail.
He stood and retrieved his water from the table. It felt
better to have his face away from the light.

"So how much do I cost?" She grew angry. "How
much are they getting paid?"

He calculated the job: travel, the two locals who
had to be eliminated, a target on the run. His hands
twitched, and he wished it was something stronger than
water in the bottle. "Fifty thousand dollars, minimum."

"Fuck." She stood and moved away from the window. The shadows scattered from her, revealing fear
and anger in her eyes. Her look hardened when she
stared at him. Had all these details helped her piece
together his past? "How much are you getting paid?"

Money wasn't going to save him anymore. "A living wage. Nothing extravagant."

"Automatik can't compete with those kinds of
prices?" She remained wary.

"Whatever extra money we come by gets donated."
His last operation had been a rush job into a town of
hostiles in Illinois that had resulted in a high school
getting a few anonymous contributions.

"No chance of you getting tempted by a bigger paycheck?" Her posture tightened.

That enticement had turned rotten years ago. "No chance." He realized he was between her and the front door and stepped back to the other side of the bed. If she wanted to leave, she could.

"I guess I haven't said it enough." She moved toward him. "Thank you." She stopped. The intimacy grew too much at eight feet away. But she still trusted him enough to stay in the same room with him.

CHAPTER SEVEN

SHE FELL DEEPER into the blood-black world that had arrived with the hack. The attack in the parking lot yesterday had set her on an entirely new course. God, one day. Only a handful of hours had sent her into a completely new orbit. James was her guide. Even with the sunlight that came in through the motel curtains, he had a way of finding the deepest shadows. Talking about the contract killers had illuminated how terrifying her situation was, but it didn't shine any light on James. He'd informed her of the details and remained opaque, unreadable.

His defenses had seemed to rise when she'd thanked him and approached. Her own voices warned her not to get closer. She and James had grown close enough by necessity. Thrown together on the chase and on the run. Entangling further would only complicate the situation.

"You're welcome," he answered, voice hollow.

"You don't want me to thank you?" He wasn't doing it for the money, or her gratitude. He didn't come off as a thrill seeker. So why was he helping her?

"It means…" The light caught his eyes, reflecting the emotion there. "Everything to me."

But there was still a piece missing. Like anything she could say wouldn't be enough. Not that he expected physical compensation. He'd been much too respectful of her space for that.

"I can't say enough for what you've done for me."
Maybe that truth would give him what he was looking for.

He shifted his weight, restless. "I haven't done
enough." His hands flexed into fists, then stretched
out again.

She wanted to reach out to him but didn't know
if she could do anything to calm him. Her own nervous energy might amp both of them up. That would
be too much for the cramped motel room to contain.
She struggled with jolts of the flight instinct in her
legs throughout the day and kept reminding herself
to breathe.

"What's left today?" she asked, trying to soothe
with her voice.

He tilted his head back and forth, loosening his
neck. "Nothing but waiting." His body slowed. An
easy sway took over his shoulders and hips, as if he
was dancing for a moment. He smiled and his restless-
ness waned. Her nerves rose as he approached. What
did he intend? The charge between them thickened.
The flashes in her body grew hotter and collected low
in her belly.

The electricity flickered in his eyes for a moment,
then he blinked it away before veering around her and
sitting on the bed. He piled pillows against the head-
board and stretched out. After adjusting the knife on
his belt and gun in his shoulder holster for comfort,
he sighed with an attempt at relaxation. He gestured
toward the front of the room. "I always sleep between
you and the door."

It was a queen bed. The other side was hers. The
heat that had diffused to warm comfort at the thought

of his protectiveness turned back to a white-hot sear. "I couldn't sleep right now."

"Me neither." He settled into the mattress, highlighting how long his body was and how he rumpled the sheets and blanket. "Just recharging the batteries."

"Cool." She sat back at the computer. "I'll try to keep it down."

"You can throw the telly on if you want." He took the remote from the bedside table and held it to her.

The man was a vision in temptation. Reclining on the bed. Reaching out. If she took his hand, followed him there, how far would that take them? Nowhere. She doused the fantasy with the cold reality of the situation. She shuddered as a wave of guilt threatened to drag her under.

"I'll find something for us." He drew the remote back. Had he seen the turmoil she'd just lived through? "But I can't guarantee it won't be a documentary about an old man making guitars." The TV clicked on, too loud, and he immediately lowered the volume.

"Luthier." She regained her footing.

"What's that?"

"A guitar maker is called a luthier."

"Brilliant." He smiled. "Let's see if we can find one." She settled into the familiar stream of content from the television as he changed channels. For moments, her interest would be completely captured by whatever was on the screen, then she'd snap back to realizing just where she was and who she was with. The danger hadn't gone away, but James's easy demeanor helped normalize it.

The tension rose to her throat and threatened to

squeeze her breath. She stood and paced to the other side of the bed. James watched her instead of the TV.

"I don't want to get used to this." She shook out her hands and her body continued to tighten.

He reassured, "It's not always going to be like this."

"Is it for you?" She was missing the release of her morning run.

He spoke calmly. "You're doing excellent. Holding up your side of the op. Letting yourself idle for a few minutes doesn't mean you've transformed into a stone-cold war machine."

That wasn't how she'd describe him. Or her father or Mark. She was learning what the soldiers knew. "I'm just pissed they did this to me." Her life and routine had been demolished without a thought.

"You'll get them back." The steel returned to his voice. "You've got some bad motherfuckers on your side of this fight. SAS, Green Beret, SEALs. A woman I know who's like a surgeon with a sniper rifle. We're not going to quit."

"I'm not trained like that." All those names he listed were indestructible. Her skin felt very fragile.

He sat up and waved his hand at her laptop. "But you're better equipped than any of us to handle the computer side. You said you needed to be in on this and you were right." But had she talked her way into something she couldn't handle? He continued, "Have you set the email up to alert you if it comes in?"

"Yeah." She nodded. "It'll be loud."

"Then you're behaving like an operator, covering your angles." He sat back onto the bed and tapped a pillow on her side. "Now the best thing to do is get your chill on so you have the energy to kick those bastards' asses as soon as they fuck up." His accent roughened as he swore. His commitment felt like more than just an assignment and vibrated into her chest.

She went to her computer and double-checked the refresh rate and notification for the email before returning to her side of the bed. His body remained neutral as she climbed on. He resumed flicking through the channels and she settled in.

He chuckled. "Now there's something I'd like to drive." The television showed a huge construction truck with tires at least twenty feet tall. "No worries about traffic."

"You want to parallel park that?" The video showed the machine hauling tons of rocks from a gigantic quarry.

"Who needs to park when you can remake the map?" A commercial came on, forcing James to change the channel a few times, finally landing on a home renovation show. "Let's see what these wankers are up to."

"I've seen this show before. They do okay stuff." The designer was walking a couple through their house, discussing the remodel in progress.

"Blind spot." James pointed at the TV with his discovery. "Right at the front door. They're putting a wall in that you can't see around when you enter the room."

"Maybe a mirror in the room to reveal that spot?" The show had moved on, but she tried to imagine the layout of the entry.

"Aces." He extended a fist out to her, and she bumped it with her knuckles.

Onscreen, the couple inspected their half-completed bathroom. "I tiled a shower once."

"Tile?" He blew out an impressed breath. "That's some patience."

"I needed the task."

James stilled, understanding.

She picked up her momentum. "I was delving deeper into coding and encryption. My body was locking up at the computer. Then the plumbing gave out in the shower. They had to break everything up to fix it." Her shoulders tightened with the memory of the intrusion. "It wasn't the best time for me to have people in my space. I couldn't do the plumbing or the walls, but I figured I could learn the tiles."

"How'd it turn out?"

"I'm sure I made rookie mistakes, but everything worked. Little flaws didn't matter." The defined order of steps and the defined grid of tiles and spacers had given her just the structure she'd needed. "I did it."

"That's sweet work. Real craftsman stuff." He rubbed his hands together, as if dusting them off. "Never did tile work." He stared at the TV as he continued, "I was slinging plasterboard after secondary school. Joined the army for the pay and travel."

His life picture became clearer in her mind. "But the SAS isn't just about a paycheck." Special Air Service was so legendary among elite units that they'd even made an impression on her. Mark had talked about their origins in counter-terrorism and their revered status in the armed forces.

James turned and stared at her. The bed felt too small. "At first I did it for the action. Then I learned I liked helping people." His eyes collected shadows. "Then I burned out from running too hot."

How deep were his shadows? They weren't always

there. "Now you're helping people again." She under-stood the struggle to lift herself out. She understood a piece of him. He knew her as well, more than just the file he'd read.

The world reduced to the space between them. A few feet. A pull toward him. A distance she couldn't cross.

He straightened his posture and turned away from her. "That I am."

The world grew again, large enough to contain the hackers, the hired killers and Mark's memory. James must've felt the connection that had grown, but hadn't challenged her space. The one person who'd learned her was the one she couldn't let too near.

They resumed watching the TV without comment. Shows came and went. News and sports fled by. None of it mattered. None of it could help their operation. His phone remained silent, without new intel. Her computer didn't alert any new emails. She tried to allow herself to rest and prepare for the next step.

But there was so much unknown. Including herself.

She got up from the bed. The rest must've helped, because her legs felt more lively as she crossed the room to her computer. A swipe across the trackpad eliminated the screen saver and revealed the email.

James killed the TV and tossed the remote on the bed. "All these bloody channels and no luthier." He swung his long legs over the side of the bed and leaned to look over her shoulder. "No bites?"

"Nothing." She almost slammed the laptop shut in frustration. "Afraid I'm not holding up my end."

"Don't think like that. We all do our part." He scooted closer. "You got us the CPAs, you got us this link."

"I wish I could just reach through the screen and punch someone until they told us what we need." She made a fist and remembered that she'd almost needed it against the man in the parking lot. She'd nearly used it on James.

"You find them." He tapped his finger on the table. "I'll punch them."

She immersed herself back in the familiar territory of her computer and the internet. As James watched, she mapped the Phoenix address within the city, then she tracked the best route from their location. "Should be about seven hours."

He groaned and massaged around his knees. "Aces."

"Can't you just call in a helicopter?" she joked.

"Ferretti doesn't dust us off unless it's a tactical situation." He lay back on the bed, hands behind his head, eyes closed.

"Seriously?" How could a tactical team operate within the U.S. without anyone knowing?

"We're stealthy and quick." As if he knew what she was thinking.

"And scary." He'd been invisible when he was following her and had appeared out of nowhere when trouble had erupted.

He smiled without opening his eyes. "That, too."

And she was glad he was on her side.

"Forty, seventeen, ten," James murmured. Some kind of code? "Hollister exit. Eighteenth street to Willow. High school on the southwest corner." He'd barely glanced at the map and had memorized every move they needed to make.

"It's like they grew you in a lab."

He laughed. "My pops takes credit for my memory. He was a tailor, remembered all the measurements."

But if James had been created in a government lab, he wouldn't reveal such human details. And he wouldn't draw her deeper self out, despite her trying to rein in the connection that grew stronger.

She looked back at the computer and all the territory they had to cover. Maybe the hackers were in Phoenix. That server she wanted could be anywhere. How far would she have to go to get her life back? Somewhere out there were the hired killers. James was her best chance at staying alive. But the two of them in the motel room was starting to feel perilous for entirely different reasons.

THEY DIDN'T SHARE the bed. After the handful of hours they'd spent watching TV, only one of them was on the mattress at a time. April kept feeling the draw toward James whenever she moved too closely. Too much silence. Too much waiting. She turned into a raw nerve that sizzled with awareness, sensitive to every shift in the air pressure between them.

James was in the chair by the computer and she sat on the bed, trying to stretch some of the tension from her neck. The late sun pushed against the curtains, rimming them with orange. Then it disappeared and the room was dark.

"Light?" James asked, hand on the lamp on his side of the bed.

"Sure." She looked away so her eyes weren't shocked. "News?"

The light cast up his face, making him look more like a demon than a rescuer. "Nothing new." He stepped away and back into the shadows she knew him for. "Automatik's working on the hitters and the IP info you captured, but no leads beyond what we already have."

"Why are they called Automatic?" And was it safe for them to remain unchecked?

"With a 'k,'" he added. Then he shrugged. "Don't know. They named it before I got there. But it makes sense. We all work together. Coordinated. No wasted movement."

The answer illuminated little, except that he didn't divulge much. "And you trust everyone there?"

"If they trust me, I trust them." Something deeper echoed in him, but she couldn't get any closer to find out.

"Dinner?" She stood from the bed and approached the snacks spread across the table. The rumpled bags didn't appeal. Hot food would've been welcome, but she understood the necessity of their situation.

James pulled his jacket on over his weapons. "Another trip to the vending machine for more variety."

"Can I come?" She couldn't calculate how long she'd been in the room.

"Of course." He moved the chair away from the front door. "I know the maître d'."

The door opened with a blast of icy air. She took her coat from the top of the dresser and hurried it on, but it was too late and the cold was trapped around her skin. At least the stagnant fatigue from being cooped up in the room was gone.

The two of them went briskly up the catwalk to the vending machines. She hopped from foot to foot, happy to have blood flowing and waiting for it to warm her.

James remained stoic, only squinting in the chill wind as he surveyed the area.

"Are we good?" She kept her words quiet through the collar of her coat.

"We're invisible." He turned his attention to the first vending machine.

"Chocolate-covered pretzels." She pointed to her choices. "Peanut butter cookies. Corn nuts and dark chocolate."

"Excellent selections, mademoiselle." He fed the machine cash and punched the buttons for her food as well as more options. "What the blazes is a corn nut?"

"I hope you have strong teeth."

"Enticing." He stepped to the next machine. "And for the lady's drink selection?"

"Water." Her body was completely off balance.

He nodded enthusiastically and bought four bottles. The two of them hurried back to the room and closed the door against the razor-sharp desert cold. They took off their jackets and reassembled themselves to eat, him at the table and her on the bed.

She flipped through the TV until they landed on yet another home makeover show they could complain about. The night settled in. The danger continued, somewhere on the other side of the heavy door. The romance in bad television and junk food warmed her too much, made her feel like she laughed too loud at times and stared too long at James when he wasn't looking. He questioned the validity of corn nuts, she put up a mock defense and the two of them were all too comfortable.

She dropped the volume on the TV as the night deepened. The light conversation was murmured across

the room. Her body needed a continuation of the growing intimacy. His weight on the bed would draw her
toward him. His chest on her back would slow her
breathing, and his arms around her would give her a
moment of security.

She got up from the bed and used the bathroom,
splashed water on her face. When she returned, he was
standing by the bedside lamp.

"Can you take first watch? Three hours is all I
need." He didn't seem tired at all.

"Of course." She was careful not to brush against
him as they switched places in the room. He came and
went from the bathroom, then settled onto the bed, still
fully armed.

He turned out the light, leaving her with only the
glow of her laptop. She'd learned more of James and
wished she hadn't. She tempted herself with additional
information, searching the internet for his name and
Automatik. He had a file on her; what did she have?
Personal details, fragments that revealed him. His
caring and determination. His shadows. The internet
didn't return any answers. The lack of information revealed more than any hard facts could. He and his organization were a deep secret.

This was how she'd saved herself. In the dark, with
the computer. But it was all different now. Outsiders
threatened her. For the first time since Mark's death,
she sat in a room with a sleeping man. A man who
trusted her. But she didn't trust herself. She didn't
know herself anymore.

CHAPTER EIGHT

HE'D BEEN AWAKE for hours, showered, packed their kit all into her carry-on bag, secured his weapons and checked himself and April out of the motel, and still he heard her smoky voice as she'd wakened him for his shift of the watch.

"James." She'd repeated, "James." It continued to echo. She'd been a lithe ghost in the ashen light of the motel room. Her hand had been real on his shoulder, gently pressing until he was awake.

He'd almost put his hand on hers, pulled her closer. But that would've just been selfish. What she really needed from him was his tactical abilities and a swift resolution to the operation. They'd switched places, her on the bed and him at the table, and that was how he'd spent the small hours of the night and into the morning.

They now sat in a diner staring at glossy menus filled with overstuffed foods. He'd eaten in this chain before and hoped the breakfast would at least be consistent, if not good. April shook her head, unsure of anything except the coffee she ordered immediately after sitting down. Her hair remained damp from her shower. He could smell the motel's shampoo and remembered how he'd busied himself looking out the edge of the drawn curtains rather than watch her finish getting dressed and prepare for the day.

"At least it's hot food." He settled on the simplest-looking combination and folded his laminated menu.

"I think we'd tried everything out of the vending machine." Her wry smile flickered off quickly. He knew she'd slept, but the day hiding out in the room and plotting their next move had taken a toll on her. She blinked weary eyes at the menu. An outsider might've thought she was tired from a motel tryst. Making love and raiding the junk food.

James had almost seduced himself in the process yesterday. Nearly believing the intimacy that had grown from the time spent together had skewed him. He'd wanted to take her hand when she'd woken him. He now wanted to lean close to her neck, breathe her in and feel as clean as she smelled.

"Hopefully we're past that necessity." They didn't have a clear idea what would happen at the Phoenix target, but it might get them a step closer to the hackers.

She spoke privately across the table. "Not that I approve of the circumstances, but it's good to get out of my comfort zone."

"As long as we don't push you too far." He glanced at the door and the diners around them. None of the people were targeting, or tracking James and April's activity. The hunters weren't in this room full of travelers.

She picked up on his caution and did her own scan of the population within her field of vision. When she was done, she gave James a little head shake to indicate she didn't sense trouble. He knew she didn't know all the signs to identify, but trusted her instinct for self-preservation.

The waitress came by with coffee, took their order, then left them alone to doctor their drinks. He paid more attention to the ominous clouds hulking in the sky than he did to whatever was in his mug.

"Is that weather going to be trouble?" He'd spent some of the night studying maps online to familiarize himself with the territory, but he'd never have the sense of a local.

She drank coffee then craned her neck to look out the windows. "Looks bad. Definitely rain."

"Can we make it through?" The coming storm seemed so extensive that there'd be no way to skirt around it without traveling to a different continent.

She shrugged. "It'll test us. You got all-wheel drive?"

"Affirmative." One of the necessities of the clean car. He mentally prepared himself for not only driving half a day, but battling the weather throughout.

"The coffee's actually not that bad." She smiled over the rim of her cup and continued to drink. With each sip, she woke up further. He'd hoped the light of day would blaze away the veiled intimacy that had been drifting between them. But the familiarity continued, and he found himself noting how she took her coffee when it wasn't her standard latte.

"Don't jinx the food."

"I'm sure the cook's doing that right now." She took out her phone and fiddled with it a moment before putting it down on the table. "Still nothing." She'd set up a relay to notify her if anything came through her anonymous phishing attempt.

For all the technology at play, this mission was still going to come down to knocking on doors or kicking down doors.

Breakfast arrived, and they both ate hungrily. They

exchanged conversation about the middling quality of the fare between bites. He explained that they needed fuel for the car after fueling themselves, then the road beckoned.

She was game, with more fire for the chase than fear in her eyes. He knew he needed to conserve his energy for the road ahead, but still his pulse moved faster. Ready. And excited by being on the hunt with April.

"THESE STORMS ARE TROUBLE." April tracked a radar map on her phone as the muted desert sped by. "They're rolling out of the west, right at us."

James drove with the same pace, just on the edge of reckless, determination on his face. "No choice but to go through." They'd already been slowed down by traffic and highway construction through Albuquerque.

Rocky hills rose up to meet the low clouds. Occasional dirt roads jutted into the wastelands, but there were no signs of human life out there. There were barely any other cars on the highway. Everyone else was smart enough to stay away. And that made her what?

On a mission. Way off the map. With a man she barely knew and knew too much.

He tugged an earbud out of his jacket and put it in before clicking the mic on the cord. "Go for James."

Her breath struggled through a tense chest. He wasn't sighing with relief or smiling, so they weren't contacting him with good news. She mouthed, *Bad?* and he held up a hand to pause her.

He murmured into the mic, "Understood," and glanced at her.

Frustration burned. She balled a fist.

James finally clicked off his call and looked at her hand. "You going to use that on me?"

"I hate not knowing."

"I understand." He fought a dry smile.

"So what the fuck is it?" If the man wasn't as hard as oak, she'd consider punching him in the shoulder so he knew she meant business.

"*Someone* was prying into Automatik last night." The smile faded. He kept his eyes on the road. "Deep, anonymous, internet searches. You wouldn't know anything about that, would you?"

Her breath loosened but turned hot with embarrassment. "I couldn't turn anything up. Not even a rumor."

"Our enemies don't know our name." He looked to her, gaze softer. "Our friends don't use our name out in the open."

"I would never..."

"I know."

"I was just looking for some context." At times, the whole situation still felt like an elaborate fiction she'd been dropped into. "I'm out here with you..." Her mouth went dry as she remembered her other searches from last night.

He knew. "Did you find anything on me?" Even though he'd caught her, he seemed cautious.

"Not a trace." It was unnatural. "Not a scrap of internet DNA."

He appeared to breathe easier. "I told you, we're invisible."

"No military record or property ownership or car registration." She'd tried all the avenues she'd known. "It's like you don't exist at all."

"I started existing the day you nearly punched your keys through me in that alley."

She couldn't hold back a laugh as she saw all the experience he carried behind his eyes. "I doubt that."

He didn't laugh. "Let's just agree that eras in my record aren't fit for public viewing." A wince of what looked like pain creased his brow. His mouth tightened, as if holding back more he wanted to say.

Could she draw it out of him? "You know me well enough to understand I don't agree to anything easily."

"That I do." But he made no change to indicate he was about to open up.

"You can't blame me for looking." Asking him directly wouldn't work.

"I'm glad you did." He loosened up enough to glance at her. "It's not smart to trust me without question."

"But I still don't have enough information." What she did know continued to move her closer to him.

"Then you shouldn't completely trust me." He shut down again. "Just know I'll carry this mission on until the end."

"Alright." Pushing too hard would only raise his defenses. She'd seen how expertly he could fight. "I learned from my forum, as we talked, we healed."

He carried a burden alone. Thick anger, like a blood clot, deepened his voice. "You, the others, deserve to heal."

Sadness tore into her chest. She wanted to reach out to him. "You don't?" But he was so far away.

"Find us some music, will you?" He stared straight ahead, down the highway, into the coming storm.

She turned on the radio and spun through the stations. Whatever James locked up, it was behind his iron will. Rain splashed against the windshield, pounded on the hood and roof. She chilled, wondering how terrible that part of his past was to be so hidden.

He plowed them further into the weather. Wind shouldered into the sides of the car and took them to the side of the lane before James forced the path back to the middle. She skipped through stations full of static and settled on pop music. Neither of them paid much attention. The storm was louder. James's silence rang in her ears.

Her phone buzzed with an alert. She felt James's attention on her as she checked the notification. "It's an email," she announced, disappointed. "Nothing from my phishing."

"Brilliant." Both his hands remained tight on the steering wheel as the storm grew stronger around the car.

Her letdown at the false alarm burned away in a rush of acid through her stomach. The subject of the email was *Albuquerque*. "Oh, fuck." She opened the message.

James tore his attention from the road to look at her. "What is it? What?"

"It's from the hackers." She felt the attack in the parking lot again, as if the man was pressing against her and she couldn't escape.

"Bloody hell." He showed his teeth in anger.

She fought a shaky voice and read, "Albuquerque was cute, but you can't cut our power. You should've stayed home. Whoever is helping you will hurt you. We can touch you whenever we want. Stop now and you will live."

He ground out, "Bastards."

"There's no signature. The sender address is just a

jumble." She dug into the email's code but only found generic details. "They covered their tracks."

Hail chattered against the car and collected in the corners of the windshield.

His voice rasped with restrained rage. "It's not a deal they'd honor."

"They're just trying to scare me off, right?" She was already scared but wasn't ready to change course.

"Like we did to them. They're sending a charge through you, see if you make a mistake."

"So we got to them." The small victory chased some of the locked dread in her joints.

"Blood's been spilled. Things can only escalate." The muscles of his neck flexed. "They won't back off."

"Neither will we." She fed off James's determination.

"We stay cool and let them burn themselves out." He battled against a crosswind that nearly sent the car skidding off the highway. Visibility was down to only a hundred yards. Everything else was smears of hostile black and gray. She braced her feet on the floor, as if she could keep the car steady. A cold sweat spread across her back.

The radio cut out to static.

She checked her phone. "No signal."

He pulled his out and swiped over the screen. "Aces." The phone dropped to his lap when he had to handle the steering wheel with both hands. "We shouldn't travel through this." Sheets of thick rain looked like high sea waves in the powerful wind.

"Take us to the shoulder." There was at least twenty yards of open ground between the interstate and a boundary fence.

He grunted disapproval. "Find us a road off. If I park too close to the highway, we could get wiped out by an errant tractor trailer."

She peered through the swirling storm and tried to draw distinctions between the asphalt, sky, desert and rivulets of water that rushed across the windows. "Coming up." He slowed, and details emerged. "Before that overpass."

"On the far side of that sign?" The storm hit harder.

"Yeah." She checked behind them to make sure no one would rush up as they eased off the highway, but everyone else had already taken shelter from the weather.

The car bounced when they hit the shoulder. James counter steered as they skidded in the gravel, then engaged the all-wheel drive. With more grip, the car lurched and bounded through a ditch. Mud sprayed up and joined the clatter of the rain and hail. James steered them past a highway marker and to a gap in the fence. A dirt road angled steeply down and away from the highway.

James warned, "Secure yourself," and plowed the car down into a culvert. The tires struggled through sandier soil. The car bounced from side to side, slamming her against the inside of the door. Her shoulder blazed with pain from the impact. She tightened herself against more blows, which came as James took them toward the far bank. Runoff carved ruts that jolted the car. "You good?" he asked tightly as he struggled to keep them moving.

"Exactly where I want to be." She spoke between strained breaths as she fought to stay in her seat. "In a ditch in a storm right before a desert flash flood washes me away."

"Cheeky bird." He managed a wild smile in the chaos. Pulling the wheel to one side, he gunned the engine and lurched them to more solid ground. He snaked from side to side until they were up the other side of the wash.

But they weren't on the road, so he had to keep them bouncing over rocky desert for a few yards. She stopped clenching her jaw once they reached the packed dirt trail. They followed it up and away from the highway and the wash. Jagged hills emerged from the low clouds.

James drove the car higher toward them. "We'll shelter there."

The stone was streaked dark with rain and looked as sharp as knife edges. "Cozy."

"You'd prefer the flooded ditch?" He leaned forward to see the road through the continuing rain.

"That hotel in Albuquerque was nice." She didn't even know where to buy towels as plush as the ones they had.

"Wasn't it?" he mused. "And a good dinner."

The warm lights had lined his face with gold as she'd learned more of him that first night. "Good company."

He glanced at her. The dim storm light carved him into obscure planes like the hills around them. Except for the electric glimmer in his eyes that inspired a quick spark to tumble down through her. "Always makes the meal."

The road flattened between two outcroppings. He turned the car until it faced the road they'd just come up. Then he backed up so they were off the path, with their rear approach protected by the jutting rocks. He brought the car to a stop, killed the lights and the engine. The rain pounded all around them.

Could he hear her voice above the din? "Like the junk food."

If he did, it didn't change his expression. He pulled the emergency brake tight, double-checked it and unfastened his seat belt. His face moved close to hers, but he was just assessing their surroundings. She moved back and let him work. That was what this was. Work. She repeated it like a mantra to remind herself of the real circumstances, not the imagined connection between them. To ice herself further, she thought about why this mission had started. The purpose of her website. The loss she'd hoped to heal.

"There goes your flood." James pointed down the hill. A wide swath of water and debris pushed along the wash they'd crossed. The turmoil tumbled under the highway, making it look like the river had been flowing for hundreds of years.

"That would've taken the car." Large rocks tumbled under the force of the water.

He whistled low. "Yeah, we would've been in trouble."

"Thanks for getting us out of there." His arm rested between them. She almost laid her hand on it.

"Thanks for navigating." He shifted to peer up and down the highway. "We would've been way too exposed down there."

Pools of water developed over the asphalt, erasing the hard lines and taking the road back to nature. "You got us off the highway at the right time."

He chuckled. "We would've needed a boat."

Had they run out of things to say? The rain continued to chatter, but they were silent. Only a couple of feet apart. Her pulse seemed to push her nearer to him with each thrum. Her body sought to complete the electric connection it had been tasting in quiet jolts.

James continued to watch out the front windows. "I'm still learning your American rain. We get plenty of rain in England, but there, it's historical. Poems and paintings, all those old buggers have covered it." He ran his finger along the upper edge of his side window and rubbed it against his thumb, checking for moisture. "This rain is primordial. Like a battle between the landscape and the water. All we need now is a volcano."

"And dinosaurs." Few human traces remained visible in the desert.

His eyes looked way beyond the view. "In that London flat, with my folks, I never imagined the different kind of rain in the world. I've learned them. Drizzle of a million needles in Vienna. Cold curtains of it in the Yemen highlands." More of his history emerged. "The panicked chaos in Los Angeles."

"Are there any you'd return to?" A part of his past drew pain, but had he lived anywhere without that agony?

"L.A. is my home now. I can make that work." He didn't address anything else.

She moved without thinking. She rested her hand on his. He started to pull out from under her. She gripped enough to let him know she didn't want to let go. The feel of his skin on hers was the heat she'd imagined between them. A slow jolt of thick lightning.

He moved his hand away.

Rejection chilled her. But she wouldn't let embarrassment choke her words. "You said we're invisible." The rain and rocks and clouds hid them.

"To the outside." He stared forward.

"You're right." She turned toward him and still couldn't draw his gaze. "I can see you. I want to."

"You…" He looked at her. The pain and gloom were closer to the surface than she'd ever seen in him. "I…" His mouth tightened, as if holding back what he wanted to reveal. "I'm not good."

"That's wrong." She ventured her hand toward him. "Everything you're doing for me…"

He smiled sadly. "Is for an old debt."

"But you'll never allow yourself to consider it paid." She understood what it was to carry a burden without question.

His eyes narrowed. She'd hit a deeper truth. "Why did I know all the answers to your questions about contract killers?"

Her hand stopped. A sudden breath caught in her throat. She'd never imagined he could be that kind of man. His moments of grim silence made more sense. The pained depth in his eyes. But that very emotion made it hard for her to imagine him as one of those stone-faced killers.

"After the SAS, before Automatik," he explained. "I never pulled the trigger, but I ran close support and surveillance for my old sergeant. He was the contractor. That doesn't excuse me."

His secret lodged in him like a bullet no one could operate on. "But you don't do it anymore." The man she'd learned about was not cold-blooded.

"Automatik showed up." He held up both hands like

a scale. "Gave me and Hathaway a way out. I took it. He didn't." One hand made a fist.

"You started over."

"You know that's impossible." Their pasts crowded with them in the car. "I tried. Even when I was doing the work, whatever money I didn't drink I sent to my parents." He took a tight breath. "There aren't enough good deeds in the world."

"Maybe just one." With herself and the other widows, there was always a despair that the pain and loss couldn't be swept away. But their shared experience let them know it wasn't about a magic doorway they could walk through to a new life. Steps counted. Small transitions. Recovery came in handfuls. Each one was prized.

The bond that had grown between her and James was as fine as gold wire. Easily broken. She should snap it. But it shone so unique, she had to know where it led. Nothing was the same from two days ago. She wasn't the same.

She pushed through her fear and reached forward. His face hardened. It seemed he might recede again after revealing too much of himself. Old pain lined the sides of his eyes. His lips parted to speak. She paused. He didn't say a word.

Her hand found his again.

CHAPTER NINE

THE GOLD WIRE she'd felt between them spun thicker.
Her fingers gripped his hand. He could pull away, but
she needed to let him know she wanted him to stay.
His gaze locked to hers; the pain remained in him. She
learned again. Like dragging herself forward, despite
a body full of broken bones.

The touch was human. The James she'd come to
know. Warm. Strong. He had calluses and scars. So
did she. Neither had arrived at this spot in a storm
without a past.

"You are good." She wanted to send the words
through her skin as well, so he could feel the truth.

He shook his head. "I haven't been."

"You are good now."

"It's still me." Emotion shined in his eyes.

"We change."

"Not enough." He started to move his hand, but
she held him.

"We don't delete anything." Her past threatened to
break her hold on James as much as he did. "We live
forward."

"*You* do." His energy rose. "*You* live."

Anger shook her words. "Because you don't deserve
to?" His stubborn torment had to stop.

His smile was that of a man relieved to finally be

falling to the burning center of the earth. "You've got it, luv." He pulled out from under her touch.

"No." Frustration choked her. She'd risked a chance and was now overexposed. Without safety. "No, James."

His eyes softened. "You don't deserve—"

"You don't get to decide that." Her hand remained between them. "I reached for you."

"The wrong man."

"You don't get to decide that." She turned her hand palm up. It trembled. He looked from her eyes to her hand and back. The tension in his neck and jaw released. He placed his hand on hers.

The connection deepened with a new trust. He curled his fingers around her. She was protected, and strong enough to hold him. Heat moved between them. Her heart pounded faster. The storm erased the world around them.

James leaned forward. His lips parted. Her trembling increased. He held her hand gently and didn't move.

She steadied her breath and told him, "I want you to kiss me."

He closed the gap between them. Her eyes shut. His mouth met hers. Tentative. Searching. Their lips slid against each other. His beard scraped her skin, making it more alive. She craved every sensation, deepened the kiss and tasted his smoky essence and rainwater.

His fingers stroked through the hair at her temple and behind her ear. Hidden places on her that hadn't glowed with this kind of attention for years. She placed her hand on his chest and felt how tight his muscles were. Together, she and James fell into the unknown.

Her mouth parted as his tongue sought hers. Waves of excitement swept up her limbs and centered in her chest. The new life in her body was shared in his. He rumbled into her mouth as she dug her fingernails into him, just below his collarbone. Her breasts became very aware of her bra against them. As she moved closer to James, her nipples rubbed on the fabric and sparked with more heat.

He pushed his fingers through her hair and held the back of her neck. The two of them were locked together. Like they'd been for the last two days. But now, they chased each other. Sliding tongues, firm lips and biting teeth.

Her body surged with the waves, hips swiveling forward. The bucket seats of the car constrained too much. Plastic and industrial fabric creaked and whined. She wanted to drag her hand down and tear his shirt with it. She wanted his skin.

She wanted too much. Her breath hitched and she broke the kiss. James pulled away and stared into her face with heavy-lidded eyes. His chest rose and fell. Slowly, he removed the hand from the back of her neck. She ended the touch on his chest. Their other hands remained clasped. She didn't tremble anymore. But she was shaken inside. Her need had come on too strong. She wasn't sure if she should ever give in to those desires, or if her life as a widow only allowed her the comfort of a simple touch.

She looked at his mouth, knowing now how firm the lips were, and the feel of his beard. She stared into his eyes and understood more of him. And he saw into her. They'd taken a chance. It hadn't killed them. But her nerves had woken up with too much ferocity. Any more would've torn her apart.

They let go of each other's hands. After a while, the rain pounded louder than her heartbeat. The storm hadn't relented. She hadn't found a release, either. James still appeared poised, body ready. She turned in her seat to face forward. Their breath had steamed the windows. The blur transformed the streaming water on the glass and the rocky hills into a completely different planet.

James turned front as well. He shifted and rearranged his jacket. She heard the metal and plastic of his weapons settling.

She broke the silence. "I'm sorry, but I couldn't…" Telling him what she'd wanted and not having it would've been agony.

"There's nothing you need to apologize for." His voice rasped. "If I went too far…"

There was so much neither was saying. "I asked you to."

"And I wanted to," he admitted.

But it couldn't go any further. They fell back into silence; the rain made all the conversation. Could she take another taste? Another test? Her blood rushed at the thought. She'd be right back at the brink if she kissed him again. Even looking at his long hand resting on his thigh made her lick her lips. Breaking out of her old life felt like it could break her.

She focused on the mission. Getting the website back. Helping all those women support each other and learn from each other. She needed to do that. But the thought of returning to her dark computer room alone set an ache deep in her chest. James sat less than two feet away from her, and she couldn't touch him. She'd stepped over borders she never thought she'd approach again. Now she was lost.

How THE HELL could he be so hot in the middle of a winter storm? Hail collected like piles of pearls at the base of the nearby rocks. Still, he wanted to tear off his jacket and release the steam under his skin.

The kiss had taken him. Just her telling him what she wanted was enough to rip him apart. He'd revealed who he was, explained his past, and she'd reached for him. Unburdening himself to her had been enough. She now knew what his closest Automatik teammate didn't. It didn't eradicate his past, but voicing it helped move the rusty nails that drove the memories into him. Even knowing, she hadn't run or shut him off. She'd offered her hand and taught him that a human touch could communicate a connection.

She'd taken the link further with the kiss. Proof that she understood who he was and didn't judge him. Her needs were clear, too. After the nervous trembling subsided, she'd grown bolder, opening her mouth to him and demanding more.

James laid the back of his hand against the window glass and hoped it would draw the heat out of him. Could April feel the fire that pulsed through him? She sat still now, hands no longer shaking. Her eyes stared into the hazy view. They had tried. The connection had lasted as long as it could before it had threatened them both. Going any further would've been overwhelming. Old scars would've torn apart.

He relied on his focus to meditate his needs down. The mission had to take priority. Find the hackers and shut them down. Protect April. When this was over, he could allow himself to think about how it might've worked out between them. If they'd just met in the parking lot, without any assailants. If the flow of time had gently moved them together, rather than smashing him into her life.

"It's not letting up." He moved his hand from the cold glass and rubbed his other fingers over the chilled skin. He'd cleared a spot of condensation and watched the rain and hail continue to sweep over them.

"This might be the second storm I saw." She used her sleeve to swipe her window and looked out. He couldn't see her expression. Her voice had been flat.

"Lunch?" Anything to return to a normal balance, though that seemed impossible.

She turned toward him, eyes alert but ringed in a sadness that ran a razor edge right through his ribs. "Do we have anything?"

"From the vending machine." He reached into the backseat and dragged forward a plastic bag from the sporting goods store. He'd transferred his kit to her luggage when they'd left the motel and had filled the bag with the remaining junk food. "It'll get us by."

She groaned. "I'm going to need a salad soon." Her hand dove into the bag and retrieved a packet of pretzels.

"We could go foraging." If there was anything green out there, it was buried in the mud.

"Do it." She nodded.

He cracked open the door and slammed it, spraying the interior of the car with a mist of icy rain. She laughed in a burst and took cover behind her arm. The air was refreshed between them.

Rainwater covered his hand. He rubbed it on his face and the back of his neck. "Beautiful day."

She held out the bag of pretzels to him. "Picnic?"

"Brilliant." He ate for calories and ignored the taste. The familiar comfort of April's company wrapped around him again. He couldn't shake it off or bury it. He tried not to think about the kiss. Maybe in time he'd be able to ignore the tug that kept him wanting to rest his hand on her shoulder or stare at her hands and look into her eyes as she spoke.

They completed their lunch. The windows steamed thicker, enclosing them in a private bubble.

"Los Angeles?" She reclined her chair a couple of notches and stretched out her legs.

"Orange County, technically." He flexed his legs in place to keep the blood flowing. "Close to a couple of airports so I'm mobile."

"House?"

"Small one." Raker had been the only Automatik member to be there. The place was barely decorated and furnished with only the necessities. Couch. TV. Bed. Gun bench. "My parents haven't even seen it."

She watched his face. "They're still in London?"

He and April couldn't go any further. But he held on to the bond they had, more valuable than any of his possessions. "I moved them to California when I joined Automatik."

"Do they know what you do?" She brushed her hair behind her ear, bringing his memory back to the silk and satin he felt there.

"They didn't before and they don't now." He was sure he owed his father an email and his mother a phone call. "After the SAS, I just told them I was a 'consultant.'"

She blinked, and he watched her remember what he'd revealed. He wouldn't have blamed her if she'd demanded he drive her through the storm back to a safe place in Albuquerque where another Automatik operator could pick her up. But she hadn't judged him. Not as harshly as he had himself. He hadn't softened the truth. Not pulling the trigger didn't make him less culpable.

He took a breath and explained, "A lot of the time we were running security around people. They liked paying for it, rather than having a government handle the logistics." Her gaze remained steady. "Other times there were individuals whose lives were only worth six figures to a government or corporation or rival."

"You left."

"I did." The past seemed further away. "Automatik unlocked that door."

"You must've made a lot of people nervous when you walked."

He chuckled. "They don't send birthday cards anymore." He hadn't seen Hathaway since leaving England. "Last time I was in a room with my old mate, he tried to pull a razor across my throat."

She shuddered. "Jesus."

"He bled more than I did that night." None of it had come as a surprise once he'd left Hathaway's employ. "It was a good motivator for me to help my folks get that little house in a nice Indian neighborhood far away from London."

"They're safe?" She showed real concern.

"Yeah."

"And you are?" Her worry deepened.

He shrugged, the pistol rubbed against his ribs. "Look at the two of us. The world's so scared of us, we've been banished to a rocky cliff surrounded by storms."

"It's breaking." She stared off to the west. A jagged white line opened over the horizon. She wiped condensation away to reveal thinning clouds over gauzy rain.

The unrelenting wind blew the weakening storm over and past them. He started the car. "On to Phoenix." Driving down the hill should've broken the spell of their private hiding place, but he was still very aware of how close she was. Their shoulders knocked together as the car bounced from side to side in new ruts.

"Can we get across that?" She tipped her head toward the wet wash they'd struggled over earlier.

He peered forward. The debris had collected by the highway overpass, leaving a path, but he couldn't tell how deep the mud was. "I'll scout once we get down there."

The car drove and skidded to the bottom of the hill, where he pulled the emergency brake and got out. The rain had stopped, but the cold wind picked up the pooled water and sprayed it against the exposed skin of his hands and face. His thighs chilled as his jeans soaked through.

The longest stick he could find at the side of the wash was only two feet long. He ventured forward in the mud, poking ahead with the soggy wood to test the depth. There wasn't a tree or shrub in sight, he had no idea where the branch came from. The storm had been strong enough to alter the landscape.

He proceeded across the thirty-foot-wide wash, marking his path by dragging the stick in a jagged line.

His boots sank into the muck. It splashed up to coat his knee. The rain had soaked into the dirt but there was firm ground beneath the layer of sludge.

At the far side he turned and retraced his steps. April waited and watched in the car, anticipation leaning her body forward. When he was closer, she asked, "It'll hold?"

He tossed the stick aside and tracked mud into the car. "Think buoyant thoughts."

The tires ground forward, spun, then caught and pulled them forward. Wet dirt sprayed up the sides of the car and streaked the windows. He battled toward the far edge of the wash in low gear. A wheel slipped and his gut sank, thinking they were stuck.

"Oh, fuck." April shared his concern.

The wheel dug deeper, found traction and kept the car moving. If his jaw wasn't clenched, he'd have sighed relief. April laughed nervously. Halfway. Two thirds. The desert brightened as the clouds cleared. Pooled water gleamed like diamonds.

The car reached the far bank. James accelerated toward the climb. Soil splashed like an explosion in front of them. Pebbles clattered against the windshield wipers. The engine strained, but the car held strong enough to get up the muddy bank. From there the dirt road was packed firm and lead them easily back to the highway.

Then James breathed. The sky was black in the rearview mirror, blue ahead of them. The wet asphalt glowed. Dirt striped backward on the side windows as the car picked up speed.

"Nicely done." April held out a fist and he bumped it.

They both settled in for the long drive. But he

really wanted to be out of that car. Running back up the path toward where they'd sheltered. Crawling through the mud. Anything to burn off the tension that wound through him. Anything to keep him from thinking about what April would look like standing in the glittering desert after the storm.

CHAPTER TEN

THE RELIEF THAT had loosened her shoulders as soon as they'd hit the highway was lost in new dread. A black State Police SUV sped up behind them. She and James had both spotted it in the mirrors and cursed under their breaths. He eased off the gas, but if the police really wanted to stop them, they could find a reason.

She didn't know if there were registration papers for the car. "Do you even have a license?"

"Of course I do." He split his attention between the road ahead and the cop behind. "But not for my sidearm."

Her mouth dried. Her legs jumped nervously. The car was caked in mud and shed pebbles onto the road. She tried to come up with some kind of explanation, but they all sounded like desperate lies. "I take it he won't know who Automatik is." The windows of the police SUV were black, hiding the driver.

"We've got contacts with some agencies, but mostly on the upper levels." He drove sensibly, with both hands on the steering wheel. "I won't have any pull with this bloke."

The police car hovered behind them for a long mile. He could be running the plates. She forced herself to stare forward and not glance suspiciously over her shoulder every two seconds. Any moment the blue and red lights could flash.

"Here he comes." James somehow managed to look calm. He shot her a look. "Give us your public face, luv."

She tried to match his casual attitude and faked a smile that felt way too gigantic and forced. "Now we look suspicious."

He surveyed her and laughed honestly. The pressure release was infectious and she chuckled with him. By the time the cop drove parallel to them, their grins were real. She peered over and saw a stern man with a shaved head. His sunglasses blocked his eyes, but she knew he stared hard at her and James.

"Mark had a couple of friends on the El Paso P.D." When those men hung out, it was usually on their own. "Intense guys."

James gave this officer a little nod. It could either set the cop off or put him at ease. The man's expression didn't change. He accelerated past her and James. Water sprayed up behind his SUV, like he was disappearing in a cloud.

"Should I race him?" James raised his eyebrows and grinned wildly.

"Do it," she encouraged with an equally reckless smile.

He maintained a sensible speed, and the trooper's SUV gained more ground ahead of them. They were safe for now. But they'd been seen. They weren't invisible. She could see herself. Guilt gnawed through the back of her head and down to her chest. Remembering Mark a moment ago, saying his name, had rattled her privacy with James. It was as if everyone could see them now. Mark's parents and hers, her friends, the people in town. Everyone knew about the kiss and how much she wanted to take it further.

She told James, "Next stop for gas, I need to get some sunglasses."

He squinted into the day. It was bright now that they'd passed the storm. "Me, too."

After a few miles, they passed the state trooper. He was parked on the median, facing the other direction, waiting. James had kept their pace reasonable, and they cruised by without worrying about being stopped. Other concerns weighed heavy. They knew they wouldn't make it to Phoenix before the school closed for the day. Each second lost was more time for the hackers to break through her encoding. She hadn't responded to their email, and there was no follow-up from them.

The hackers knew about Albuquerque, so the hired killers had to be somewhere within two hundred miles of her and James. He explained that they might be trying to track her credit card usage, or the GPS on her phone, anything to get an indication of their position. She turned off the location services on her phone but kept the data alive for research.

"Phoenix looks like a big city, but they'll probably have lookouts at the major hotels." It was clear James knew the process. "We'll want to weather the night somewhere they're not looking. A small town outside the borders, maybe."

"I know someone in Phoenix." She had at least one email from Silvia she hadn't responded to. The woman would be worrying by now. "She might be able to put us up."

"A good friend?" James remained guarded. "You trust her?"

"Yeah. She and I went through the same thing. We met on the forum and talk privately, too." Silvia's energy and enthusiasm for experiences always revived April. "We visit each other when we can."

"Can you call her? No email."

"She's probably still at work, but might answer."

He took his phone from his coat, punched in the security code and handed it to her. "Use mine. Won't leave a trace."

She looked up Silvia's number on her phone and dialed it on James's. Before it rang she told him, "At the gas station—sunglasses and a burner phone."

"Good idea." He smiled at her, impressed.

Silvia picked up with a cautious, "Hello?"

Of course there'd be no caller I.D. on James's phone, and Silvia didn't know him anyway. "Silvia, it's April."

"Hey, you okay?" She kept her voice down, so she was still at her desk at the law firm. "Haven't heard from you. You on a new phone?"

"I'm okay, but things are a bit…hectic." How could she explain everything without sounding like a paranoid insane person? "I'm coming in to Phoenix today. Any possibility you could put me up?"

Silvia didn't hesitate. "Absolutely. What time you getting in?"

April asked James, "What time?"

"Three, maybe four hours." He glanced at his watch.

Silvia spoke lower. "You have someone with you?"

"Yes." Again, she had no idea of how to illuminate the situation.

"Do you need help?" Silvia switched into battle

mode. "If you need me to call the police, just say, 'Give or take a half hour.'"

April reassured her friend, "I'm not in danger." But that wasn't true. "I mean, not with James. He's…" She looked at him and caught him sneaking his attention back at her. "He's one of the good guys."

"Okay, babe. I trust you to know." Silvia dialed her intensity down, but not much. "I'll be home by the time you get there. I'll have food. What else?"

"That's plenty. Thank you." But what was April bringing into Silvia's life? "If we're imposing, if you don't want the drama, let me know and we'll find another way."

"There's no other way." Silvia held firm. "You're coming here."

"Thanks." This kind of ferocious protectiveness was common on her website. James had it, too. A bubble of sadness wrapped around the warm appreciation he inspired in her. "I'll call if anything changes."

"Be safe. See you soon." Silvia hung up. April knew the danger that had shaken her world now extended to her friend. She hated involving her, but they were always there for each other and it was a place that no one would be looking.

April handed the phone back to James. "I can give you directions to her place once we get closer."

He stowed the phone. "Sounds good. Thanks for securing us a roof."

"Sure." They'd been seen by the police officer and in a few hours they'd be seen by her friend. How much would Silvia know? April felt like she still wore all the need she'd found for James like a red blush across her face.

They exited the highway at the next opportunity and pulled into a gas station. While James filled up, she took a few bills of his cash toward the store. He leaned against the car, casual, though she knew he tracked every vehicle and person who came and went. With his arms crossed over his chest, he was an imposing figure. The caked mud on his boots and the bottoms of his jeans revealed he was up to no good. She walked on glass shoes, thinking that everyone was watching her, aware of the danger, crime and desire that surrounded her.

In the store, she picked out sunglasses for her and him. She was tempted to wear hers while buying the prepaid phone and extra calling cards. The clerk rang her up, business as usual. April hid her secrets well.

Back outside, she masked her eyes with the sunglasses. James still leaned against the car and worked on his phone, presumably updating Automatik with their status. She handed James his sunglasses.

"Cheers." He covered his eyes with them, looking extra mysterious.

"The aviators suit you." They were both very clandestine now and could scan the area freely without anyone knowing.

His angular face remained dead serious. "James motherfucking Bond." A private smile crossed his lips for her. Warmth spread down the center of her chest. She tried to keep it from reaching between her legs, but remembering just what those lips had done to hers was too much. A needy ache carved through her. She swallowed hard and couldn't be fulfilled. He topped the car off and got in.

She closed herself in next to him. He took them

back onto the highway. The need continued to pulse through her. She tried to bury it in rational thoughts, all the reasons she couldn't act on the yearning. She hadn't even known James for three days. The memory of her husband loomed. There was too much peril, too close to her. But the desire persisted. If it wasn't satisfied, it would wreck her.

JAMES DROVE THE highways he'd memorized as April set up her burner phone. With each stage of the mission, she became more of an operator. A partner. Not that he wanted to clear a room of hostiles with her, but the two of them were a good balance. She handled the tech expertly and explained what she needed to in terms he could understand. He was content being the muscle.

They turned south to Phoenix. The low sun glowed around April's silhouette. Her large sunglasses gave her a dangerous sophistication. She navigated them through the gigantic city toward her friend's house.

"Silvia?" he asked to remind himself.

"Silvia," she confirmed. "Husband was a marine. IED, just like Mark."

Many men and women he'd known had lost their lives and limbs to those bastardized explosives. He'd always held the sappers who dismantled them in high respect. "Terrible business. I'm sorry."

She was quiet for a few blocks. "Right turn at the light." The sun was down, the sky deep blue. She took off her sunglasses. "She's a paralegal. Switched careers like I did."

"Is there a man in the house?" He needed to know how secure the location was. "Anyone else?"

"She dates. No one serious right now."

"Kids?"

She grew somber. "They never found the right time."

He realized this information wasn't covered in April's file. There was no tactical use to the knowledge. That wasn't why he asked, "And you?"

"We didn't want." She looked at him, honest and open, then returned her gaze to the streets. A small, sardonic laugh cut through her. "You're not married, are you?"

"Not ever." He laughed back. "I don't even have a jar of mustard in the refrigerator." He didn't let the thought of her in his house linger. She deserved something fully furnished and comfortable.

"Automatik keeps you busy." She directed them through another two intersections.

"There are married people in Automatik." The former recon marine, Art, had found someone special in the chef he'd hijacked into his Mexican desert mission. And James had seen plenty of sparks between Ben Jackson and "Bolt Action" Mary on the helicopter ride out of Morris Flats. "Even a couple of operators hooked up with each other."

"Sounds…dangerous."

"They are." He'd be more relaxed traveling these unknown avenues if the rest of the strike team was close. "Mary can pick a lock with a bullet from a mile away."

April turned to scan out the windows. "Is she out here?"

"I wish. The storms restricted travel." He brought the car to a stop outside the modest two-story house she indicated. "We're on our own in Phoenix."

"We have Silvia." April smiled as she looked at the open front door. A Latina woman with a long ponytail, wearing jeans and a sweater, stood there. She pointed at herself, then at April, as if to ask if she could come out to them. April nodded, and the woman who appeared around April's age approached.

James got out of the car and hauled the carry-on from the backseat. April skipped across the narrow lawn and embraced Silvia. The two women parted but held each other's arms and spoke quietly between them. April nodded emphatically and gave her friend a gentle, reassuring shake.

He advanced toward them, and Silvia tipped her head toward the house. "Come in." She maintained her hold on April as the two women led the way. He turned a quick circle and assessed the street. Medium-sized houses. Working class. Some chimneys smoked; other houses were completely dark. A car drove down the street and parked in a driveway. Business as usual. But he didn't trust the area completely, because a skilled operator could conceal himself or herself behind the squat palm trees, or in the shady hedges between houses half a block away. It was what he'd do.

Silvia closed the door behind him, sealing the cold out, and extended her hand. "Silvia."

"James." He shook hers and noted her extra pressure. "I'm doing everything to protect her."

"Good." Silvia still eyed him with wariness.

"He is." April stroked down her friend's arm.

Silvia punched a code into a home alarm control box by the door, setting it, before turning to April. "So what the hell is going on?"

April took a long breath and ran her hands through her hair. "It's the hack."

Silvia held up a hand to stop her. "Are you hungry?"

"Yes." April sighed in relief and followed Silvia into the kitchen. James left the luggage in the front entry and joined them. The place was clean and orderly. A well-stocked bar on one counter and a pass-through to a comfortable-looking dining area. The art on the walls was a mix of black-and-white photography and abstract swaths of glossy color.

Silvia unfurled the lids off foil containers on the kitchen island, releasing steam and the spiced aromas of Mexican food. "I got takeout on the way home. Grab a plate."

April took one from a stack next to the food and piled beans and chicken and rice on it. James hadn't realized he was starving until he saw the crackling, darkened skin of the chicken. April pulled warm tortillas from a plastic bag and gave herself two and James two.

She instructed slowly, "Now, this is a tortilla. You eat it with the other food."

He played along. "Like naan, but flatter."

Silvia looked at them, dumbfounded. "Are you serious?" She pointed at his plate. "This is Mexican. Do you have that in England?"

He took a long smell of the food. "Not as good as this."

Her eyes narrowed when she realized the joke was on her. "Enjoy. Both of you." She followed behind them, filling her plate then herding them into the dining room. Silvia poured lemonade from a pitcher, and they all set into the food. The taste lived up to the look and aroma. One plate wasn't going to be enough.

After a few bites, April gave Silvia an account of what was happening. James worried she'd reveal too much about Automatik, but April stayed nimble and manufactured a story that James worked for a security firm that was hired by another victim of the hackers. They were going to interview her when the attack happened. From there, they were on the road, tracking the hackers. She touched on the storm but didn't mention anything that had happened between them. He couldn't look at her when she recounted weathering the worst of it, lest he entertain the more carnal thoughts, and the rush of heat to his crotch, that rose each time he thought of the kiss.

Silvia took it all in, sometimes shocked, other times calculating. She was smart and stayed at speed. She also seemed to read between the facts and assessed April and James sitting next to each other. Her perceptive gaze dissected and observed, but she didn't interrupt to ask any personal questions. James saw that she wanted to, though.

"Holy shit." Silvia leaned back in her chair and rubbed her temples. "Serious business. I'll bet you guys could use a drink."

April answered first. "You know me. I'm useless after a sip. Another time."

"Thank you, but not while I'm working." James took a gulp of the lemonade instead.

Silvia nodded. "Another time." She refilled his glass. "Military?"

"SAS." There was no need to hide these facts. "Retired."

"So you know your business." If she was impressed, she didn't show it.

He was never one to boast. "I can close a deal."

April was more emphatic. "He's very good at this."

"Glad to know." Silvia still didn't seem convinced. "Because it's not just a job."

He met her pointed gaze. "No, it isn't." He finished his plate of food and stood to refill it, but Silvia was quick to take it from his hand.

"What can I get you?"

"I can handle it. You don't need to." The hospitality was extraordinary, but he wasn't there to be served.

"I know you can handle it." Silvia was already walking to the kitchen. "I just don't want you tracking any more mud than necessary."

"Damn." He'd forgotten about the mud on his boots and pants. "Sorry."

She threw over her shoulder, "*De nada.* That's what washing machines are for."

He sat back down and ate the new food when it arrived. Silvia and April cleared their plates, then brought a laptop to the table and huddled around it. They scoured through every piece of information they could find on the assassinated men in El Paso, but found no leads or details beyond the basic story. The authorities were investigating and were at the point where they were asking the public for help. James knew the local cops wouldn't find a trace. The hitters were professionals. The only link between the victims and the killers were James and April and the hackers.

He kept that knowledge to himself. April knew what he was and didn't judge him. Silvia might. The two women continued their search, targeting everything from the CPA firm in Albuquerque to the school in Phoenix. No patterns or direct connections emerged. Silvia didn't dig into what security firm he worked for, or who his original client was. If she didn't believe the story, she trusted April to have her reasons for lying.

James bussed his plate while they were busy, careful not to dislodge too much caked mud from his legs. On the way back into the dining room, a shadow slipped into his peripheral vision with the sound of soft movement. His combat instinct triggered in a flash of adrenaline. He spun toward the inky shape and pulled his knife, sure to be between the attacker and April.

"Don't!" Silvia shouted.

James faced off with a black cat on a side table. Its narrow yellow eyes and predatory stance inspired a primal fight-or-flight urge in James. He glared back at the animal and didn't give ground.

Silvia stood and approached cautiously. "Don't mess with my cat."

James lowered the knife but kept it in his hand. "She snuck up on me."

"He's supposed to." She edged in front of James and went to the cat. "He does that to everyone." She put her hand out to the cat, who kept one eye on James as he bumped her palm with his head.

"Nice knife." April was on her feet, alert to the danger that had just passed.

He sheathed the blade behind him. "Italian." It was a good thing he'd had the sense not to draw his pistol in this house full of friendlies.

Silvia petted the cat, and the beast continued to rub against her hand. When James stepped closer, the animal recoiled.

"He was feral and eventually moved in." Silvia gave the cat a respectful distance. "You have to let Diablo come to you."

"I get that." He stepped away. A silent truce arose between him and Diablo. The cat receded into the shadows he'd come from and completely disappeared from view.

April approached Silvia. "Can we wash up?"

"Of course." The woman waved them to a hallway that stretched to the back of the house. James picked up the carry-on and followed. Silvia pointed in an open doorway. "Guest room." James put the bag in there and came out to find April and Silvia standing at an open linen closet, selecting towels. "Bathroom on the other side of the laundry." The washer and dryer stood in a nook in the hallway. Silvia tossed him a somewhat ragged towel. "Use this for the mud. I have a stiff brush for your boots."

"Cheers." He took the towel to the guest room.

April trailed in after him with a nicer-looking towel. "For the shower." She placed it on the immaculately made bed. "We'll throw your pants in the laundry."

He placed the weathered towel on the ground and stood on it to take off his boots, but stopped. "I don't have another pair to wear."

April's assessing gaze went from his feet to his face, making him feel very naked in front of her. Her eyes flared with the need she'd shown in the car. She cleared her throat and appeared to collect herself before leaning back into the hallway to ask, "Do you have a spare pair of pants?"

Silvia appeared in the doorway. "Nothing that'll fit." She smiled. "I burn all my victims' clothes."

April groaned and left the room, pushing her friend as she went and throwing back to James, "Just hand the pants out, and I'll take care of them."

She closed the door, forcing James to raise his voice. "I can do my own blasted laundry."

April must've been close to the door and murmured, "I don't want a pantsless man walking around my friend's house."

Silvia mumbled something about it not being the first time, making April chuckle. James removed his boots and pants, careful to keep the dried mud within the borders of the old towel. He also shucked his jacket and had to take off the shoulder holster to pull off the admittedly stale T-shirt. He balled everything up and kept the holstered pistol in one hand as he passed the clothes through the barely cracked door.

April retrieved the clothes and called for the luggage too. He rolled it to her, blocking himself with the door, and it disappeared into the hallway. A stiff utility brush was pressed into his palm in return. He wound the holster back around his shoulders and sat on the edge of the bed.

"Bloody hell." The strangest position he'd ever been in during a mission. Wearing nothing but his briefs and sidearm, brushing the mud from his boots in a guest room decorated with black-and-white photos of roses. The woman he needed to guard was on the other side of the door, but he could hear enough of the surroundings to be aware of any trouble. That wasn't the only reason he wanted April in the room with him. The relative safety of Silvia's house allowed his needs to surface. His exposed skin burned for her cool fingers. He wondered if the taste of lemonade remained on her mouth. For the first time, being protected felt very dangerous.

CHAPTER ELEVEN

"THIS IS FUCKING WEIRD." April loaded James's dirty clothes, along with hers from the luggage, into the washing machine.

"You sure you're okay?" Silvia remained close and lowered her voice for just the two of them.

"How should I know? I don't have a reference anymore." Doing the laundry felt like way too domestic a task in the midst of these insane circumstances. It was also incredibly personal to mingle hers and James's clothing together.

She closed the machine. Silvia spoke a little louder over the initial rush of water. "Do you want to sleep in my room with me?"

April was very aware that James was just a few feet away behind a closed, but unlocked, door. Barely wearing any clothes. As soon as he'd handed over his pants and shirt, she'd been tormented with the question of what his naked body looked like. She'd felt the lean muscles, seen how they moved him, but to actually see them, or touch his exposed skin, made her breath rush faster.

"I feel...safer with him." Was that the complete truth? "We've been together through all this. He's prepared for this kind of thing."

Her friend caught on one word. "Together?"

"Not like that." But there was the kiss. The potential for more continued to echo.

Silvia nodded. "You can if you want to." She placed her hand on April's arm. "No one's judging you."

"Thanks." The harshest judgment came from within. "I don't know."

Silvia picked up April's fresh towel and handed it to her. "I have a gun. Do you want it?"

"I'm not trained to deal with pressure situations." April waved off the idea. "I'd be more dangerous than helpful with it."

"Soap and shampoo are in the shower. Anything else you need?" Silvia leaned toward the stairs that led to the master suite on the second floor.

April didn't have the answer. "Thanks for everything, babe."

"Any time, babe." Silvia smiled warmly and added, "Anything." She departed upstairs.

April collected clean clothes and toiletries from her carry-on and took them into the bathroom. The shower wasn't hot enough to loosen the muscles that knotted at the base of her neck. She soaped her skin and thought about James. She tried to ignore the fantasy, but it only grew stronger when she wondered what his hands would feel like on her slick body. The last stages of the shower were rushed, and she shut it down to dry off. She dressed for sleep, put her glasses on and exited the bathroom to find the washing machine nearing the end of its cycle.

The door to the guest room was ajar, but there were no lights on inside. She approached cautiously. "James?"

He spoke from the shadows inside. "The shower

and the washing machine were running. I opened the door to hear better."

"Can I come in?"

"I'm… I'm only wearing a towel."

She swallowed hard. "The shower's all yours."

"Okay." He warned, "Incoming."

She considered taking off her glasses but determined she couldn't stand to miss the beautiful details. It was the best decision. James moved quickly into the hall. His dusky skin highlighted the curves and angles of his defined muscles. The shoulder holster he still wore framed his chest and back perfectly. In a blur, he was in the bathroom and the door closed.

It was the worst decision. She wanted to move with him, to feel how the length of his body fit against the curves of hers. It wasn't the steamy air from the shower that made her head spin. She busied herself with moving the laundry from the washer to the dryer, but saw how her hands trembled. He was so close. So possible. The shower ran and she could imagine more of his details now that she'd seen him with his shirt off.

Was Silvia right? Could April simply take what she wanted? Nothing was simple.

The kiss had told her that the connection was real. It had set off a need that persisted and persisted. The more she tried to suppress it, the stronger it grew. She couldn't hide from it anymore. She didn't want to. She had to know what it was to live out a desire.

She went into the bedroom. The ajar door put a stripe of light across the floor and up a wall. James's boots were relatively clean and stowed on the spare towel in a far corner. The only other trace of him was the rumpled impression on the edge of the bed where he'd sat. She seated herself next to it and waited. A tremble moved through her, peaking at the top of her breaths.

James's shower was quick and he was soon padding back to the room. He peeked into the bedroom. "Can I grab my clothes?"

"You can come in," she told him. The air heated with his presence; his body must've still been warm from the shower. Or it was her who produced the new fire, blushing with her boldness. "Close the door."

He did, and as the last of the hall light blinked across him, she glimpsed his naked chest and the holstered gun in his hand. "Is everything alright?"

The shutters were closed over the single window in the room. Her eyes adjusted and collected what light seeped around the edges. His shape emerged. Broad shoulders, narrow waist, wearing only a towel. He moved closer with concern.

"Yes." He was close enough to touch, but she couldn't reach for him yet. Nerves pounded in her. Her heart raced on excitement tightened with fear. "Can you sit? Without the gun."

He placed the holster on the floor by the corner of the bed and sat near it. "What's going on?"

"I don't know. I don't want to think about what it is." She slid her hand across the foot of the bed toward him. "But I don't want to ignore it."

"April, it seemed like we…" His words stopped and he grew still. His hand extended out and rested on top of hers. The connection shocked her. She'd tried to deny their attraction and ignore their bond. But there it was, like a common pulse they shared.

She turned her hand over to grip his, hard to stop the trembling. "I can't tell you to kiss me."

She'd never heard his voice so low, rumbling from his chest. "I won't take what you're not willing to give."

"I can't tell you to do everything." She moved closer to him. "I have to feel what you need."

He pulled his hand out from under hers. The fear and desire that had been rushing through her stumbled, leaving her without equilibrium. Had she been too bold? Asked too much of him? Maybe his need didn't match hers. She choked back a gulp of embarrassment. James turned toward her and held her by the shoulders. Her tumult fell into place again, drawing her closer to him. He leaned in, bringing their faces close. The dark erased most of his features, but she saw the serious depth in his eyes.

James kissed her. His hesitation was gone, replaced by undisguised hunger. He gripped her tighter, drew her near. His mouth opened, inviting her into his need. Instinct moved her without thought. She teased her tongue out, and he slid his against hers. But her mind turned, thoughts of doubt clouding the sensations. She reached forward, still shaking and hoping to share his confidence. His muscles jumped as her hands smoothed across his ribs. Both of them were learning.

The kiss drove more heat through her. Touching his bare skin took her breath. Her days had been so planned and regular. With his vitality so close, she had to shake out her fear and live without thinking. The two of them locked together. He pressed her against his chest. She wore only a T-shirt, and the fabric allowed her breasts to rub against his firm ridges. Her nipples tightened, seeking more sensation.

James eased her deeper onto the bed and turned to face her fully. His hands skimmed across her back. She arched with the warm and careful touch. The pleasure carried an edge of newness. Her skin and muscles had been for workouts and daily necessity. She didn't want to think about how long since this kind of intimacy. Too much of that reflection would take her away from the moment. She needed to experience all the sensations James surrounded her with.

His fingers traced the hem of her shirt and found the flesh of her waist. A shiver shook her again, and he drew his hands away. The kiss parted. Was the moment so fragile that this could shatter it?

She whispered, "I'll stop you if I have to." She took his hands and placed them on her hips. His hold grew tighter again. "I haven't…been…" How could she say it? She didn't even know where they were headed.

"I understand." His voice rumbled on the side of her neck.

"Go slow." She stroked her fingers down his cheek. "But don't stop."

He pressed into her touch. She didn't know how long it had been for him. A man with his face and physique and confidence, not to mention his accent, wouldn't have too much trouble finding a hookup. But the way he sighed out when she scratched lightly through his tight beard, it seemed that he was as starving as she.

His fingers resumed their search around her waist. Like he was drawing a new map, illuminating places she'd forgotten. Her breath rushed and her voice caught in her throat when he ran a broad palm up her back and paused between her shoulder blades. He kissed the side of her neck, freeing her voice in a moan that rocked her. She couldn't worry if Silvia heard her. There was too much distance between the floors. And the worries of the outside world had held April back for too long.

James's other hand caressed down between her breasts. Her T-shirt moved with him, tugging across her sensitive nipples and making them blaze for more. He grew more purposeful and his muscles tightened against her. She leaned into him as he kissed her throat. Delicate skin burst alive with giddy sparks. She nearly shrunk away, too sensitive, but breathed and found herself relishing the heightened awareness. And the trust she'd given him.

His palm slid over her breast. She reached out and clutched his shoulder for support. His breath rushed and rumbled in his chest. He surged closer, incredibly potent but careful enough to temper his strength for her. Small circles with his hand drew her nipple to a firmer point. The blaze of sensation shot down between her legs, where she felt herself growing wet.

The lightest touch of his teeth on her throat had her moaning again. And again, louder, when she pressed her breast against his hand. He kissed her jaw and cheek. She leaned her head down so their mouths could meet again. This kiss built on all the fires they'd been burning. Her mouth was open to his, tongues probing deep.

Tears welled in her eyes. She wanted this pleasure, to chase it to the end. But what if it was wrong? He tugged up on her shirt, and the kiss parted so he could swipe the fabric away. Cold judgment threatened to kill the moment. She wanted to cross her arms over her chest. Had she gone too far?

"Lovely," he whispered, chasing the chill. His eyes

flashed in the dim light as he looked her up and down. "You're lovely, April." He waited, and didn't rush her.

"It's too dark. You can't see me." But she wanted to believe him.

"I've good night vision." His hand rested casually on her knee. "I can see you're skeptical. And I can see that tattoo over your left breast. A little bird with a long beak."

She wiped the tears away. "A hummingbird." She'd been in Phoenix with Silvia when she'd gotten it.

"Of course." His voice smiled.

Amazing that he could pick out that much detail. "It was an impulse, six months in the making." Maybe the last thing she'd done that was outside of herself. But she hadn't regretted seeing the little symbol of freedom and flight in the mirror.

Another benefit of the decision was having James reach toward the tattoo. The memory of the buzzing, prickly pain was wiped away by the new sensation of the rough pads of his fingers over the bird. She didn't want to cover up anymore.

"I can feel its wings beating." He moved his hand away so he could kiss the tattoo. She wrapped her arms around his shoulders and held him close. His mouth moved across the top of her chest, down between her breasts. His beard prickled on sensitive skin. A sense of panic cut into her. She felt too good, was too ready for the next experience. A long breath brought her focus back on the immediate moment: James kissing her chest, his body in her arms, his hands on her waist.

He licked a warm circle around her nipple. She shuddered a sigh, dug her fingernails into his back, then gasped when he bit gently on the tight point. His teeth held the tip in place and his tongue flicked against the very end. Electric pleasure kicked her pulse faster with each touch. She ground her hips against the bed, stirring the heat that had gathered in her pussy.

James lay them down on the mattress, stretching her out next to him. He skimmed his hands from her wrists all the way to her waist. He shifted to bring himself closer to her and his towel fell open. It was too dark for specifics, and her glasses were probably fogged anyway, but she couldn't mistake the contrast between his skin and the light towel. He started to bring it back around him, but she stopped him with a hand on his arm.

She murmured, "I wish my night vision was better."

He chuckled. "You'll have to feel your way."

"Cheeky bastard." Before he could answer, she placed her hand on his chest and moved it slowly down. She learned more details of his landscape. Muscles, bone, scars and rough areas. The body of a man who'd lived in conflict and survived. He wasn't doing battle now. The potent energy was focused on pleasure. She searched further across his ribs and abs. There, she detected a quake, as if he was just as nervous as she was. It was reassuring to know they were in this together and he wasn't in complete control.

Her resolve was challenged as she caressed over his hip and along the top of his thigh. He tensed as well. The side of his erect cock brushed against her fingers. She glided the back of her hand along it. He sighed out and arched toward her. She wrapped her hand around his erection. Smooth skin. Firm. She stroked up and down while he moved with her, pushing forward and back. Having him react to her touch, so carnal and ready, deepened her need.

"April." Her name in his hurried breath made her body shudder. Sweat glossed her chest. He pulled her closer so they could kiss. She glided over his length. He filled her mouth with his tongue.

His hand slicked over her sweat and the center of his palm hovered over her nipple, gently brushing the sensitive point and teasing her for more. She bit his lip, and his touch firmed so she could fully rub against him. The kiss parted and their faces remained close. The pace of their breath matched. Their bodies moved in rhythm.

His hand trailed from her breast, past the center of her belly and to the edge of her yoga pants. His fingers paused there, at the border of her clothing. She surged forward, inviting him to proceed.

The strokes on his cock slowed as her attention drew down to his hand skimming under her pants and over the skin at the top of her thigh. It almost seemed impossible, like it was happening to someone else, but the jump of her nerves was too real. He brought warmth everywhere he touched, and it joined with the needy heat of her pussy. The panties seemed so ordinary, though. A sliver of her worried they would ruin the mood. James wasn't deterred by them, his fingers gliding over the cotton and down between her legs.

His touch was so close to where she thrummed with need. She rolled her hips forward, encouraging him, but the yoga pants were too tight and bound the movement too much. The two of them released each other and he used both hands to swipe her pants away. He left her panties on.

She turned back toward him, but he gathered her, sat them up and spun her so her back leaned against his chest and shoulder. His legs bracketed her and his cock lined the back of her hip. Drops of fire rained with his hand down her belly and to her crotch. She spread her legs. He pressed his fingers over her panties and along her wet cleft.

"Ah, fuck..." She needed the support of his body as she jolted with the contact. With shivering legs, she dug her heels into the mattress so she could press harder back into him. He slowly rubbed up and down her pussy, drawing more moisture and heat from her.

She held his thighs to brace herself. His breath tumbled over her bare shoulder and his mouth found her neck, just below the ear. All of her was aware of his motion and touch. The need for release that grew in her pussy extended out. It seemed like she could come just from the feeling of her naked thighs rubbing against his.

He tugged her panties to one side and brought his wet touch directly to her lips. She rolled her hips to bring him up and down the folds. Her pulse thundered, and her breath clipped with her quick moans. His finger circled higher and rubbed along her clit.

She froze. She gasped. The tremble struck through her. James stopped and placed his hand on her waist. Was she afraid? Was it just too much sensation all at once? When the initial shock diminished, she felt the desire still charging through her. But she didn't know if she could satisfy it, or if her body was just too unaccustomed to this kind of intimacy.

"We can stop." He continued to hold her.

She didn't want to, but she didn't know how to proceed. "Do you want to?"

His erection and the tension in his body told her he didn't. "I want you to feel good. I want to bring some pleasure to this clever, fierce, strong and brave woman I'm still learning."

"Tell me how you'll do it." So she could ready herself and not be shocked blind by the sudden pleasure.

He murmured, "I'll touch you again, along your pussy. Up and back, up and back again." She could almost feel it and started moving her body. "I'll circle your clit, test it. Rub my fingers down it."

"Now," she told him. He complied, exactly as he'd described. First his fingers slipped over her lips and collected her moisture. He slicked along the folds, building her need higher. The tip of one of his fingers drew around her clit, sending electricity through the surrounding nerves. He paused at the top, allowing her to ready herself. Slowly, he ventured two fingers down over her clit. A reflex brought her legs together, and he immediately drew his hand back.

Frustration choked her. She pulled off her glasses and tossed them onto the bed so she could rub at her eyes. Her body demanded his touch, her release, then betrayed her when she dove too deep into the pleasure. She was torn between allowing this private moment with James to self-destruct in disaster, or chasing it down no matter the cost. If he was as exasperated as she, he didn't show it. He continued to hold her and support her with his steady body.

She bit back tears. "I feel like I've ruined it."

"You haven't ruined anything," he reassured her.

"Maybe I'm broken." She hated the thought.

"You're not." His hands grew stronger on her hip and shoulder. "You're not at all. This is what makes you lovely. The way you feel. Sensitive to the world. To yourself." He stroked gently down her arm. "You paint with very vivid colors."

Her frustration receded, but trepidation still gripped her. "Can we...try?"

"We can," he replied. His kisses on her cheek and temple were as soft as his words. She breathed deep and sank into his support. He stroked down from her hip and along her thigh. His other hand moved up to draw a delicate line between her breasts and back down again.

She realized how tight her hands on his legs were and relaxed her fingers so she could trace the definition of his muscles. He growled a sigh that vibrated through his whole body. The rumble loosened her as well. She parted her legs. He dragged his fingers up the inside of her thigh. Nervousness rose with his hand, but his pace allowed her to acclimate herself with each inch higher. He reached her pussy and barely glanced his finger over her lips. She angled herself for him, as he grew bolder. With each stroke he increased the pressure. She moaned in time with him.

"There you are," he encouraged her. His fingers never reached her clit, only skimmed close and circled around so the hyper-sensitive bud wasn't shocked.

She reached back and found his cock. He moaned and nodded, his cheek on hers. She stroked up his length and rocked her body so her hip rubbed against it as well. Confidence grew. They could find pleasure however they needed. Her hand circled his head. He tested a finger into her opening. Warmth, edged with hot white, spread up into her chest and made her heart beat faster. She turned her head and coaxed him on with her mouth on his neck.

He entered her again, deeper. And again, in and out. The pleasure she'd feared was gone rushed back. The two of them surged together. Their sweat mingled where her back met his chest. A climax approached, but swirled just out of reach. Her pace broke, with every part of her in disarray.

James started to slip away from her, but she held his leg. "Wait, please."

"I'm not leaving." He kissed her shoulder and disconnected his body from hers. He was quickly facing her, expression intense. "Lean back and take off your panties. I'm going to put my mouth on you."

The image alone sent jolts of yearning from her fingertips to her toes. Worry persisted in the corners of her mind. She tried to push it away as she reclined and arched her back to remove her panties. James shifted around her until his shadow hovered over her legs.

He moved lower, and she opened to him. His hands caressed her legs, hips. One hand cupped her ass. His other fingers found her pussy again and slicked along the folds. Bright heat bloomed when he entered her. The blankets gathered in her hands. His kisses arced across her lower belly and spread the center of her warmth further out. She drew her knees up and braced her feet on the bed. The hazy shadow shapes disappeared from her vision when she closed her eyes. He continued to move in and out of her. The climax tantalized her from a distance.

James's kisses reached her mons, then dove lower. His tongue slicked through her folds to just below her clit. She quaked with the pleasure while the heat took her over in stronger and stronger waves. His finger plunged a little deeper, and his tongue swept up and above her bud. Fear burned away. It could've cost her the searing intimacy of James's kiss. He tested the flat of his tongue across the tip of her clit. Pleading moans and demands filled her throat as the climax stormed closer. He swept over her another time, firmer. She encouraged him with words she could barely speak. The hard muscles of James's shoulders and arms pressed against the insides of her thighs. Doubt couldn't ruin her; the momentum had built too high. James continued to lick her and plunge deeper. She ran out of words and pulled the blanket from the bed as her body contracted before the release.

He licked across her clit, then placed his lips around it and captured every sensitive nerve in her body. The orgasm slammed into her. Breath rushed. She sweated and gripped harder on the blankets and gathered them around her and James. Every fast heartbeat pulsed white in her closed eyes. Pleasure sped from where he kissed her to the far points of her body. The waves slowed as she caught her breath. He moved his finger slightly and shifted his mouth, sending out new sparks that renewed the rush. The bursts of heat evened to a steady glow.

She reached down and stroked over James's hair. He was real, not imagined. Solid and careful. He pulled his finger from her and kissed once more over her pussy before bringing his body next to hers.

"April." He placed his palm between her breasts, over her heart. She felt how fast it beat. The release had shaken the nerves from her body. She was naked and exposed and loved being that free.

She put her hand on his and held him. Her voice was husky. "Thank you. For being patient."

"Anything for you." He settled next to her and stroked through her hair.

It should've been enough. Her body had wound tight, threatened to break and finally found release. Her spent muscles should've sunk into the mattress, relaxed. But an excited need still buzzed through her. She'd been daring and free and didn't want to stop. Her hunger hadn't been sated.

She turned to James. "We're not done." To prove it, she slipped her hand over his waist and rolled him toward her. When they kissed she was nearly put off by tasting herself on his mouth. But it was so carnal that it made her feel more real and raw. She reached for his cock and found it still erect and ready. He thrust forward as she stroked over him. Her body yearned to know what he'd be like inside her. She whispered, "Do you have a condom?"

His answer was tight with frustration. "I bought more bullets, not condoms. Never expected this. Or you."

"Maybe Silvia?" Going on the hunt threatened to stall her momentum.

"Go up and ask her for one?" He sounded astounded at the idea. "What about in here?" He moved away from her, and she pawed over the rumpled bed for her glasses. She got them on and saw his shape standing over his boots.

Red light pierced through the room. James stalked to the bedside table, holding a small flashlight. His body caught the glow and looked like a carving on an ancient temple dedicated to sex. Long, powerful limbs. Curved erection.

"There we are," he murmured victoriously. She scooted up the bed and saw an open box of condoms behind the open door of the cabinet beneath the bedside table. Silvia didn't limit herself to one bedroom. "Shall I?" James reached for one.

"Hurry." She rolled back onto the bed. The foil crinkled as it tore. She watched James, cut in relief by the red glow, roll the condom on his cock. Incredibly erotic. Her pussy ached to know that length. "Leave the light on."

A devilish smile curled on his lips. He left the flashlight on the bedside table and crawled on the bed with her. Their bodies wound together. There was no momentum lost in the interlude. Her breath rushed in excited anticipation. She gasped with the flood of contact when he took her against his chest. His arms tightened around her, and she felt his desire match hers. He rolled them so she was on top.

"I need to see you, too," his low growl commanded gently. She blushed at being this open. But she had to obey his craving and her own. She sat up to straddle him, pressing his cock between them. She drew it along her pussy and had to brace her hands on his chest when the pleasure thrummed up through her.

More. She needed more and angled herself so his tip parted her lips. He remained still, gripping her thighs and staring into her face. The smile persisted on his mouth, but his eyes were focused. She eased back and drew him inside. Her pleasure strained as he stretched her. She slowed the pace; her body learned to accommodate him. It took more time than she wanted and only reminded her of how long she'd been dormant. But that memory faded as she was swept back into the now. James moved the backs of his fingers across one of her nipples in an even rhythm. He captured it as it firmed and rolled it and pinched it. The pleasure opened her, allowing her to sink deeper onto him.

They sighed out together. He entered her completely. She paused, steadied herself and rocked her hips to move him in and out. She quickened. He thrust up to meet her. Where they met, she sparkled. Grinding blazed the pleasure higher.

James watched her, rapt. She leaned down and brought their chests together. He coiled his arms around her and kissed her. She moaned into his mouth. Their bodies locked deeper. His heat glowed inside her and all around her. The kiss parted so she could breathe. She bit into his neck. They pushed harder and harder until another climax gathered around her like a storm.

He must've sensed her impending release and urged her, "Yes, April. Yes, luv."

The orgasm rolled through her with a softer edge than the last. She gasped and bucked, sank him deeper into her so she could savor the deep glow. When she opened her eyes, she saw James's intensity blazing.

He rolled them and took the top. She hooked her legs around him and coaxed him with her nails in his shoulders. He thrust, and the remnants of her climax took her breath away. His brow knit and he bared his teeth, moving faster in and out of her.

She barely found the air to speak. "Now, James... In me..."

His muscles tensed and he buried himself in her. The release thundered through him and pulsed within her. She languished in the blaze. He collapsed toward her and turned so they lay on their sides, still intertwined.

With her lips on his throat, she felt his pulse ease. Hers matched it. They disentangled themselves and she sighed as he exited her. He rested his hand over her pussy, a warm comfort for the ache. They lay next to each other, facing the red ceiling. She took her glasses off and stroked across his hair.

At some point, she'd need to thank Silvia for having condoms in the guest bedroom. Her friend had experienced the same loss as April. A life and love cut off in an instant. It had taken time, but Silvia had reemerged, learned who she was again and lived. Could April do that? Had she just stepped into a new self? Or was this not herself, only a brief flash in the night?

CHAPTER TWELVE

JAMES WOKE THROUGHOUT the night and couldn't believe each time that April was in the bed next to him. The experience they'd shared felt unreal because it was so real. She knew him, accepted him and invited him closer. His hookups over the last few years had felt like a rush to a finish. With April, he had to focus on her and her pace. He learned not only what she responded to physically, but also how her mind was involved in the pleasure. Taking their time allowed him to savor each touch. Maybe because somewhere in his thoughts he knew that it might be the last time they allowed themselves this kind of freedom.

House alarms weren't impenetrable. Each creak of the structure or gust of wind outside surfaced him from a thin sleep. The gun was on the nightstand. His knife was nearby on the floor. None of the noises escalated so he needed to investigate. He was glad to leave the flashlight off. It was better to preserve the memory of her glowing body and ecstatic face in the red light.

After they'd regained the use of their limbs post-sex, they'd cleaned up and collected their clothes from the dryer. His jeans and shirt were ready next to the bed, and he dressed in the dark before the dawn. April stirred. She'd put on her sleep shirt and yoga pants, but the sound of her moving through the sheets tore at his soldier's resolve. He'd planned to gear up and start the day with planning and mapping and tactics.

Instead, he sat on the bed amid a delicate calm that made his body feel lighter, the aroma of her soap and herself surrounding him. She turned away and pawed at the bedside table until she found her glasses and put them on. The dim light from the shuttered window revealed her bleary, but concerned, face. "Everything alright?"

"Just getting started." He put his hand on hers, very conscious of the touch. He wanted the latent slow heat of her in the bed, but maybe their moment of intimacy had passed.

"What time is it?" She didn't pull her hand away, but the contact felt awkward and unknown.

"Early." He checked his phone. "Not yet zero six. Sunrise in an hour and a half."

"The school won't be open until around eight." Her smoky voice made him want to wrap her and the blankets around him.

"You can keep sleeping." He was up for the day and needed to steer his mind to the op.

She moved her hand out from under his and rubbed at her eyes. "I'm up." Not a convincing display, especially after she yawned and stretched out her arms. He made a fist and tried to hold the gravity of the touch, but it might've already been gone.

April got off the bed with a long, mournful sigh. A pang of sadness knifed down him. He wanted it all to stay the same, for time to stop, containing just the two of them in this room. She dressed as he shrugged on his shoulder holster and clipped his knife to the back of his belt. His boots were clean enough for indoor use, and he sat in a side chair to lace them up. When April finished dressing, she leaned against the edge of the bed.

"What now?" Her voice was flat and there wasn't enough light to piece together her expression.

Was she asking about them? He didn't have the answer to any of those questions, just the desire to stay close to her and the source of the new energy that pumped through him. "We track down our lead at the school."

She didn't move, and he felt like he was staring at a picture he'd be seeing the rest of his life. April in shadows, next to the bed they'd shared, neither of them knowing if they were over or if they'd just begun.

The shower turned on upstairs. Silvia began her day. The tableau snapped when April walked about the bed, collecting her clothes. He covered his weapons with his leather jacket and helped April pack their bag.

They weren't cold with each other, but the unspoken connection they'd had wavered, uncertain. April made the bed, and he lost a part of himself. At least he'd helped her find pleasure. It was unfair to imagine he could be anything more than a temporary relief from the pain of her past. Once they'd collected all their things and erased their presence from the room, he turned on the light.

She squinted and didn't look him in the eye. "I'm going to put in my contacts."

"Right." He watched her leave and stood in the middle of the room, listening to the sounds of the waking house. The urge to action revved high. He understood the mission, even if all the steps were still hidden. Picking a lock, smashing through a window, running a car through a barricade, he knew exactly what to do. He was lost with April. If the end of the night brought her the realization that he wasn't the kind of man for her, then he had to accept it. The price of a life he'd tried to leave behind. It haunted him.

The shower turned off upstairs. April returned. "It's all yours."

He used the bathroom for his morning routine. His kit was in place and mission ready. He splashed cold water on his face to center himself. *Get the job done.* Then he could move on to the next op, and April would be free to pursue her life. He exited to find her standing in the hall.

"Coffee?" she asked, neutral.

"Hell, yeah."

He followed her into the kitchen. She and Silvia were obviously close enough to comfortably share a cooking space. April knew where all the ingredients and implements for coffee making were. The roasted aroma soon filled the room.

Silvia descended the stairs wearing the components of a business casual outfit, as if conjured by the brew. Her long hair was still damp, but pulled into a ponytail. "You got it going?"

April checked her work. "Couple of minutes."

James drifted aimlessly in the kitchen. "What can I do?"

Silvia thought, then answered, "Toast."

The task helped relieve the tension of uncertainty that made each word he wanted to tell her too brittle. "Point me in the direction."

Silvia indicated the toaster and showed him the bread and butter. He absorbed himself in the production line, but not so much that he missed Silvia questioning

April with a look. April shook her head to get away from the subject, and Silvia backed off. What would she say if the two friends were alone? A cold sweat spread on the back of his neck. He hated being lost.

"You know how to get to the school?" Silvia took them all into safer territory.

James tapped his temple. "Got it."

April collected mugs. "He sees something once and it's set." She was impressed, but he still couldn't bask in her praise.

Silvia sliced avocados into vivid green slabs. "I wish I could do that." Diablo the cat stalked into the kitchen, glared at the three humans busy with their tasks, turned and disappeared back to whatever corner he'd come from.

James shrugged. "A lot of training."

"You know..." Silvia paused with the knife in her hand. "I can take a personal day and go with you."

April looked from her to James for the answer.

He dipped his head politely. "Thank you, but you shouldn't. The less you're involved, the better. Go about your day. Act like nothing's changed." But everything had changed. It was going to be a struggle to pretend otherwise. "Plausible deniability and all that."

"I get it." Silvia brought the avocados over to James's stack of toast. "If you need something, I'm on the other end of the phone." She took over at his station and lined the toast with the avocado slices before sprinkling salt and pepper on them.

April handed Silvia a mug and hesitated in front of James. "Cream, no sugar, right?"

"That's right." Damn, it wasn't going to be easy to walk away from her when this was all over.

She smiled, sly with victory, and handed him a mug. "You didn't think I noticed at the diner in New Mexico."

"I think you notice everything." That perception made her unique. A long second drew out between them. She looked into his eyes, giving him the tug of their link. But how far it went, he still didn't know.

"Are you coming back here?" Silvia carried her mug and a large plate of the toast into the dining area. James and April followed with their coffee.

April answered first. "I don't think we can plan that far ahead."

"Right," he agreed. "We haven't been able to plan more than one move at a time."

They ate and finished their breakfast as the rising sun sliced pale yellow light around the dining room shutters. After a brief cleanup of dishes, James brought his and April's gear to the front door. She stood with Silvia and told her, "We'll let you know when we know."

"Okay." Silvia looked at April with deep sympathy and fierce friendship. "You be safe, babe."

"I will." April put her hand on Silvia's arm and held it.

"She will," James vowed.

Silvia disarmed the alarm, and April let go of her friend to open the front door. The frigid morning rushed in. The safety of Silvia's home was over. The real danger resumed.

He and April wasted no time hurrying to the car and shutting themselves in. The outsides of the windows were frosted. The inside immediately steamed with their presence. He turned the engine over, knowing it would take too damn long for the heater to kick in.

They'd driven a block when April exclaimed, "Oh, shit."

Adrenaline rushed up through him, and he scanned all the angles for trouble. "What is it?" Nothing seemed out of the ordinary.

"What if they're on winter break?" She searched out the windows with concerned eyes. "When is that?"

"Hell if I know." He relaxed away from full battle mode. "We'll find out soon enough."

"If they're closed," she planned, "we'll have to use those lock picks of yours."

"That would be long after sunset." He glanced at her. She almost looked eager for it, bless the determined woman. "And I would be alone."

"But you'll need me at the servers." The woman was persistent.

"I'll send you a picture." His tactical mind chafed at the possibility. "Disabling alarms, breaking and entering, getting chased by the authorities would put you too far in harm's way. I won't have that."

"I'm in harm's way," she reminded him.

"Not because of me," he countered.

She reached over and put her hand on his leg. "That's right." The touch spun him, confused. He'd convinced himself the intimacy was done, and yet it immediately sprang back to life. He connected to her and last night and what they shared.

"Do you want me to move my hand?" She looked at him with concern.

"I don't." But it was selfish.

"This morning," she ventured, "I couldn't tell."

"We're back on the clock." He chose his sentences and knew they were too clumsy. "And I thought you... sent a distant message."

"You'd disappeared." Her hand pulled away slightly but remained on his thigh.

"I'll have to." The pain of the lost possibility split him. "I'll disappear so you can live a normal life."

"What if I don't want you to?" She drew out the question so each word landed with growing impact.

He pulled the car to the curb and turned toward her. Hope hammered through him. He stared at her face, seeing that she spoke the truth, and gave her the same in return. "Then you have me," he promised.

She tipped her chin up and met his gaze, brave. "That's what I want."

"Truly?" He'd bounced between too many emotions to keep up. "Because you know what I am."

"I do." She moved her hand to his cheek. "And that's why." His heart jumped as she looked at him, honest and aware. Without judgment. "Don't make me tell you to kiss me."

He didn't wait, and brought them together in a kiss. The sting of tearing himself from her washed away. The night before rushed back. The possibility, the chance at tomorrow, was all he needed. Knots of doubt that had bound around his ribs released. He tasted sweet coffee on her lips and breathed her in until he was filled with her fire. She stroked down his face and placed her hand on his chest. The connection was like an electric shock that started his pulse after long lying dormant. They broke the kiss and sat, inches apart for a few breaths.

His motor turned. The op waited. After it was complete, the real possibilities opened. "Let's tear that school down."

She smiled, ready. "Let's."

They separated and he drove them back into the mission. His past actions weren't gone, or forgiven. But with her, he was allowed to move forward. They drove toward the unknown, with hostiles hunting them. James dedicated himself to protecting her, and the sliver of hope she'd given him.

CHAPTER THIRTEEN

THE TENSION OF the morning had soured April's night. James's distance in the dark of the bedroom had made her wonder if their sex and connection had been some sort of needy dream. But she'd known it was real. The effect remained in the sweet ache of her body. Their job in Phoenix remained. How could she perform with cold blood after running so hot with him?

It would've been impossible to proceed without knowing what had happened and where she stood. At times it was maddening how careful he was of her. But that was also what made him so unique. Still, she'd had to reach out first. And she was glad she had. It didn't even matter she didn't know exactly where the two of them were headed. Just the possibility of more time together made her feel the fresh air in her lungs.

The atmosphere cleared between them to bright blue, leaving a clear path to their task at hand. He found the school, circled it twice as they watched the buses arrive and students pour into the entrances. The closest street parking was two blocks away, and they walked quickly through the frigid morning toward the large main brick building.

She jammed her hands in her coat pockets. "Should've brought coffee to go."

He blew into his fist. "I could go for a three-hour shower."

A realization hit her and she slowed, taking him with her. "Are you wearing your gun?"

He nodded and sighed, then glanced at the school. "I don't like it. I know it's not right. But we're in the crosshairs."

"You mean I am." She looked about, but didn't know the area well enough to recognize signs of danger.

"*We* are," he corrected her. "I'm with you in this."

He was the only thing that made this insanity seem possible. "Keep your jacket zipped."

"Roger that." He patted the front of the leather.

They picked up their pace again toward the school. A block away, the first bell of the day rang. The area cleared of students as if they'd never been there, and quiet descended. Anxiety tugged at the muscles between her shoulders, but she didn't know if it was because of the current mission or because she was stepping back into a high school.

"I was really happy to graduate." She reminded herself of her accomplishments since those days, including creating a website that helped countless women. That community steeled her nerves toward the task at hand.

"Didn't take to school, myself." James's precise attention took in the environment. "I learn better on my feet." He arrived at the front doors and opened one side for her.

The smell of unclean lockers and thousands of students and institutional linoleum hit her with a wave of unwelcome teenage angst-filled nostalgia. "Fuck, it's been a long time…"

"Agreed." A sour expression crossed his face. "Here we are." He pointed the way to a heavy wooden door with an aging brass sign above that read *Administra-tion*. "Plan in mind?"

She'd been toying with a concept and rolled it out. "We're thinking of enrolling our daughter."

"Bloody hell." He put on a strained smile. "You take point."

She walked into the administration offices before him and proceeded to a broad wooden counter that divided the entrance from the several old steel desks where men and women worked on computers and spoke on phones.

"How can I help you?" A young African-American man who looked like he was fresh out of college approached the counter. He wore a crisp plaid shirt, tucked in, and oversized glasses.

James leaned close to her and muttered in her ear, "Braces."

She whispered back, trying to figure out what he meant, "On his teeth?"

"What do you call them?" James sounded frustrated. The man had almost reached them. "Suspenders."

It was true, the man wore trim leather suspenders. She was sure there was a girl or two at the school with a crush on this hip administrator. She gave James an elbow on his arm. "Try it sometime. It would look good on you." The picture of him in a white collared shirt, chest framed by the suspenders, gave her a delicious shiver.

James chuckled, she joined him and the mood was bright when the man arrived at the desk. "I'm Ollie Bower." He extended his hand. "Assistant dean of students."

She shook his hand, "Yvonne Pandya."

James was next, with his smoother accent. "Simon Pandya."

Ollie maintained his bright curiosity. "I don't recognize the names, so I know you don't have a student here. What is it you need today?"

She started lying and hoped it would get her where she wanted to go. "We moved into town about three months ago, and we're interested in enrolling our daughter."

"Great." Ollie clapped his hands together and fished out a binder from under the desk. "If I could get your address, I can see if you're in our district."

"We checked," James interjected. "And we are."

She kept the momentum going. "But what we're really looking for is to see if your school would be a good fit for Delia."

Ollie was game. "Sure. Well, it's too bad she isn't here to see firsthand, but I have a few minutes." He pulled out his cell phone and checked the screen. "And can walk you around."

"She's at home," April explained, "working on an end-of-semester project to close out her last school."

Ollie nodded knowingly. "This time of year, right? We're all going to need that winter break." He walked to the side of the counter and lifted a hinged flap so he could join April and James. "Does Delia have any particular interests or activities?"

James looked to April with the same question in his eyes.

"Computers," she answered.

"Ah." Ollie deflated slightly. "Truth be told," he tried to rally, "budgetary concerns in the district have limited our computer literacy classes to just the basics."

She clicked her tongue, disappointed. "So coding, 3D modeling and printing, web design…nothing like that?"

Ollie winced like she was pulling a splinter from his finger. "I wish. I really do."

"Here's the thing." April turned to make the conversation more private with Ollie. "She's very computer savvy. Like, scary savvy. We might still put her in your school for all her other classes, and I need to know how good your computer security is."

"Oh, it's very good," Ollie reassured. Then a thought crossed his face and his brow knit. Was he informed of her phishing attempt? "Do you think she'd get into our servers?"

"It's a possibility." James added his authority.

April admitted, "She's been known to find her way in remotely, or even through the hardware."

"We refresh our logins regularly, so that shouldn't be an issue." Ollie glanced toward the back of the room, where there were two doors, one wood and one metal, with a dead bolt. "And our servers are behind lock and key."

The computers in the administration room were attached via Ethernet cables; they didn't trust Wi-Fi. All those lines ran to a metal conduit that had been retrofitted up one wall, across the ceiling and through a patched hole near the server room door. Her heart sank. This wasn't the hackers' main operation.

She tried to mask her disappointment. "That's a relief." Turning to James, she gave him a small shake of the head. He blinked understanding.

"Especially after what happened in Denver." James laughed nervously.

Ollie looked from James to her. "What happened in Denver?"

"I'm sure we can't say," James equivocated. "What with the lawyers and the government involved."

Ollie's eyes widened. "Really?"

She furthered the mystery. "Why do you think we had to move?"

"Oh…" Ollie's smile crumbled. "Let me give you my card, and you can call or email if any other questions crop up." He tried to sound positive. "We're looking forward to meeting Delia if you'd like to bring her by sometime."

"We'll be in touch." James shook his hand and took the card Ollie pulled from his breast pocket.

April gave him a small wave. "Thanks for your time, Mr. Bower."

Once she and James were outside the administration office, she spoke in a low voice. "I'm sure he's glad to be rid of us." They walked across the main hall toward the front doors.

"So this location is a no go?" His accent returned to the rougher one she was used to. He strode with more purpose, too.

"Just another relay." Aggravation clouded her thoughts, obscuring what the next step should be.

James was undeterred and pushed open the front doors. "Back on the hunt."

ANOTHER DEAD END. He'd have to update Automatik as soon as he and April were back in the car. Maybe his team had come up with a lead they could chase down. Spinning aimlessly would drive him insane. He desperately wanted to put his boot in the face of the hackers who fucked up April's life.

At least she was next to him in this mission, proving herself to be quite the asset. "You did brilliantly in there."

"Thanks." She smiled and tugged her coat collar tighter around her as they crossed the street away from the school. "I think it was easier being Yvonne than being me."

He rubbed his hand across her back. "It's all you."

"You're the expert in undercover." She walked briskly up the block.

"For that you'll have to talk to my bloke, Art." He had tons of respect for the former marine. "The man infiltrated the Russian mob…"

Menace stilled the air.

"Whoa." She kept walking. She didn't feel it.

James knew death was coming. Birds and bugs were silent. The nearest traffic was two blocks away. He surged forward and threw his left arm around April, keeping his right free. "Trouble," he explained before she had a chance to ask. They sped toward the car, but it was fifty yards away. He buzzed with adrenaline, and his awareness spread to assess the landscape. Anything could happen in that distance.

April tensed next to him, her movement stiff and jerky. He heard her rushed breathing and hated that she had to go through this. Again. It hadn't been that long since the attack in the parking lot.

Footsteps echoed. Clothes rustled. James looked back to see a white man pursuing them up the sidewalk. He wore all black. Softshell jacket with a bulge under one arm. But he didn't have a pistol in his hand. He had a long combat knife.

James raged that the weapon was there for April. They wouldn't be able to outrun this fight. The neighborhood was too dense for firearms. He drew his blade and clipped to April, "Watch our backs." He released his hold on her and turned to face the man.

She gasped when she saw the attacker. The man looked through James to her, his real target. From the way he held the knife, comfortable, like an extension of his thumb, James knew he was military trained. This was one of the hitters who'd taken out the men from the parking lot.

The man tried to circle around James to get to April, but James kept himself between her and the aggressor. April's feet scraped on the sidewalk behind James, reassuring him that she was keeping active and ready to move.

This man wasn't there to intimidate or try to get April to quit her search. He didn't speak or smile. James knew what he was. He'd worked with these men and had been very close to being one himself. A killer.

He attacked. The first jab with his knife was a test to see how James would react. The man kept his attention on James's blade, but James responded with minimal tactic to keep his own skills a secret.

The man swiped again, lunging closer. James let the blow pass, then sliced forward, driving the man back a step. During the dance, a clock spun wildly in James. Another killer was out there somewhere. No one would work alone on a job like this.

After a feint to one side, the man cut back to the other in a broad swipe. James put up his left arm and let his jacket take the blow. The leather was slashed, but his skin was intact. Before the man gained his balance again, James kicked him on the front of his hip and spun him back.

James pressed the advantage, leading with his knife. The man made a defensive slash to keep James at bay and left his face exposed. James threw a quick jab into his jaw but had to recoil when the attacker's knife swept back toward him.

The impact of the punch jarred up James's arm and his knuckles would be bruised, but goddamn, he'd gladly lose the skin on his hand if it meant beating this man to the ground. The hired killer proceeded with more caution. Hate gleamed in his hard eyes. James had made this personal.

The man circled. James turned, facing him. He caught a sliver of April in the corner of his eye. She remained poised to run, her burner phone in her hand.

"Nine-one-one?" She was nearly breathless.

He threw over his shoulder, "Not yet." If the police descended, there would be no way to explain everything, including his sidearm. This fight was just a battle in the war against the hackers.

The next attack came in a flurry. The man swiped with his knife and knocked James in the chest with his elbow when he countered. James lost a breath with the burst of pain. He maintained his footing enough to dodge the next slash as it came back around. The man wasn't done and kicked into the side of James's shin.

His leg threatened to buckle, and he lifted it off the ground to absorb the strike. But he was still off equilibrium and vulnerable. The man took advantage of this with a direct stab toward James's gut.

James chopped down with his left hand, caught the man's wrist and swiped him off line. The blade barely missed James's hip. The smallest opening had to be exploited. James stabbed toward the inside of the man's exposed elbow. Before his knife could pierce the attacker, the man grabbed James's forearm and stalled his momentum. James pivoted quickly and drove his elbow into the man's temple. Hard bone thudded. The man didn't let go, and James smacked him again in the same spot.

What would it take to put this fighter down? The man grimaced and blinked and swung his knife back up toward James. The tip angled up for under James's chin. He kicked the man in the knee, wrenched his arm from his grip and stabbed him through the jacket and into his right shoulder.

It was a testament to the man's experience and training that he barely made a noise. Just a strained grunt. He'd been stabbed before. So had James. He knew that first wet panic of blood when the wound was fresh and he couldn't tell if it would kill him or not. The gash he put in the man wouldn't put the killer in a grave, but it would slow him down.

"Another one!" April called out behind him.

He put the sole of his boot on the first attacker's chest and kicked him off the sidewalk and into the street, freeing James's knife. April shifted her stance, giving James a read on the next assailant's position. The second man crashed through a hedge between tall apartment buildings. He was a blur. The only details James could make out were the olive-green military jacket and the black knife in his hand.

Green Jacket went straight for April, leading with

the knife. She scrambled away and dodged where the man in black was still collecting himself. James kicked into the legs of Green Jacket to slow him. The man rolled quickly and lunged at April. James jumped at the man, crashing his shoulder into his and throwing him off target.

They tumbled and scraped on the ground. James got his legs under him and crouched, knife ready for the next strike. Green Jacket gathered himself and stood.

James's blood iced with shock. His breath locked and his limbs shook. Before him was Hathaway.

"Bloody fucking hell." His old sergeant and mercenary partner recognized James as well. Two years had aged Hathaway further. More time in the sun, more pints between gigs. His stubble was salt and pepper, same as his close-cropped hair. Teeth yellow from cigarettes of all nationalities. Hathaway's squinting eyes flicked between James and April. He spoke in his thick Northern accent. "Don't mess with this, James."

James brought himself to full height. "It's best you disappear, Sergeant." But he'd never let him go. Once April was safe, James would dedicate himself to making Hathaway pay for coming after her.

She remained on the edge of the action, phone in hand. The Man in Black stepped off the street and onto the sidewalk. He stood and transferred his knife to his left hand and clutched his right arm to his chest. April moved closer to James. They were bracketed by the two men.

Hathaway kept his knife at the ready, but held out his other palm as if making peace. "I don't know what those other wankers are paying you, but I can double it. Or more." He smiled, showing off those teeth. "You know I'm good for it and I've got other jobs lined up."

"Take the other jobs," James told him. "Leave this one."

Hathaway shook his head. "You know I never quit until I'm finished."

James stared him down and anger burned his words black. "I will finish you."

Hathaway laughed. James didn't.

"Ohhh," Hathaway continued to wheeze a chuckle. "It's personal." His jacket was open. James knew he'd be carrying at least one 9mm under it. And a revolver on his ankle. Lunging at him would expose April to the Man in Black. But staying at this distance only gave Hathaway and his partner the advantage. Rage churned in James.

A miniature voice came from a speaker at James's side. Without looking at her phone, April had dialed 911, and the female operator asked again and again what the emergency was. She'd learn soon enough.

He faked toward Hathaway with his blade. Hathaway recoiled and switched his knife to his left hand, surely so he could draw his pistol. But James was already spinning to counter the attack the Man in Black launched.

That man's knife stabbed toward April, and she bent out of the way. James chilled, seeing the steel threaten April. He wanted to kill but took the closest opportunity and slashed into the back of the man's hand. Skin and tendons split. This time, the man screamed out. James continued his offensive with a chop to the man's throat. The Man in Black's knife fell from his hand, and James caught it.

"Run," he commanded April. She took off in the direction of the car as Hathaway was just pulling his automatic. The escalation in lethality ramped up James's pulse. He threw the Man in Black's knife at Hathaway. The mercenary flinched to the side, so it only tore a line in the shoulder of his coat. But it slowed him taking aim and made him scurry for cover behind a short cinderblock wall.

James sheathed his knife and sped after April on legs charged to run. He zipped open his jacket and drew his pistol. The buildings around could be populated. The school wasn't that far off. An errant bullet would be devastating. He saw Hathaway brace himself against the wall, gun extended. April was the target. James suppressed his rage to steady his hand and fired first. The bullet slapped into the wall with a spray of brick chips.

Hathaway ducked for cover, giving James time to fish out his car keys. He caught up with April. Terror widened her eyes, but she hadn't succumbed to complete panic.

He pressed the keys into her hand as they ran. "You drive."

She nodded, more focused. He looked back to see Hathaway peek quickly up from the wall. Imminent danger pushed quick urgency through James. He veered April off the sidewalk and between parked cars into the street. When Hathaway broke cover again, he was aiming where James and April used to be. He swung his gun around toward them. James fired at the same time Hathaway did at them.

The rear window of a parked car exploded. April yelped in fear and ducked. James hunched over her and kept them both moving. "Are you hit?" The shot shouldn't have reached her, but physics weren't always predictable on the battlefield.

"No…no…" she rasped.

The car was only a few yards away. From their crouch, he couldn't see where Hathaway or the other man were. The sound of shots surely brought attention, and April's phone was probably still live. The police would arrive soon. He and April had to be long gone by then.

She unlocked the car from a few feet away; they both threw open the left-hand side doors. She pulled herself into the driver's seat and started the engine. He dove into the backseat and left the door open so he could lie below the window level and cover their retreat. The engine screamed as she stood on the gas, screeching tires carrying them away as fast as they could. He leaned out of the car and saw Hathaway rush into the street, gun at the ready.

James sent a bullet toward him, but Hathaway was already ducking out of the way. A parked car absorbed the attack with the sound of tearing metal. Hathaway stuck his gun out from his hiding place and started spraying blindly. Bullets skipped over the asphalt and blew car tires. James maintained a steady breath, despite his body wanting to scatter in panic. Any one of those rounds could hit him and April.

She gritted out, "Hold on," and turned the car hard to the right. He braced himself with one hand on the seat and jammed his elbow against the open door to keep it from smashing his head. They swerved off the street Hathaway shot along and he couldn't get to them.

James sat up and closed the door, keeping the gun

in his hand. He found April's phone on the passenger seat and hung up the call with 911 before asking her, "Are you alright?"

"I don't know." Her knuckles were white as she gripped the steering wheel, and she didn't take her eyes off the road. "Are you?"

"Yes." No. He was uninjured, but felt like every scar on his body had opened up and oozed life out of it. "Ease off the accelerator, get us to the highway."

She slowed the car to a civilian pace. "I'm not sure how to get there," she stammered.

He watched their rear and saw no sign of pursuit. Fear and danger still rushed in his blood. He forced himself to recall the map. "Left at the next big street. Then a right two blocks later. That should take us to the highway."

Sirens swirled through the city, but there were no signs of the police yet. A helicopter sped toward the area from the south.

"Then what?" she asked. Her voice was tight, like she was close to breaking.

He put his hand on her shoulder and felt her shuddered breath. "West," he said as calmly as he could. He took his hand away and opened the carry-on in the backseat. He found the box of ammunition.

"West?" She sounded more like herself, aggravated not to have all the information. "Where west?"

He ejected the magazine from his pistol. "West. To California." The op had been fucked sideways, and he had to regroup with friendlies. "San Diego." He reloaded two rounds into the magazine, racked one of them into the pistol and ejected the mag to fill the last spot. The gun locked back into his shoulder holster. He hid the rig under his jacket and climbed into the passenger seat.

April followed the directions he gave. Highway signs directed them toward an on-ramp, but traffic was backed up.

He checked behind them and scanned the sky. The helicopter circled over the school area. "What a bloody mess. A lot of parents are going to get a very frightening phone call."

"Oh, God..." She pulled on her seat belt, face drawn. "Do you think anyone was hurt?"

"Only the bastard I put on the ground." His injuries would take him out of the hunt for a while. "My bullets didn't stray." They hadn't killed Hathaway, either.

"What about his?" Her gaze flicked nervously to the rearview mirror.

"Shouldn't be a problem. Except for the parked cars." He wanted to get out of the car and carry it through the traffic that clogged the on-ramp. They inched forward. "They won't be coming right away. He'll have to tend to his wounded mate, somewhere under the table."

She trembled. "But they'll be coming eventually."

There was nothing he could do to stop her fear. His bullets had missed their mark. Hathaway was alive and wouldn't quit. James still reeled from seeing the man. The hackers had hired one of the best to protect their business. From the shock in Hathaway's eyes, James knew the killer had no idea who he was going against. But it hadn't altered his course. The job took precedence. Hathaway had blood money to make, and it didn't matter if his former partner was between him and the target. Rage as black as a blood clot clouded his vision. James's past had come back to kill her. "Yes, they will."

CHAPTER FOURTEEN

THE TRAFFIC PERSISTED after the on-ramp, threatening to shatter April's nerves apart. Her heart only thumped a little less rapidly than it had when she'd been running for the car with James. She'd been shot at. Witnessing the fight with James had been terrifying. His proficiency was amazing, and still he took blows. But with the gun, everything felt final. No chance to talk her way out of it or puzzle through the problem. One bullet, then death.

After the immediate danger had passed, her head cleared enough to absorb that James knew the second man. He was a killer from the era of James's history that haunted him. James had never forgiven himself for that part of himself. She had no idea how he'd react now that he was faced with it.

She wanted to ask, to do whatever she could to protect him the way he had her, but the words caught in her throat. James maintained the stern exterior of a seasoned soldier in combat. It didn't seem like she could reach through his body armor. He spun through the AM radio stations until they landed on local news.

The first report detailed the traffic they were sitting in. The woman on the radio gave some hope for it clearing after a certain street, but April didn't know how far up that was or how long it would take to get there.

After the traffic came the weather, then a man

spoke in clear, clipped sentences about the breaking news. The high school was under lockdown as officers cleared the area after reports of shots fired a block away. She thought about what James said about the parents. Everyone must be terrified.

The radio announced that no injuries were reported, but ambulances were on the way as a precaution. Eyewitnesses had hazy accounts of three men and a woman involved in the conflict. "It appears that the woman fled with one man while the other two men left the scene together."

April looked about at the other cars on the highway and imagined that all the people were listening to the same report. Prickles of nervous awareness swept over her skin. She searched the sky, expecting to see a helicopter hovering over her and James. He, too, scanned around them. If the witnesses had seen their car and it was reported, all eyes would turn to them. There would be nowhere to go on the gridlocked highway. Her breath strained, like she was slowly being suffocated.

The radio continued, "One of the men was wearing military clothing, but there is no word on the kinds of weapons they had."

Her heart pounded. Her palms sweat on the steering wheel. James had his hand on the door latch, like he was ready to bolt. Did the radio have a description of the car?

The radio man went on. "The situation continues to evolve, and the police are asking residents to be alert and report any unusual activity. Anyone with information should call 911 immediately."

She let out a long breath. No word about the car. James released the latch and rubbed his hand over his forehead. They moved through the traffic sludge and he kept an eye on the helicopter action over the school.

"One police helo, three news at higher elevations." His situation report was strictly military. He pulled out his phone and punched through the apps. "I have to update Automatik."

"Is that where we're going in California?" She imagined a high-tech hangar at the end of an unmarked airstrip.

James typed and talked. "Part of the team. A place to lay low."

If they could ever get there. The highway rose to a crest about a half a mile ahead, and it was taillights all the way. "Then?"

He clipped, "I don't know." The end of that conversation.

She released the steering wheel and her fingers creaked. Rubbing her palms together dislodged the gravel that had dented into her flesh during the scrabbling run for the car.

"Are you hurt?" James looked at her with pained, worried eyes.

She flexed her hands, stretched her arms out a bit and wiggled her legs. "Just bruises."

"Good." He checked the left sleeve of his jacket and revealed a six-inch gash in the leather. Her stomach turned with the thought of that being in his skin. The scream of the man he'd stabbed would haunt her for a long time.

"It didn't get you?" She reached over to check his arm.

He pulled away and ran his fingers in the opening. "No blood." His distance reminded her of the gloom between them this morning. But deeper. His eyes were almost lost. His face stony. He'd receded to a very private place, and it didn't seem like she could reach him there.

But she had to try. "Mark never told me what it was like to get shot at."

"He probably never wanted you to know." James brought his brows together, pained. "I wish you didn't know."

"Thanks for saving my ass." They were still too damn close to where it had all happened. "Again."

"My pleasure." His smile faded quickly. "You were in on it, too, getaway driver. Well done."

"I had good motivation." She still hadn't come down from the rush of fear. Her legs prickled with the need to run or kick.

"But you kept your head and got us out of there like a pro." His mood lightened, but a storm cloud continued to swirl deep in his look.

She extended her fist to him, and he stared at it for a moment before bumping her knuckles with his. The small touch didn't last long enough. He receded again while maintaining his activity by watching the unfolding scenario over the school. She focused on driving and took long breaths to keep from getting too nervous.

They crested the ridge on the highway. She expected to see another hundred miles of stopped cars, but they were only an exit away from road construction and the freeing of traffic. The radio cycled through the story again, with no new details.

She still didn't feel safe. "I was hoping there'd be news about…them…being apprehended."

"Hired killers." He filled in what she couldn't say, mouth turned down in a scowl.

She ventured, "That was the man you worked with?"

He nodded and reseated his pistol in the holster. "I lived and died with him. He was the sergeant of my SAS troop." James looked everywhere but at her. "After discharge, I went freelance with him." That was all. He fell silent. The remote expression on his face told her there would be no more information.

They finally reached the break in the traffic. She wanted to stand on the gas and put as much distance between them and the scene of the fight as possible, but she restrained herself and kept the car at a reasonable speed to avoid suspicion. It didn't matter how many miles to the west they made it, though; James's reserve was impenetrable.

HIS PISTOL HAD been reloaded. He'd updated Automatik with the latest operational developments. April was secure and in motion toward a safe place. She hadn't been hurt. They hadn't been identified by the authorities and weren't being followed by either the police or the hunters. But he still hadn't done enough. Hathaway was still out there. He'd shot at April with the intent to kill, and James hadn't ended him for that.

"He'll regroup," James explained to April as she drove. It was a way of lining up all the moving pieces in his mind. "The bloke I cut will get patched up and sidelined. There are others Hathaway can call in, and he'll move out." He used to be one of those perimeter men. "They might've been in close support already."

She checked the rearview mirror, but James had

already scanned for an unwanted shadow. "How long will that take?"

"We have a couple-hour head start on him." But he seethed, knowing Hathaway was out there, picking the scenery apart with his squinting eyes. "And he doesn't know what direction to search."

"But he knows we're still looking for the hackers." Though they had no current leads, she maintained her energy. "It might turn into a protection detail for him."

"It could." The price would go up; Hathaway preferred to be hunting on the loose. "He probably doesn't know where they are at this point. Just anonymous wired funds." An exit approached on the desert highway, leading to what looked like the only civilization for a million miles. "Get off here. We'll fuel and food."

Compared to the congestion of Phoenix, this little stretch of gas stations and drive-through restaurants was absolutely desolate. He kept expecting the iconic American desert to be hot, but the winter wind cut bitterly.

April brought the car to a stop at a gas station and peeled her hands from the steering wheel. She was still rattled from the encounter, and could fry herself revving that high for too long.

"I'll take over driving," he told her. "Get the battery out of that burner phone and trash everything. We'll pick up a new one here."

He got out and set about fueling the car. April seemed a bit wobbly on her legs for a moment, but steadied herself and discreetly pulled the phone apart and threw it in the garbage.

"Cash for the new phone?" she asked, hand outstretched.

He gave her the money and kept watch while she entered the store. Damn it all. They'd learned each other so well and operated great together. In the field, in bed. After a rough start, the communication had flowed easily. But now it choked down to the bare necessities, and he felt his own chest constricting. He'd been an idiot to think he could escape his past with Hathaway.

The car fueled quickly. His nerves jumped to get back on the road. It wasn't the answer, and there was no clear next step to the mission, but at least it was movement.

April returned with a bag from the shop, her expression neutral. "We're too far north." She got into the passenger seat and he joined her in the car. "They had a map on the counter. We have to jump down to Highway 8 to get to San Diego. In about thirty miles, there's a north-south highway that'll get us there."

"Good navigating." He pulled them out of the gas station and to a drive-through for lunch. "Any strange looks? Anyone marking you?"

"It didn't seem like it." She adjusted her sunglasses. He couldn't read her. Those eyes could be looking at him and only seeing what he used to be, a cold gun for hire.

They got their food and hit the highway again. AM radio still came in, giving them the news reports out of Phoenix. So far, April and James had remained unidentified, with none of their specifics announced for the public. The school had been cleared, all the students released to their parents safely.

"Silvia will be worried." April put her food down and dug through the gas station bag for the burner phone. She hadn't set it up yet, so he pulled out his phone, keyed the code and handed it over. "Thanks." She turned down the radio and dialed. "Silvia, it's April. We're fine." The most important info first. She paused as Silvia talked, then explained, "I know how bad it sounds. It's not what we wanted down there. We were ambushed."

His gut clenched. Fucking Hathaway.

Silvia's concerned tone came through the line. April heard her out. "We're okay. Really. No injuries. James is…amazing. He got us out of there."

"You drove," he reminded her.

Her brief smile reminded him of how they'd been learning to communicate. But that was lost.

"You need to be safe," April told Silvia. "I don't think they know we saw you, but I don't trust anything anymore."

That should include James. He brought the worst of the world to her. "Can she stay somewhere else?"

April repeated the question to Silvia, then told James, "She has a friend she can go to."

"Good. Have her text the address to this number." He had to make sure the violence didn't spread too far. "Any sign of trouble, she can call the authorities. Don't worry about our status. She has to be safe."

April started to speak into the phone, then turned to him. "I… Can you just tell her?" She handed him the phone, and he went over the same information with Silvia.

"I understand, James," Silvia replied, voice serious. "Thanks for taking care of her."

"Doing my best." He gave the phone back to April. His best barely kept them alive. He hadn't stopped the killer who wanted her dead.

"We're going to a friend's as well." April wrapped up her call with Silvia. "I'll check in and let you know… Absolutely… You, too, babe…" She hung up and handed his phone back.

He secured it and stared ahead for the highway interchange marker. Nothing on the horizon.

April resumed her lunch, then asked, "Food?"

His sandwich was still wrapped in his lap. "No appetite right now." He seethed with no outlet. How many people had he helped terrorize with Hathaway? People like April, with lives and friends and dreams worth chasing. Some of them, Hathaway had killed as part of the contract. That blood was on James's hands.

April motioned for his sandwich. "Give it to me. I'll keep it in the bag."

"It's fine."

"It'll get cold."

"It's fine." Was she trying to draw him out like before? She should be cursing him for being part of her horror.

"Cold fast food is never fine." She waved her fingers for the sandwich.

He pushed it into her hand and refocused on the road. "I've lived for weeks off cold ORPs made in muddy water."

"ORP?" She bundled his sandwich in the food bag and set it behind his seat.

"Operational Ration Pack."

"Like an MRE." She wrinkled her nose. "Tried those once. I don't know how you guys do it."

He scoffed. "American rations are so unrefined. No tea powder sachet in sight."

"Delicious." She stuck her pinky up ironically.

"Quite." His phone buzzed, and he checked the screen. "Silvia texted me her friend's address." He keyed the phone's code and split his attention between it and the road and forwarded the text to Automatik.

"Is she going to be okay?" April watched the side mirror, as if she could see her friend in the distance.

"She will." A buzz on his phone indicated a return response from Automatik. He paraphrased, "Two of our best are inbound to keep an eye on her. A former SEAL and that woman sniper I told you about."

"Thanks." She turned to him, eyes blocked by her sunglasses. "Like you were watching me."

"Exactly." Ben and Mary would be invisible, but ready. "She won't know unless she has to." He looked at the next section of the text. "No news on Hathaway or his team. No blips on the injuries at any of the hospitals."

She crumpled the last of her food into her bag and tossed it in the backseat. "They probably just glued him together."

"I've done that." He tugged the collar of his T-shirt down to reveal a jagged scar under his collarbone. "Bullet creased me, and we didn't have time for stitches."

She shuddered. "God."

"Wasn't as bad as the shrapnel in my thigh." He flexed the leg, glad that pain had passed. "Had to hike out quite a few klicks with a tampon stuck in the hole."

Her mouth hung open. "Why did you have a tampon?"

"To plug wounds. Why else?" He pointed with his thumb to the back. "Can I get my food?"

She retrieved it with a queasy look on her face. "Now you're hungry?"

"All that talk about ORPs made me thankful I don't have to eat them anymore." He opened the bag and dug into the food. She'd been right. As it cooled, all the flaws in flavor and texture were highlighted. But he needed the fuel.

Yes, he wasn't a soldier anymore. Not in the way he'd been when he served Her Majesty. The days of those rations were over. He wasn't a merc either. He couldn't afford hundred-dollar bottles of Irish whiskey anymore. Even if someone gifted him one, it would take him months to drink it, instead of one night.

The thought of the whiskey on his tongue was worse than the waxy fast food. He ate everything for the necessary calories and balled up the trash. April took it from him and stowed it with hers.

If he wasn't a soldier or a merc, what was he? Automatik had recruited him to be a protector, and his missions for them had felt like a success. Never enough to outweigh what he'd done with Hathaway, though. Even a well-placed bullet couldn't change that past. Only April had helped him ease the tension of those scars. Whatever she thought of him now, he knew he wouldn't stop until she was completely safe.

CHAPTER FIFTEEN

PART OF HER recognized that the desert in winter was beautiful. They'd seen thick rogue clouds in the distance. Small storms had collected quickly to rain angrily, then dispersed on the wind. None of it left an impression on her soul, the way nature should. In the past, on trips, she'd seen landscapes that had made her feel incredibly small and expansive all at once. Mountains that took her breath away and rivers that made her want to run forever like the water. But as they headed west, the last of the sun in their eyes, she was merely mechanical. The world broke down into safety or danger, with no pleasure in between.

James remained mostly silent. He'd made a phone call when they'd been about an hour away from San Diego, but since then, his face had been stern. There were times during their earlier communication that she'd thought she could find him again. He'd receded, giving her no opportunity to access him.

Had it only been three days? Four? Barely any time. But also so much time. In danger. Thrown together. Fighting. Searching. And finding each other. That was why it felt so hollow not being able to talk to him or see the quick understanding in his eyes she'd grown accustomed to. She'd just discovered this man, and now she'd lost him again.

She killed time setting up the second burner phone.

When they were lucky enough to get phone service, she searched for news on the Phoenix incident. She scanned and reported, "No new leads. Traffic was fucked for a while around the school, but that's all they're talking about now."

"If they don't have anything after this much time, they won't pick up any trails." He took off his sunglasses and tossed them in the center console. Efficient reserve showed in his eyes. No way in.

"We're invisible." Would she ever be able to live in normal society again?

"To some." James remained grim. "A ghost can hunt a ghost."

Hathaway was still out there. From the way he'd spoken during the fight, he wasn't going to quit. She shivered. She was the target. "How long?"

"If he catches a lead, he's a day away at most." James drove them into the city of San Diego. "We don't know what our next step is, so he won't." He continued to be terse and remote. She expected more of the same from whatever safe place they were going. In El Paso, she'd only gotten a glimpse of his partner, the man with the red hair. Who were these soldiers of Automatik?

A few miles into the city, James slowed and entered a neighborhood of nice, small houses on narrow streets. It reminded her of home, making a cool sweat break out over her skin. What was happening at her house? It could be burning, her life in ashes. Or Hathaway and his men could be ransacking it for clues. All her secrets and privacy torn apart, while she was hundreds of miles away.

James pulled into the driveway of one house and followed it around back until they were hidden from the street. A man opened a door and stepped out onto a small porch. The only light came from within the house, silhouetting his broad, muscular frame and bald head.

"That'll be Art." James shut down the car. The engine ticked down, and she realized that she and the machine had been redlining since Phoenix. She wanted to stay inside the metal shell, the only place that had been safe, but James opened his door and swept the cold air inside.

She got out and breathed in the salty air. James collected their gear, and she walked with him to the back porch. Art's face was still obscured. He cocked his head for them to enter and stepped into the warm house.

Past a little laundry room, the place opened into a decent-sized kitchen and dining area. The house seemed to be from the '40s, with upgrades to take away from the cramped architecture of that era. Instead of quaint, the kitchen was functional with industrial fixtures and well-used pots and pans stacked in organized rows. The door closed behind her. Art locked it. He joined them in the kitchen, where she finally saw his stern face. But a clever light shined in his eyes, and she knew there was more to him than just muscle.

He motioned to the open dining room. "I took a wall down." He turned to James, brow furrowed. "But you never saw this place before."

Sadness flickered across James, echoing into her own loneliness. "Never been to the restaurant either."

Art moved deeper into the house, past a small living room, to where a narrow hallway led to a master bedroom at the end. He pointed at doorways in the hall. "Guest bedroom. Bathroom."

James placed their luggage in the guest bedroom. When he stepped back into the hall, the wooden floor groaned.

Art walked away, explaining, "I left that creak there so we'd know if someone was in the hall. Do you need any ammo?"

"I'm full, thanks." James moved with him back toward the kitchen.

She added her small voice to the space. "I'm going to use the restroom."

Art turned to her. "Everything works like it should in there." His hard features softened with sympathy. "You hungry?"

"I think?" Her body was completely out of sorts.

"There are leftovers when you're ready." He didn't smile outright, but she did feel welcome in his home.

She used the bathroom and washed her hands for the first time since Phoenix. The tremors of that conflict continued, though the dirt from the street swirled down the drain. She rubbed water over her face in an attempt to return to humanity, but the last few days couldn't be undone. Hell, since Mark's death she'd been on the outside, looking in at other people's normal lives.

All her business in the bathroom was finished, but she stayed inside and leaned against the small vanity sink. A little silence. Solitude. James's recent distance had left her raw and alone. But she couldn't pull completely away from him. Everything was a knot, and she couldn't find the beginning or the end of the thread to unravel it.

She returned to the dining room to find James at

the table and Art in the kitchen, spooning food onto plates from a casserole dish. Art asked James, "You see what he was carrying?"

"Glock, .40." James sipped a glass of water and stared at the table. Did Art know that James had a history with Hathaway? Or was that something he'd only shared with her?

"Pro," Art responded, stoic. "Ex-military."

"Coordinated." James stood to accept the plates and placed them on the table. "Police don't have a trace." He pulled a chair out for April.

She removed her coat, body stretching tight against long-held tension, and hung it on the chair before sitting. Was she just one of the soldiers, hitting chow because it was necessary before getting back in the fight? The home around her wasn't a barracks. There was life here. She picked up a fork and looked at the food, trying to sort herself out.

"I like it cold." Art came to the counter that divided the kitchen from the dining area. "But I can warm it up if you like."

James watched her, as if to follow her lead. She cut a piece of the casserole with her fork and tried a bite. Rich flavors of cheese and chicken and potatoes helped ground her. Paprika spice hit the back of her tongue and helped her circulation find all the places she'd shut down since the fight.

"This is amazing," she said after swallowing. "Never had leftovers like this."

This was the first real smile she'd seen from Art. "I'll tell the chef."

She and James ate in silence. Art put the rest of the food away and joined them at the table. Her world was in too much turmoil to feel completely safe, but she trusted the capabilities of the men around her.

James finished his plate with a satisfied sigh. "You definitely have to make a reservation for me at the restaurant."

Art cleared the plates. "No reservation necessary. There's always a table for the team."

With a belly full of food, she succumbed to a bone-dragging fatigue. She felt her breath slow and her eyelids were heavy.

James asked across the dining room to Art, "Do you have any denatured alcohol and a rag for burning?"

"Blood?" Art put the dishes in the sink and opened a cabinet further back toward the laundry room.

"The bloke held his knife like a marine." James cracked a wry grin. "He didn't have a chance."

Art returned with a can of alcohol and a rag. "Sounds like a royal marine to me." He plunked the goods down in front of James. They sassed each other, but didn't puff up with any real offense.

"Cheers." James pulled his knife.

She saw the congealed and crusted blood on the steel and stood from the table. "I'm going to lie down for a bit."

James stood. "You alright?"

"Just tired." She edged out of the dining room. "Thanks for the food." Art gave her a nod. "I'm fine," she reassured James as he continued to look at her with concern.

"We'll be right out here." He hadn't broken out of the reserve that had distanced him from her, but it was clear he was still committed to her safety. Tears loomed just below the surface. She couldn't steady her voice to answer James.

Fatigue scraped her nerves raw. She closed herself into the guest bedroom and tried to find her balance. A pile of hand weights took over one corner, and a bookshelf along one wall was filled with all varieties of books. She reached for one, just to get out of her head for a minute, but her weary eyes couldn't even focus on the title. It took all her energy to get her shoes off and dim the overhead light before falling backward onto the made bed.

James's and Art's voices rumbled like distant thunder, bouncing back and forth as they conversed in the other room. She couldn't make out the words. Were they talking about her? Or the mission? The blood on the knife had been too much for her to see, and she focused on the memory of one of the desert clouds in order to distract herself. She drifted up with it, toward a deep blue sky. She was surrounded by James's echo and fell asleep.

"YOU WERE NEVER the trigger man?" Art bore holes through James with his stare.

"Would that make a difference?" James ragged the blood from his knife. He worked the soaked fabric into the seam where the grip met the blade, carrying away any trace of the man he'd stabbed.

Art glanced at the knife. "It makes a difference."

James felt like he was cleaning his own blood from the steel after performing surgery on himself. Telling Art about his past opened a lot of wounds. Art just kept staring at him. His body was still, but James knew his mind was turning. The man could explode in a split second. Art had that kind of trigger. James wouldn't blame him at all.

Art stood. James readied himself to be berated or hated. Art should be contacting the rest of the Automatik team to let them know the worst of James's redacted file. "I have an old barbecue out back. We can burn that there."

He started walking without another word, and James sheathed his knife to follow. They stepped into the cold night and Art searched through tall grass in his small yard until he found a small grill. He lifted the lid for James. James pulled a lighter from his jacket, lit the edge of the rags and tossed them in the grill. The alcohol caught in a hot gulp. The fabric curled and blackened. A few moments later there was no traceable evidence left.

Art replaced the lid but didn't return to the house. "Does she know?"

"She does." James tried to hold on to the hope he'd felt after he'd told her and she'd still accepted him, but that was before his past had come alive and pointed a gun at her.

Art still didn't move. "You and her…?"

"For a minute." James wished he had a pint in his hand and could wet his dry throat. "Before the bullets. Now…" He lost his voice.

Art crossed his arms over his chest. "No thoughts about going back to that life?" He cocked his head and eyed James. "You're not double booking?"

The first impulse of anger urged James closer to Art, who uncrossed his arms. James was prepared to list all the ops he'd done with Automatik, and Art. But he understood Art's mistrust and backed off. "I'm never going back."

"Bueno." Art rolled his shoulder, his body loose as he returned to his house. James went in with him and tried to let this acceptance sink in. Once they were back in the kitchen, Art motioned toward a high liquor cabinet. "No drink, right?"

"Not on the job." He really wanted the mission to be over so he could raise a glass with Art and the other Automatik operators. And April.

Art opened a lower cabinet and retrieved a covered bin. "Hayley baked yesterday." He removed the lid. "Cookie?"

THE MATTRESS CURLED next to April, drawing her body toward someone who sat there.

"James?" She couldn't remember where she'd gone to sleep and blinked and blinked against her dried contacts in an attempt to see.

"I'm Hayley," a woman's voice whispered. "This is my house, with Art."

April sat up and focused on the blonde with the sharp eyes. "Thanks for putting us up. And that casserole was absolutely the best."

Hayley smiled. "Thanks." She smelled of cumin and pepper. "Is there anything that you need?"

"Is James alright?" She hadn't been separated from him for this long since they'd met.

"They're fine." Hayley stood. "But if you want any of my cookies, you might want to get in there now."

April's mouth watered. A simple pleasure like a homemade cookie had seemed impossible. She pulled herself from the bed.

Hayley led the way toward the kitchen. "Hot tea?"

"Perfect, thanks."

Hayley paused in the living room and looked April over with compassion. "I know where you are. I've been there and we'll all get you through." The rawness of her nerves had receded, but tears still welled in her eyes when Hayley's care wrapped around her. April took a second, and a breath, before following the woman into the rest of the house.

James and Art huddled at the dining room table like they were planning an assault on a beachhead. But in front of them was a glass container of cookies. Or what was left of them. When James saw April, he stood. "Good sleep?" He'd taken his jacket off, but still wore his gun.

"Like I hit the off switch." No dreams. But no comfort either. She felt rested but not refreshed. It would've been different if James had lain next to her.

Art pushed the cookies toward her and joined Hayley in the kitchen. She murmured to him about the tea, and the two of them went about putting it together. They moved easily in the kitchen, sometimes bumping against one another, lingering with the touch.

April sat at the table and smelled the cookies. Lavish brown sugar and butter draped like a cloak around her, with an extra edge she couldn't identify. Burnt caramel? "What are these?" She took one of the marvels in her hand.

Hayley answered from the stove. "Bourbon brown sugar browned butter chocolate chip cookies."

"Fuck…" April whispered reverently.

James was absorbed with an intricate process on a piece of cardboard on the table. "They're bloody good."

His mood hadn't completely shifted, but she sensed a shift. Like a strong wind that might chase the storm. He squeezed out two tubes of glue on the cardboard and mixed the thick pools with a plastic knife.

The odor wasn't strong enough to overpower the taste of the cookie as she took her first bite. The warmth of the sugar and bourbon were pervasive, picked up and smoothed out by the chocolate. The flavors went deeper and deeper as she ate. In three bites, the cookie was gone.

"Unbelievable." April was already reaching for another.

"Thanks." Hayley smiled, and Art stood behind her and kissed the side of her neck.

April tried to let the cookie overwhelm the lonely pang in her chest. James was just a few feet away, but so much farther. He was too absorbed in his task to see her staring at him. Or he was ignoring her as she tried to reach him. The glue was mixed, then he pulled his jacket from the back of the chair and proceeded to spread the opaque mixture on the gash in the sleeve.

Art chuckled as he lined up mugs. "I've been there. Except it was on my arm." He held up a heavily tattooed forearm and traced a thin white line. "Old rusty bridge cable got me as we scrambled down a ravine."

James matched Art's story with his own glued-up chest injury. The water boiled, and Hayley stepped up to the mugs, pouring and nodding. "Glued the tip of my finger back on once. Fucking seafood restaurant was the worst. I don't know if it was the knife or the oyster shell that did it, but I had to keep working or they'd give my job to someone else."

"I'm kind of not sorry I've never glued parts of my

body back on." April felt soft in the midst of these soldiers and tough chef.

James continued to work on his jacket. "You've put yourself back together."

Hayley arrived with tea for April and herself. "And a lot of other people. Your website is amazing."

April could only half smile her thanks. The website was dead, its revival a fading possibility. The leads were gone, and Hathaway still wanted to kill her to keep it that way. She sipped her tea and ate another cookie and wished it was just a friendly visit that had brought her to Art and Hayley's home.

James completed his task and laid the jacket across a side table with the arm extended to dry. He returned to the table and sat, but seemed restless without something to do. Hayley watched him, then turned her attention to April.

"When I met Art, he was on a mission." Hayley wrapped her hands around her mug. "I didn't know anything about this stuff. Automatik. Secrets." She leaned into Art when he sat next to her. "I know that when you're in the middle of it, the beginning seems like some kind of nightmare dream thing you can't escape, and there's no end in sight."

April felt that trap tight around her.

Hayley continued with a sardonic chuckle. "I was just a desperate chef trying to gig and I thought Art was a goon with the Russian mob. But he turned out to be Automatik. And those men and women come through." She put her hand on April's arm. "We're all going to get you through."

"They take a shot at one of us, it's a shot at all of us." Art spoke to James as well. "No one gets away with that. No one." If she hadn't shared cookies with the man, April would be downright scared of Art's stainless-steel determination.

James seemed to pick up on Art's resolve and straightened. "There's a way at them, and I'll find it." He turned to her. A thread of their connection wound through her. But the energy didn't flow completely between them. An ache of sadness filled the distance. "We're not done."

Was he only talking about the mission, or about the intimacy they'd found and lost? "Are we planning tactics tonight?" Her nap hadn't done enough to revive her. After the cookies and hot tea, she felt the call of the bed again.

"Sleep." James considered her face, his eyes warming. "By morning I'm sure you'll figure out a way to wreck those bastards."

She couldn't argue with the notion of sleep and stood. The room wobbled around her, and she knew she wouldn't be sharp and helpful if she forced herself to stay awake much longer.

Hayley walked with her back to the bedroom. "You good?"

"Yeah." April sat heavily on the bed and removed her shoes. "Just burnt."

"I feel you." Hayley patted extra towels on the top of a small dresser. "It's hard to stay cranking for that long." She tipped her head back toward the other room. "I don't know how they do it."

"Training. I watched my husband learn it." She'd met Mark just after he'd enlisted, and he'd told her what they were put through.

"Right." Hayley sighed. "I'm sorry about that."

"Thank you." The mattress tugged at April like a welcome black hole.

"Extra toothpaste and a new toothbrush in the bathroom. Towels." Hayley hovered in the doorway. "Is there anything else you need?"

James. April didn't want to sleep alone. She wanted that link they'd found, that understanding. But she didn't know how to get it back. Her throat tightened with frustration. "No."

Hayley closed the door behind her. April stood to turn out the light and returned to the bed, alone in the unknown.

CHAPTER SIXTEEN

THE HOUSE WAS locked tight and quiet. James lay awake on the couch in the living room, mind buzzing, body restless. Art and Hayley had gone to bed not long after April. There was no way that Hathaway or the hackers knew where to find April. She was safe here, but he couldn't stop spinning terrible scenarios. A strike team through the windows. A battering ram through the front door. Or an armored car crashing into the corner of the house and taking the walls down so armed operatives could move in. In each action, he couldn't come up with a way to protect April.

The floorboards creaked in the hall, and he sat up, hand on the grip of his pistol. April walked across the hall to the bathroom. He tried to let the initial rush of danger pass, but his legs had to act. He stood. A weight pushed down on his shoulders. The burden could crush him.

A couple of minutes passed, then April stepped back into the hall, foot hitting the groaning floorboard again. She paused and stared at him. She wore her glasses now, making her eyes unreadable from the distance in the shadows. After a moment, she disappeared into the bedroom.

He couldn't just stand there. He couldn't move. He had to. After the attack, pulling away from April had been agony. He'd thought it was for her good, her safety, but there'd only been an unending sense of loss. Through it, she hadn't changed. The woman had never judged him, while he was sending his soul straight to hell.

James walked to the hall, stepped around the weak point on the floor, and entered the guest bedroom.

April sat up in the bed and found her glasses on the side table. "Is there trouble?" she whispered.

"No." He remained in the doorway. "I'm here because..." He was a part of Automatik. He wasn't a mercenary anymore. As April's protector he couldn't stand being so far away from her anymore. "I don't know how to fix this."

"The mission? The hackers?" Sleep remained raspy in her voice.

"Me...and you." He took a step toward her. "You know who I am. You've seen it. Who I've been."

"Yes." She drew herself up so she was kneeling on the bed.

"And you let me in the room?" Any sign of fear from her, he'd leave.

"Yes." In the dark, she was a collection of calm clouds.

"I don't want to leave," he confessed.

"Don't." She tipped her chin up like a queen staying his execution.

"I want you." He was completely exposed.

"Come here." She put out her arms, and he moved to her. Her hands glided over his shoulders and around his back. He kneeled on the bed with her and breathed in the desert storms on her hair and skin. They coiled together. A tremble rose through him and dissipated.

He kissed her, and she returned it tenderly. Silent acceptance that confirmed everything she'd said.

They parted. "You're amazing," he told her.

"Lay down." She pushed on his body with her palms.

He removed his shoulder holster, boots and socks and jeans. She pulled the blankets back as he piled everything on the floor, his pistol at the top. He climbed into bed, between her and the door. She curled into his body, wrapping her legs around his and twining one arm behind his shoulders. The other hand rested on his chest. His breathing slowed.

Her lips brushed against his shoulder when she spoke. "We have our pasts. We can't let them have us."

The night stilled. The quiet surrounded them and seemed to expand beyond the walls and roof and city. He placed his hand on hers and held her. Yesterday couldn't be changed. Tomorrow was unknown. He gripped her tighter. She wound her fingers through his. One second. That was all he needed. One second with her, then the next. He lived each one, feeling her strong and brave presence next to him. He allowed sleep to approach, knowing that after sunrise, he'd fight like hell for her.

SHE WOKE TO find herself still wrapped around James. The quiet of falling asleep together had been as restorative as the sleep itself. Having him next to her now felt right. She didn't want to fight against their histories any longer. Holding James, trusting him, didn't take away from what she had with Mark. That life, that marriage, couldn't be altered. This life had to start now.

Of course James was already awake. She couldn't see without her glasses but felt his breathing, steady but not deep. Heavy curtains blocked all but a sliver of light at one edge of the small window in the guest bedroom. A kiss on James's arm turned his head toward her.

"Good morning," his voice rumbled.

"Good morning," she squeaked, then cleared her throat. "Did you sleep?"

"I did." He sounded impressed. "Better than in a long time."

She stroked over his chest. He rolled over for a brief kiss. Neither had brushed their teeth, but it conveyed that the risk he'd taken to find her last night continued. After hours under the covers together, their hot bodies sweat, and skin clung to skin. His erection glanced across her thigh. Her body responded with a quickening of her pulse and a blaze of awareness between her breasts and around her hips. But neither moved further. The moment wasn't right and the circumstances of the mission were too unsettled.

James ran his fingers through her hair. "Another morning, and you're mine." His conviction wrapped her in heat. A thirst she could never satisfy scratched her throat.

"Another night, when we can take our time." His beard prickled against her fingers.

"We will," he promised.

Another kiss, then they unknotted their bodies. Cold air moved in where she no longer touched him, but parting this time didn't make her feel like she'd lost him. He got out of the bed and dressed. She got her glasses on in time to see him pull his shirt over the muscles of his back.

"No tattoos?" she asked, though she hadn't done a full inspection of his skin. Yet.

"None." He shrugged on his shoulder holster. "But the idea's growing on me. A dagger through a skull." He swiped a hand across his chest. "Or Kali, with all of her arms."

She stepped from the bed and collected her clothes. "Maybe start small."

"I'll consult Art. Have you seen his work?"

"It's bold." Art conveyed a lot of attitude through his ink.

"Hayley, too." James sat to pull on his boots. She steadied herself on his shoulder as she balanced on one leg to dress. When he stood again, they were both fully clothed. He unplugged his phone from a charger on the side table. "Bathroom's yours. I'm going to check in."

She stepped into the hallway to find Art on one end, near the master bedroom. Even dressed in something as casual as jeans and a sweatshirt, he looked dangerous. But there was nothing mean about his face.

"All good?" he queried.

"Yeah." She pointed toward the bathroom to indicate her destination. He nodded understanding, and she went in. She brushed her teeth, put in her contacts and took care of her other morning needs. By the time she was out, sounds in the kitchen indicated the house was completely awake.

James walked from the dining area and past her, toward the bathroom. He tapped his phone. "Ben and Mary have eyes on Silvia and there are no signs of trouble." He closed the door behind him, and she proceeded to the dining area.

Hayley moved with relaxed efficiency in the kitchen

while Art backed her and helped with supplemental tasks. "Coffee, right?" Hayley indicated a kettle over a flame on the stove and a French press standing by.

"Absolutely." There was no room for April in the kitchen. She remained in the dining area and leaned on the separating bar to watch Hayley's mastery. Eggs were cracked and vegetables sliced. Art brought Hayley a package of sausages, which she cut into discs and scraped into a large pan with sliced onions.

Hayley looked up from her cooking with concern. "No allergies?"

"None," April responded.

"Anything you won't eat?"

"Liver." April's stomach flipped just thinking about it. "Stuff like that."

Hayley pointed at her with a wooden spoon. "I'll change your mind about liver sometime, but not for breakfast."

April hesitated with a doubtful whimper.

Art pointed at himself. "It worked for me, and I never thought it would."

"I'll try it," April acquiesced. "And if you ever want me to take a look at your website, I'd be happy to."

"Shit, that would be awesome." Hayley nodded emphatically as she threw more food in the sizzling skillet. The caramelized hot edge of the onions reached April's nose, as well as sweet peppers and voluptuous tomatoes. Hayley stirred and talked. "We used one of those do-it-yourself site builders, and there's all kinds of stuff that's not working."

Art brought a stack of plates next to the stove. "The mobile site's jacked."

"I can fix that." April already went through the check-

list of things to look for in the code. "That's how everyone's looking at things these days. We'll get you up to
date."

"Sweet." Hayley whisked eggs in a large bowl. "It'll
be a liver and website party."

"Can't wait." James returned with a wry smile. He
leaned on the counter next to her, shoulder to shoulder.
"Sounds like a hell of a time."

Hayley shot him a look. "You and Art can mud
wrestle or something."

Art flexed and stated, "I'd win."

James straightened and stared him down. "Probably." After they seemed to reach a truce, James joined
her again.

Someone knocked on the front door. James wrapped
his hand around his pistol. Art pulled a revolver down
from the top of the refrigerator. Hayley winced, and
April scanned for cover in the dining room. Silently,
James and Art communicated with their eyes and hand
gestures. They moved toward the front door. April's
breath tightened and her sweating hands clenched into
fists.

A voice came from outside. "Raker, reporting for
duty." James and Art visibly relaxed.

Hayley blew out her tension, whispering under her
breath, "Jesus."

Even though they knew who it was, when Art opened
the door, James stood off to the side, covering him. A
lean, red-haired man with a trim mustache walked in
with his hands raised in mock surrender. He was around
James and Art's age, face weathered from time in the
sun, and wearing jeans, a flannel shirt and down jacket.

The door closed, he bumped fists with Art and James before coming over to her.

If he'd been wearing a hat, he would've taken it off with polite charm. He spoke with a country twang. "I'm Raker." He put out his hand, and she shook it. He had the calluses of a career soldier.

"April, but you know that."

He looked away, sheepish. "Yeah, part of the job." His face brightened when he brought his look back to her. "Glad to hear you've been out there kicking ass. Looks like Sant doesn't need his old partner no more."

James drew attention moving into the dining room. "We're going to need everyone for what I have in mind."

Art and Raker joined him at the table. The tension that had just released came back.

April came to his side, feeling her jaw clench. "You thought of something?"

Hayley continued to cook and listened in.

James took a long breath and put his hands on the table. "We can't find the hackers. The mercs are in the wind." He smiled, vicious. "We let them find us."

Hayley commented from the kitchen, "Not here."

"Not at all," James reassured her. "We bait them. Draw them out." He turned to April. "I think that address you found in Phoenix might've been a setup. They knew we were going to be there at some point."

Art and Raker considered the plan, both staring at the table as if there was a map complete with flags and miniature tanks. Her stomach churned. She tried to remain as stoic as the men, but fear trembled out through her fingers. "We saw what happened the last time they found us."

James growled bitterly. "We weren't ready."

"Two teams." Raker smoothed the corners of his mustache.

Art looked up at the ceiling, thinking, calculating. "Target and a wingman close enough to get in when things heat up."

April swallowed hard. "How hot?"

James put his hand on her arm. "As soon as he shows himself, we strike."

"I'm bait." She tried to fill her confidence with his.

"*We're* bait," he told her. "Hathaway's going to bring everything he's got now that he's been bled."

Raker regarded his partner warily. "You know his name?"

James tipped his head toward the back of the house. "A word."

"Alright." Raker remained reserved. He followed James through the kitchen and out the back door.

Hayley announced tightly, "Food's up." She spooned the scrambled-egg mixture onto the plates. Art added a butter-slathered piece of crusty bread to each before passing it over the bar to April. She set the food around the table, while Hayley brought out the coffee and mugs.

Ordinary business. But nothing felt normal. How could she go out there and put herself in danger? It didn't matter. She was in the crosshairs no matter what. If it meant taking the fight to them, punishing those sons of bitches, then she could do it.

James and Raker returned as Hayley was pouring the coffee. Raker had a slightly stunned look on his face, and James was grim. He must've told his partner about his past with Hathaway. They loosened up again when they rejoined the group and sat at the table.

Art pushed a mug of coffee toward Raker. "You drive all night?"

"Handful of sleep in a highway motel." He shrugged. "Not too bad."

Everyone ate the hearty yet deft food and complimented Hayley, who accepted graciously. Art collected the plates as they were emptied. April and the others were on their second cups of coffee when she brought them back to the mission. "I know how we can hook them."

All eyes were on her, especially James, who regarded her with admiration. "The idea is to put you in harm's way as little as possible. If at all."

"I'm in harm's way," she told him flatly.

Anger flashed in his eyes, but not for her. "So what's your plan?"

"The library," she said. Blank stares all around. "I'll use their computers to log on, check my email, snoop around for clues on the hackers. It'll ping on their side, and they'll pick up the IP address for the library."

Hayley muttered, impressed, over her coffee, "You do know your business."

James's eyes narrowed. He thought about it and scratched his jaw through his beard. "Library's too populated."

Raker leaned back in his chair. "You can draw them away. Give them time to scramble toward the target, then head them off somewhere."

"The freeway." Art leaned his elbows on the table. "He shows, you split, lead him to the freeway and we're in business."

James's energy built. "It can't be too close to your home."

"Oceanside?" Hayley ventured.

"That's good," Art agreed.

April asked her, "Do you have a laptop?" Hayley stood and went into the living room while the men continued to stare into the distance and strategize. She came back with a laptop and set it in front of April. The library in Oceanside was easy enough to find, and she zoomed in on the map. "Here it is."

The men huddled behind her and pointed out ingress and egress routes. Freeway options and lookout points. They identified choke points and dead ends. She watched James memorize it all. "Bloody brilliant," he murmured close to her. His appreciation of her brought a comfortable blush across her chest and up her neck.

"When do we do it?" she asked, wishing she could just soak in his admiration and not face the hazards of the mission again. But part of her was ready to take it on, knowing he'd be fighting at her side the whole way.

"Today," he answered, standing tall. "Now."

CHAPTER SEVENTEEN

SHE'D LEFT PHOENIX in fear. Driving up to Oceanside, April flexed her muscles and steeled herself for a fight. She wanted it. She wanted to scare Hathaway and his men off on the way to ending the hackers' control over her.

James drove and discussed the rules of engagement. Raker and Art were the primary shooters. James and April were merely planted to draw the enemy out. His job was to keep her safe throughout, not to go after the mercenaries. His dedication to her didn't go unnoticed. She knew how strongly he felt about Hathaway and understood it must've taken a lot of self-control to not place himself at the front of the hunting party.

It had been difficult to leave Art and Hayley's house behind. That spot had been such a center of community, more than she'd felt with more than one person in the same room in a long time. Art and Raker had argued about who was going to drive, with Art winning out because he knew the territory.

Hayley had said her goodbyes with April and somberly wished her good luck. April knew this woman had been thrown into similar circumstances and told her she'd like to hear her story sometime.

"When you come back." Hayley squeezed her hand.

"I'll come back." April said it for Hayley and to

convince herself. She had to return, safe and whole
and with James.

Whatever Hayley and Art spoke about was unheard
as they'd huddled close before the group embarked on
the next stage of the mission. Within a block of driving away from the house, April lost sight of Art and
Raker's car. They never reappeared on the freeway,
but she knew they hovered within striking distance.

Off the freeway and into the medium-sized city of
Oceanside, she quieted and watched. James navigated
them to the library without a map. His eyes didn't rest,
registering everything as they approached and passed.
She tried to do the same, tracking the best way back
to the freeway and noting which streets seemed more
congested than others.

They were on the south side of the Marine Camp
Pendleton. Men and women in BDUs walked on the
sidewalks and got in and out of cars, going about their
business. Seeing the uniforms only reinforced the idea
that the town wasn't a normal place. It was her war-
zone.

James parked the car and turned to her, solemn.
"There's a ritual Raker and I have before we rope in.
He puts his hand on my crotch, gives it a squeeze, then
I kiss him on the mouth."

She was shocked into a laugh that loosened some
of her nerves. "Well, I can't jinx the operation." She
teased her hand up the inside of his thigh and rested
it on his groin. He leaned to her and they kissed with
a simple promise that they were there for each other.

The kiss parted, and she steeled herself.

James smiled like a predator. "Let's fuck them up."

Shivers of fear diminished into her own thirst for revenge. They got out of the car and walked to the library. Inside, she was surrounded by normal life. Children tried to keep their voices down in the kids' reading area, people walked the stacks, while others spread out newspapers and magazines on the central tables. Along one wall was a long counter with the computers.

She angled James toward the customer service area next to the circulation desk. "We'll need a library card."

"Simon can take care of that." He pulled his wallet and the fake ID. Within a few minutes with the helpful library staff member, they had a card and instructions for how to get started on the computers. They picked the one farthest from any of the other patrons, where both of them could sit in the heavy institutional chairs.

She used the new card to open the computer terminal, then browsed to her email client. "Here we go." She logged in and watched her old life populate in front of her. Online shopping advertisements racked up. Political emails. And some personal ones, friends checking in or venting about their trials. Her mom had written twice and her father once. All the emails had come through her phone once they'd hit the road, but she'd ignored them, knowing to answer would leave a dangerous breadcrumb. "My parents are worried."

"Can you check in with them without telling them too much?" James split his attention between the computer and keeping an eye on the rest of the room.

"I think." Her mother had a way of reading between the lines and drawing her out if she was being obtuse, but she'd try not to give her the chance this time. She wrote an email to both of them, explaining that she'd gone on a road trip with some out-of-town friends who came to get her. The cell phone reception had been spotty, making this her first chance to email back. She sent it, and a realization sank into her. "I might not ever tell them the truth."

"It keeps them safer." James leaned his shoulder into hers. He was strong and he was also willing to trust her. "Sometimes, the more people who carry a secret, the heavier it is."

"You told Raker." The two men hadn't been in Art and Hayley's backyard for long.

"He wasn't as surprised as you'd think." James smirked. "None of us would've joined unless we were trying to fix something somewhere."

She pushed back with her shoulder. "I'm glad you joined."

"I'm glad I got out of the car before Raker in the supermarket parking lot." He smiled warmly.

"That's all it took? Coincidence?" It felt like much stronger forces had been at play.

He mulled the question. "We would've met, one way or the other." He scanned across the library, then brought his gaze back to her. "I can't imagine not having met you."

She blushed as he regarded her. But the flames couldn't burn her down. They were fuel. She reached forward, brave and open, curled her hand in the collar of his zipped-up jacket and tugged him into a blistering kiss. They parted, breathless.

James collected himself and refocused on the computer. "Was that enough to lure them?"

"Not yet." At no point had her email been compromised, so she couldn't be sure they'd ping off her latest activity. She opened another tab and searched for news on the incident outside the Phoenix high school.

"Anything new?" James read over her shoulder.

"No. But if the hackers are set up to ping off these searches, they'll see this one." She dove deeper and went to her forum website. At the top right was a small "Admin" link. "And this will set off all their alarms." She entered her user name and password, opening the dashboard of the website.

James tensed. "I thought that would get them past your encryption."

She clicked to the control panel for the forum, where a secondary login was necessary. "This is what stopped those fuckers."

He whispered reverently, "Sexy."

"It's as far as I can go." She logged out of the site and the internet and pushed her chair away from the computer. James stood and headed toward the closest unoccupied table by the door. The earbud connected to his phone threaded up through his jacket and was barely noticeable. There'd been no communication with the others since they'd left San Diego.

They sat on opposite sides of one corner of the table, both of them facing the exit. He muttered under his breath as he drew a discarded magazine toward him. "Now we learn one of the most important skills of soldiering: being more ready than the enemy after a long wait."

JAMES WATCHED THE strain rise and fall in April and wished he could do more to help her through this stage of the mission. They both flipped aimlessly through magazines and day-old newspapers, occasionally pointing out an interesting photo or ridiculous advertisement. Her nerves would rise when the front doors opened, then she'd breathe again after scrutinizing whoever entered.

He reassured her, "Art and Raker will see them long before they get in the door."

"Right." She tipped her head from side to side to stretch the tension from her neck. "I'm not used to being bait."

"You're the hunter now." He had his own difficulty waiting while Hathaway was out there, searching for her. But he reined it in, funneled it into productive anger that would help him in the fight. "He thinks it's going to be easy, but you're laying the trap that's going to end him."

She sneered with the power. Mean and ready.

"That's the look." A flare of awareness gathered in his cock. There were a lot of possibilities with April. Later, when they had the time to discover more of each other. He was reassured, too, when the feral expression dimmed from her face. She had enough of it in her to survive, but it wasn't in her nature. And that made her that much more beautiful.

He picked her hand up from the table and kissed the back of her wrist. A blush stained her cheeks, and a deeper heat showed in her eyes. "More soldiering?" she whispered.

"You're remarkable." He wished he knew all the words to describe her. He wished he could communicate everything without having to talk at all.

"Good Lord." Raker groaned in James's earpiece. "Ain't that a little thick?"

"Learn from that man," Art interjected. "He knows what he's doing."

James laughed, and April cocked her head to question it. He surreptitiously pointed at his earbud.

Raker didn't let it go. "I've already got a wife."

"Is she happy?" James muttered, blocking his mouth with his arm.

"I'll say," Raker replied.

"What does *she* say?" Art pressed.

"She says," Raker drawled, "'Mr. Raker, I like you.' Then I tell her I like her and we're all squared away. Nothing unnecessary like our verbose British friend here."

James brought his cheek to April's and whispered, "Tell me, April, do you like the words I say to you?" He leaned the earpiece close to her mouth.

She smiled, knowing his intent. Her husky murmur sent a shiver down his spine. "I do, James. You're quite a man."

Art laughed on the other end of the line.

Raker chirped with mock reproof, "Do you two know you're in a library?"

"You should see what we're reading." James kept his voice down and made it seem like he was still speaking to April lowly. "I'm translating the *Kama Sutra* for her."

She chuckled. "Did you invent that, too?"

"Of course." He pretended to brush dust from his shoulder. Their antics drew a couple of glances from the other patrons, but nothing sharp enough from the staff to warrant them coming over. The radio chatter died down, but it had helped to break up the waiting and he and April sat a little more comfortably at the table.

She tipped her chin up and stared at the ceiling.

Her finger tapped quickly, then she retrieved a small pad and pen from her purse. "Some ideas for Hayley and Art's website." She sketched diagrams, accompanied by cryptic symbols he couldn't decipher. When she was finished, she put the pen down with a look of satisfaction. Her finger no longer tapped. Her brows came together in a question when she looked at him. "Do you need a website?"

"Not at all." He'd never thought about it.

She started hesitantly, "What…what do you do when you're not doing…this?"

"I help out a couple of auto shops I know, doing electrical work for cars."

Her brows lifted. "So Simon's kind of real."

"The less you lie, the easier it is to keep the stories straight." But he had no more secrets to keep from her. "You ever need an in-dash entertainment system, I can hook you up."

"I'll let you know." She kept staring at him with a question. "That takes up all your time?"

"We're in the field a lot." It seemed like at least once a month he was in another city, planning an op, hitting the target. "Or I'll be at the gym. An MMA place I can walk to."

She lit up. "I'd like to learn some of that."

"You've got cardio. That's a good start."

She burned him with a glare. "Of course, you know that because you were trailing me."

"Doing my job." He wouldn't apologize. "Just like we're doing now."

Her eyes sharpened and addressed each person in the library. "I don't see anything strange," she reported.

"Just me." He held up his arm to display the line of glue that held the sleeve together.

"You could use a shower, too." She ran her fingers over his hair.

"The both of us." He waggled his eyebrows. "And lunch."

She leaned back in her chair and put her hands on her stomach. "Why'd you have to say that? Now I'm thinking about food. And Hayley's cookies." A delicious groan came from the back of her throat.

Art broke radio silence. "Probable targets inbound." James tensed and put his hand around April's arm. She looked at him, nerves rising, and waited. Art continued, "I count two cars. Four men visible. Lead car has a man in green M65 jacket, buzz cut."

Hathaway. "That's them," James announced.

"Three blocks out." Art sounded like he was moving. "I'm on foot, tracking to rendezvous with Raker."

"Just picked them up," Raker jumped in.

James stood, April with him. "We're moving out." He hated the strain of fear in her eyes and wanted to stay and take care of Hathaway himself, but he couldn't lead her into that much danger.

They walked quickly for the doors, and even though Raker tracked, "Two blocks," James pictured Hathaway bursting into the library any second.

"That was fast." April's voice wavered, tight. "Why were they so close?"

Chilly ocean mist hazed the sunlight outside. James and April rushed to the car. He had the motor started before they'd closed the doors and buckled themselves in.

"One block." Raker maintained his battlefield cool. "Art has rendezvoused, and we're at full force."

James peeled out of the parking lot. April tugged on her seat belt and helped him with his. Her question bit him. There was no way Hathaway could've tracked them to California. He and April had been airtight.

Into the city, the traffic grew thicker. He reported on the radio, "On the move. Freeway bound."

Art updated, "Two black SUVs. Livery markings, so they're probably custom, maybe bulletproof."

James glanced one block parallel and saw the two target cars hurrying toward the library. "Eyes on." Then he lost sight.

"They saw you, too." Raker grew excited. "Illegal U-turns across traffic. They're coming in hot."

James tried to keep his tone even when he caught April up. "Two black SUVs. They've spotted us."

She turned and watched out the back. "I see them." Her breath rushed. "Weaving through traffic. They're not being subtle."

One block until the freeway on-ramp.

Art gritted, frustrated, "We're following, but are getting caught up in the wake of their fucked-up driving."

James hit the on-ramp and floored the car, blowing through the traffic signal at the end of it and merging hard onto the freeway. A few seconds behind, the SUVs charged on after them. He figured out how they'd been so quick to respond to the bait. "Hathaway wasn't hunting after Phoenix," he told April and the radio. "The bastard pulled back. He was on guard duty."

April's eyes were wide with understanding. "The hackers…"

"They must be within a couple of hours of here." There was no indication of where, and the territory in California was vast, but even a single spot of blood on the trail could keep him on the hunt. "The hackers are close."

CHAPTER EIGHTEEN

SHE'D NEVER BEEN in a car going this fast. Even as a teenager, when everyone else thought they were immortal, she'd been very aware of the limits of life. She gripped anything she could in the car and hoped she didn't test those limits now. James dodged through light traffic, jaw clenched, mouth tight. The SUVs continued their pursuit about ten car lengths behind.

"They were afraid." She was, too, and couldn't look at the speedometer.

James showed his teeth. "They don't know fear yet."

If only she could revel in the panic that must've made the hackers want the mercenaries close by. The perils of the high-speed chase narrowed the scope of her thoughts to basic survival. "How close are Art and Raker?" She still couldn't see them behind.

"Not within striking distance." He swerved across two lanes to get around a slow-moving work van. She banged against the door and swallowed the pain in her arm and shoulder.

The black SUVs split up, one veering high, closer to them, while the other maintained a position closer to the slow lane. "They're cutting off our exit."

James swiveled his head, tracking them. "I see it."

She watched both SUVs edge nearer. Four car lengths away. "This wasn't part of the plan." Her throat closed on her words. The world blurred by. James was the only thing clear and in focus.

He stole a glance at her, fierce determination in his face. "We will end them."

How, she had no idea. But she couldn't doubt James's abilities and willpower. The windows rolled down on the SUV closest to them in the fast lane. The black steel of a killing machine protruded from the opening. Cold fear racked her body. "They have guns."

James spat, "Bloody monsters." He steered with one hand and drew his pistol with the other. "They're not even worried about collateral." All she could do was watch. He barked, "Weapons free. Weapons free," presumably to Art and Raker.

The SUV charged past a sedan and sped one lane parallel to James and April. Two car lengths. James countered by moving into their lane, directly in front of them. Giant concrete pillars for an overpass flew by, seemingly inches away from James's door. Her heart pounded and she fought to slow her breathing. The smallest bump, a bottle cap in the road, would wreck them completely at this speed.

She checked the SUV behind them at the same moment a flame flashed from the barrel of the passenger's gun. She ducked as the pop cracked. The bullet didn't impact their car. She had no idea where it landed.

"Contact. Contact," James repeated. The freeway curved. He yanked the car out of the lane, away from the SUV. He switched his pistol to his left hand and aimed out the open window. "Steer," he commanded.

She grabbed the juddering wheel and fought to keep them tracking with the curve. James fired three shots, then pulled back to face front, taking the wheel again.

She hoped to see the SUV engulfed in flames and slowing to a stop in the distance behind them. But the machine continued its pursuit.

"Bulletproof windscreen and panels." James steered to the center of the freeway. Once the shots had gone off, many of the drivers hit the brakes and backed off. But she and James still rushed into new traffic that had no idea what was coming.

"The police will be out soon." She scanned as far as she could, but there were no flashing lights yet.

"Roger that." James peeked in the rearview mirror. "Welcome to the ball."

She looked back to see Raker and Art's compact SUV powering into the mix. They approached the car on the far right of the freeway.

James spoke to them, "Copy that. We'll call them Car two. Car one has Hathaway."

The men in the SUV by them were obscured by the tinted windshield. "He's there?"

James's lip curled. "He's the one shooting at us."

Now she saw the man. He leaned further out of the car to aim toward them, his face a mask of deadly rage. His pistol fired again in a wild barrage. She dove low in the seat. A bullet blasted through the side window behind James. Another punched a hole in the door frame and roof.

"Stay down." James switched his gun to his left hand again and aimed while driving. His answering salvo chattered. He returned to driving for a moment, then shot again. She couldn't see the effect, but didn't hear any great damage to the SUV.

More gunfire popped to her right. She stole a quick

look at Art in the passenger seat of his car, trading fire with the other SUV. Both cars sped on.

James fired again and again, then turned back to face front, cursing. "The worst thing about bloody driving on the wrong side of the road is that I have to shoot with my left hand."

She saw the slide of his pistol was locked open and put her hand out. "Reload." As he handed her the gun she reached past his jacket to one of the fresh magazines on his shoulder holster. She ejected the old, slammed in the fresh and snapped the slide forward.

He took the pistol and immediately fired back at Hathaway's SUV. More bullets responded; one pinged off a rear wheel. "Switch, switch!" James called out. "He's trying for the tires."

She braced herself as James pulled hard to the right. The car screeched across the freeway, narrowly missing the trailer of a large semi. The truck helped block the SUV from staying on them. Raker and Art veered opposite, toward Hathaway.

A confused look took over James's face. "What the fuck is a do-si-do, Raker?"

"It's a dance move," she was compelled to explain. The second SUV came into view when they cleared past the semi. The driver was bearded, in a baseball cap and sunglasses. He steered with one hand and held a submachine gun with the other. The barrel rested on the window frame, aiming right at them.

James hit the brakes as the gun chattered. Bullets ripped into the tires of the semi. They exploded with a boom that resonated in April's chest. Chunks of rubber rained down over the windshield of her and James's car.

The second SUV was slightly ahead of them now.

James slowed more and swerved to get behind them. He extended his gun out the window and fired into the back of the SUV. Sparks erupted and the metal dented, but the car kept moving. James shot again, this time at the rear tire. Some rubber tore away. She excitedly anticipated the tire blowing and knocking the SUV out of the chase. The wheel kept turning. The fight wasn't over.

On the other side of the freeway, Raker and Art dodged cars and traded shots with Hathaway. A police helicopter quickly approached in the sky behind them. "Helicopter," she said.

James hissed a curse. "Eyes in the sky. Wrap it up." He hit the gas and rammed the back of the SUV. "We're taking the next exit we can."

"We are?" She braced for another impact and was still jarred forward. Glass and plastic broke and scattered past.

"Negative!" James shouted. "Break off pursuit." She followed his glance back to where Hathaway screeched across two lanes to wedge himself onto an off-ramp. "Police'll be swarming. Then no one wins." Art and Raker's car hurried to catch up to James and April. He warned, "Stay back." Then to her, "Hold on."

"What're you going to do?" Nothing had worked against the black SUV so far.

"Send a message." He rammed the SUV again. They pulled ahead, forcing him to speed up to hit them on the left of their bumper. The SUV screeched and started to fishtail. James kept pressing until the black car spun around in front of them, then next to them. But the driver was fast and put the car in reverse. The cars rubbed, door to door. In an instant she was directly across from the passenger in the SUV.

He wore sunglasses and a bandana pulled up over his mouth and nose. An expressionless killer who raised a submachine gun toward April and James.

"Lean!" James extended his pistol across the car. She yanked on the seat lever and fell back and out of the way. He fired twice, the gunshots deafening. Acrid smoke filled her nose, and the concussion rattled her ribs.

The hit man screamed out and dropped his weapon between the cars. He slumped over the open windows, hands dangling on her leg. Blood spread on the front and back of his denim jacket. She saw the impression of a rectangle in one of the inside pockets and suppressed her rising bile to paw inside. The SUV started to pull away, dragging his body with it. Her heart leaped. She searched more frantically for what she hoped was in his pocket.

"Are you done?" James clipped, struggling with the wheel. His voice seemed very far away. Her ears rang from the gunshots.

"Wait…" The man's phone slipped into her hand. "Done!"

James jammed their car into the SUV, sending it across the shoulder and into a large cinderblock sound barrier. The man whipped out of her window and was wrapped up in the black car as it screeched along the wall, buckled and flipped onto its side.

She spun away from the carnage. "I have his phone." The screen was open to the dialer, indicating a call had ended a minute ago. "It's unlocked." She closed that app, opened the settings and adjusted the sleep function so the phone would never time out.

The phone nearly flew out of her hand when James swerved hard to the next exit. He drove across the shoulder, kicking up debris that rattled against the car, and bumped over a curb on the way to the city streets.

Raker and Art were close behind. At the first intersection, James veered left and the other Automatik operators headed right. She checked the sky and saw the helicopter track with Raker and Art. "The helicopter's following them."

"Helo on you." James swerved through another intersection. "That car sterile?" Three blocks away from the freeway, he slowed to fit in with the traffic around them. "Roger that. Good luck." He told her, "They had to bail out of the car. They're on foot, and we have no backup until they secure another car."

"Are we good?" The car had several bullet holes in it and the engine complained, even at the slower speeds.

"We'll switch this out when we can." He headed north on city streets, running parallel to the freeway. Cold rage tightened his face. "And I need a bigger gun."

The exit where Hathaway had ducked off the freeway was only a mile behind the one they'd used. He could come down on them any second. She searched the streets for the SUV. "He's still hunting."

"He's scrambling." James finally put his pistol back in the holster. He shrugged his shoulders high, then released them with a breath. "He's down a team and took a big risk with a public assault. He'll ditch the car and go underground."

"Back to the hackers." She tried his relaxation technique, but it barely dialed down the churning adrenaline in her. High-pitched ringing still pierced her ears. Her pulse raced. *Focus. Control*, she commanded herself. No use. A task might help. She flipped through the emails on the phone, but it was filled with innocuous communications.

"Most likely." He punched the steering wheel. "Fuck!"

Her alert peaked and her muscles tensed, though she couldn't see the next threat. "What?"

"A bloody waste." He grunted in frustration. "All we bought was another delay. And that bastard motherfucker got another shot at you."

"We got this." She held up the phone.

"You did good to get it, but there won't be anything on there. Hathaway's men are too experienced." The cords of his neck flexed and his jaw set like iron. "I know."

She dug deeper into the emails. "The man was from Akron, Ohio. Not very communicative." A minor victory bloomed. "But he does have some bank notifications of electronic payments."

James got back on track with the mission. "We'll send those amounts and account numbers to Automatik. They should be able to track them down."

"That'll take too long. The hackers know how close we are." She looked over the other apps, probing for where the man might've slipped up. "They could be packing up right now." His web search history revealed a list of recent activity, mostly sports scores. "I've got them." She was nearly giddy. "I got them."

James matched her excitement, showing his teeth in carnivorous anticipation. "Give them to me."

"Two days ago he searched for pizza restaurants

in Quartz Hill, California." She switched to the map app and found the city. "It's north, on the other side of Los Angeles."

He lit up. "You are the most brilliant and vicious hunting hummingbird." He waved her toward him. "Give me a kiss."

She leaned close and kissed his cheek while he drove. He gripped her leg with an appreciative squeeze. She kissed him again and took her seat, buzzing with the small victory and James's enthusiasm.

He retrieved his phone. "We're going to destroy them." After dialing, he related to Automatik the information she'd found, then signed off with, "We're closest and inbound after resupply."

"It's us?" Fear and a brutal thrill mixed in her.

"If you want it?" He glanced to her, checking.

When the hackers had first taken her site weeks ago, she'd felt helpless. Every avenue she'd tried to combat them had terminated in a dead end. The hopelessness had dragged her down. James changed that. She had an ally. A partner. And a hunger for the fight. "I want it."

CHAPTER NINETEEN

SHE DIDN'T KNOW any of the cities they passed through. It felt like James had been driving for hours and they hadn't even reached Los Angeles yet. She watched the sky for helicopters and scanned the streets for Hathaway. AM news radio recounted the shootout on the freeway over and over, but the details remained sketchy. Art and Raker's car had been found, but no occupants. The second black SUV disappeared. Her and James's car hadn't been identified.

James navigated without directions away from large streets and into a family neighborhood. His demeanor pulled taut and ready. She prepared to meet efficient, capable special operators when he pulled up to a medium-sized two-story house on the middle of the block.

"Another Automatik soldier?" she asked, slipping the mercenary's phone in her coat pocket and pulling the heavy fabric around her for protection.

James answered, barely audible. "My parents."

TAKING POINT ON an assault of an enemy tunnel system cut into the side of a mountain had been easier than walking up the front steps of his parents' house and punching the doorbell. At least then there'd been a plan with contingency escape routes. He had no idea what he was going to say to his parents. There were things he needed from the house, but would he lie? Again?

Footsteps approached on the other side of the door. April huddled close to James's shoulder, incredulous. "Are you serious?"

His father's voice called out, muffled. "One moment. *Dheeraj.* One moment."

"Very serious." He brushed his hand over his hair and straightened his jacket.

The door opened and there stood his father, Sunil. The man goggled, surprised at his son, then brightened with a smile. "James!" He stepped onto the front porch and embraced his son. James hugged him back. His fifty-plus-year-old father's muscles were still ropy under his T-shirt.

Sunil stepped away from James and turned his attention to April. "And we haven't met."

"April Banks." She hesitated, uncertain, then extended her hand.

His father gave it a welcoming shake and waved them both inside. "Your mother is with her friends today, but I can call her to get her here." He closed the front door and angled toward a phone on a small table by the sofa in the living room. A TV opposite it showed local news helicopter shots of the aftermath of the freeway action. "She'd hate to miss a visit."

James intercepted him. "We won't be long, Papa."

Sunil's smile flickered. He looked at his son with a more critical eye. "Is everything alright?" His questioning gaze jumped to April.

James's gut tightened. What could he say? "There's trouble."

Sunil stepped closer with concern. "What is it?"

The news report continued on the television, braying and sensational. James tipped his head toward the TV. Sunil's eyes stretched wide.

"That's you?" His father moved away from him. Anger then flared in his face and he extended a long finger to James's chest. "Are you a criminal?"

"No, Papa." James was suddenly sixteen again and trying to explain what he'd been doing out so late with all his friends.

Sunil wasn't convinced. He kept his finger on James and addressed April. "Are you alright? Did he take you?"

"Not at all." She was emphatic. "He's helping me."

Sunil's skeptical eyes narrowed. "You're both criminals."

James gave his father credit for being brave and confrontational, if not completely frustrating. It was obvious that James was bigger and stronger than him—it had been that way since he'd hit his teen years—but Sunil didn't back down. James put his hand on his father's and lowered it from his chest. "We're not criminals."

Sunil made use of the finger to point at the TV. "Gunshots? On the freeway?"

"They were shooting at us." James still burned to make Hathaway pay for that.

"What did you do to make them shoot at you?" Sunil crossed his arms over his chest and waited.

James threw up his hands in frustration and stalked toward the kitchen. His father followed, April close behind. She displayed more patience than James could muster. "Mr. Sant, we're not doing anything wrong."

"I've heard that from James before," Sunil barked, disappointed.

"When I was a kid." James entered the kitchen and was surrounded by the aromas of his mother's cooking. Warm spices and sharp onion. The stove was clean, but he was sure a meal was packaged into tidy containers in the refrigerator. "What about when I was in the SAS, Papa? Did you trust me then? Or when I helped you emigrate and buy this house?" He tugged open the junk drawer and pulled out the heaviest hammer he could find.

Sunil stepped back, hands raised defensively.

James cornered his father, keeping the hammer at his side. "I'm not a criminal. I'm the good guy."

"It's true." April stood as a buffer between them. "It's true, Mr. Sant." To hear her avow it made the truth sink in. Like she'd picked the lock to a chain hanging around his neck. He was making right what he'd done wrong.

Sunil put his hands on his hips and stood, defiant. "Explain to me what's happening."

James sidestepped his father and ventured deeper into the house, where the guest bedroom was by the door to the backyard. Sunil thundered after him on bare feet.

"James Sant!" His father used his name like a lasso and tried to drag him back into the hall. But James was already in the room and threw open the door to the closet that protruded in one corner. Shoved the extra clothes aside and got into the closet. "James." Sunil stood before him, pointing at the ground where he wanted his son to report.

Things were about to get worse. James swung the hammer into the wall next to the door on the inside of the closet. Plaster cracked and dust flew. He pounded again and again, cutting a trench, despite his father's protests of, "Oh my goodness!"

Even April looked distressed. "What are you doing?"

The hole was large enough, and James dropped the hammer to the floor. He reached inside the wall and pulled out exactly what he needed. Sunil retreated to the other side of the room when James emerged from the closet with a pump action shotgun half wrapped in fabric and a box of extra shells.

Sunil whispered, heartbroken, "These are the actions of a good guy?"

James shrugged. "I built you a closet, didn't I?" He left the room, knowing his father remained on the trail. "I'll fix the hole later." He went out the back door and obscured the shotgun as best he could on the way to the detached garage behind the house.

The side door was unlocked, and he entered into the dry shade. A switch on the wall turned on a hanging fluorescent light, illuminating a two-car garage with only one car at the moment. He opened the back door to his father's immaculate sedan and placed the shotgun in the wheel well.

Sunil put his hands on the trunk, as if he could stop the car with his will. "I am not loaning you my car until you tell me what's going on."

James went to the small workbench on the side of the garage, pulled out one of the drawers and lifted a false bottom. "You're not loaning me the car. I'm stealing it." Under the bottom was a large envelope, right where he'd left it.

He found a screwdriver on the workbench and tried to return to the car, but Sunil blocked him. "No, James."

"Where I'm taking this car, I don't want it connected to you at all, so give me two hours, then call 911 and report the car stolen." He tried to snake around his father, but the man remained nimble and shifted to bar the path.

True worry joined the frustration on Sunil's face. "You must tell me."

There wasn't time to tell him everything. "I'm still a soldier." Down the road, he'd have a meal with his father and mother and tell them everything, including his time with Hathaway.

"For who?" Sunil squinted, like he was trying to piece the last few years together.

"For the good guys, Papa." James stepped to the side of his father and returned to the car. He handed April the envelope and unscrewed the license plates. She tore the paper open, revealing another set of plates with sterile numbers that Automatik had supplied him months ago. She gave them to him, and he attached them to the car.

Sunil rubbed his forehead. "This isn't the kind of thing good guys do."

James put the legitimate plates on the workbench and tossed April the keys to their car. "Bring it in here." He hit a button on the wall and opened the garage door. She hurried down the driveway, leaving him alone with Sunil. James confessed as much as he could. "You're right. I used to be a bad guy. After the SAS." Emotions sheened in his father's eyes. Hurting this man drove a barbed spike through James's chest. He had to clear his throat to continue. "But not anymore."

The two men stepped behind the sedan when April drove toward them, then parked the small, battered

SUV in the empty space. James put his hand on his father's shoulder. "After we leave, close the garage door and don't open it until I get in touch." James let his father go and retrieved the spare key for the sedan from a jar full of rusty nails on the workbench. April dragged the carry-on from the old car and put it in the backseat of the sedan.

James reiterated to Sunil. "Two hours. Report the car as stolen. Say it was parked on the street when it disappeared."

His father just stared at him, hurt and sadness still in his eyes.

James took the time to breathe and address Sunil directly. "You don't have to believe me, but please believe me. I'm part of a team of ex-special forces men and women." He held his hand out toward April. "She's part of this team." Her lips parted with a question she kept to herself. James continued to his father, "We help people. Did you hear about the gunrunner gangs who destroyed each other in the Midwest?"

Sunil nodded slowly.

"That was us," James told him. "We protect people when they can't protect themselves."

His father pointed vaguely to the south. "The freeway?"

"Mercenaries," James answered, his anger churning again. "Paid to hurt her." He looked to April, ready to fight for as long as it took to make her safe.

All was silent in the garage. Sunil looked at April and at James with his wise perception. He finally replied. "Two hours, then I call the police."

"Thank you, Papa." James gave his father a quick

hug and hurried into the sedan. April strapped herself into the passenger seat, and James started the engine.

Sunil leaned into the open driver's side window. "You are coming back to clean up this mess." He waved at the battered car April had just parked. "This cannot stay. And the hole in the closet must be repaired."

"I will take care of everything." He patted his father's hand.

"Miss Banks." Sunil gave her a small bow.

She waved back. "Thank you for everything, Mr. Sant. I'm sorry about the circumstances."

"Be safe." Sunil turned his tearing eyes back to his son. "You be safe. And you come back."

Emotion rose and tightened in James's chest. "I will." He put the car into reverse and backed out of the driveway. By the time they hit the street, the garage door was closed and he no longer saw his father.

THE QUIET AROUND James was thick with meaning. Watching some of his interactions with his father reminded April of her family dynamic. No matter how old she was, there were always the old ruts of communication to rely on, rather than actually saying what they meant. Beneath it, though, was real love. She saw that too with James and Sunil.

She tracked the map on her burner phone, seeing how far it was from their location to Quartz Hill. James didn't need directions yet and drove them from the neighborhood to more populated streets lined with businesses. Most of the shops and restaurants were Indian.

James scanned over the businesses and ended his

silence. "That's why I moved them to Artesia. Good community."

She watched the ebb and flow of emotion in his eyes. "So if you ever offer to do some home improvement for me, I should expect to have a shotgun sealed into the walls?"

"Life in Automatik." He tapped the steering wheel. "Contingencies everywhere, and you hope you never need them."

Was that her life now? She couldn't exist under that much fear. "When you told your father that I'm a member of the team, was that because it was easier to explain?"

"As soon as you told me you wouldn't go to the safe house, and you had to pursue the hackers yourself, you became a member of Automatik." He smiled warmly at her, but she remained unsettled.

"Does that mean I have to stash guns everywhere?" She didn't even know if her house was still standing. "Make contingency plans for abandoning my life at a moment's notice and starting a new identity?"

"That's not you," he insisted. "It's me. That's what I'd been living."

With the way things had happened so quickly, throwing her and James together into the danger, into the desire, she hadn't thought about what the next step after the mission would look like. If they survived the mission.

"It's always like this for you?" she asked.

"This op is…different." He drove them from the streets onto a freeway. Traffic thickened and slowed their northern progress. "A lot of unexpected turns."

"After the op?" She knew everything beyond the moment was unknown.

"I've been running and gunning for quite a bit." He stared past the distance ahead. "Never been one to plan too far ahead."

"You planned the shotgun and the license plates." She didn't blame his lack of structure beyond the mission. She'd designed her life once, then found out how quickly everything can change.

"That's tactical." He waved it off. "That comes easy."

"I know the rest is hard."

"That's what makes you remarkable." He brought his focus from the distance and to her. She warmed with his look. "You never stop fighting."

"I've stopped." She chewed her lip. At her lowest point, she'd done nothing, just stared at the shadows made by the windows on the walls.

"I've never seen it." He extended his hand, turned his palm up and laid out facts. "We get hit, we go down. Some people stay down. You took a huge hit, you healed, you fought your way back." His hand remained out. He looked at it, then her hand, and back to his.

She placed her palm on his. He curled his fingers around her. The connection went beyond his words. His admiration and caring sank through to her bones and deeper into her chest. His fierce protectiveness lit her own fires.

He continued to hold her hand and looked at her, determined. "Once the op is over, we'll return to my parents' house. I'll introduce you as not only my teammate and partner, but my girlfriend."

Planning beyond the latest second took bravery. She tightened her hold of him. But the term "girlfriend" seemed out of date for people their age. "How about your lover?"

"Yes, we'll do that." He smiled, with a wicked edge. "It's so avant-garde."

"And it makes people more uncomfortable when you say it." She imagined her sculptress alter ego swanning through his parents' house in oversized glasses.

"Even better." He drew her wrist to his lips for a kiss. It sealed a pact. Not a somber one, but alive with the quick energy they shared. The grave mood came shortly after. All the promises would only count if the op was a success. If they made it out alive.

CHAPTER TWENTY

"BLOODY LOS ANGELES goes on forever." Traffic loosened and tightened with no causality, making the target of Quartz Hill seem impossibly far away.

"This is still Los Angeles?" April looked about in shock.

"The people who live in these outlying cities will tell you some other names, but it's all one giant cluster fuck." He pounded on the steering wheel in an attempt to spur the cars around them.

"Charlie Foxtrot," she said, melancholy in her voice. He imagined her husband had taught her the military lingo.

"That's right." He scanned the darkening hills around them. The sun would soon set behind them and bring on the yellow shadows of city night. "The whole basin is Charlie Foxtrot."

She checked her burner phone. "The map says we should pick up speed after the next off-ramp."

"But it doesn't say why." He sped up just to slow down behind the car ahead of them. "It never says why." His frustration was amplified by the lack of tactical knowledge of their destination. He hadn't ventured to this area. There was no time to recon and plan. He and April took point and would have to act and adapt as the situation unfolded.

Her nerves appeared calm, but he couldn't read what

went on beneath her surface. She held up the phone for him to see the map. "We exit in five miles. Highway 14."

"Roger that." One pistol and one shotgun. No body armor he could wrap April in. Or an armored car where she could stand by until he'd cleared the hostiles from wherever it was they were headed. The sun fell behind the mountains. Their peaks cut a crisp, jagged line in the sky. He welcomed the night. "We're invisible again."

Her tension revealed itself in an uneasy smile. "Around a half hour until your dad reports the car stolen."

"That's mostly for insurance and to sever any suspicion of him." He adjusted the air freshener clipped to a vent. "The cops will take forever to find it."

"I thought it was part of a big plan." Her smile completely disappeared.

"Nothing that crafty." He couldn't afford to lose her to the anxiety of the unknown. "Do you know how to load pistol magazines?"

"Yeah." She perked up with more resolve.

"The rounds are in the suitcase." He drew his pistol and ejected the magazine. She climbed back and rummaged through the carry-on, returning a moment later with the spare ammunition and the large flashlight she'd taken from her home. He handed her the magazine, and the empty one he'd stored in his shoulder holster after the firefight on the freeway.

At first she fumbled with the mechanism, but soon managed it. She leaned over her task, meditative. The bullets clicked into the magazines in a regular rhythm.

The first full one she handed him went into the pistol, the second into his holster rig.

He pointed with his thumb behind him. "There's a box of shotgun shells on the floor. Can you open it and stuff some in my pockets?"

Her jacket and shirt lifted up, revealing a crescent of flesh above the waist of her jeans as she stretched her body between the chairs. Her curves had fit so right along his body, sometimes moving with him, sometimes making him move. The circumstances of the car ride into blackout territory didn't stop a jolt of attention in his cock.

He reached a hand out, then paused to ask, "I see some skin and I'd like it."

She twisted and looked back. A knowing grin grew on her face. "Take it."

His fingers glanced across her smooth skin. He moved his hand further to the small of her back. With the touch came more memories of her wrapped around him and her sleeping next to him, her warmth like a shield against the rest of the world. That they'd found this within only a few days didn't mean it was rushed. It meant he'd been starving for her and hadn't met her yet. April sighed and swiveled so he rubbed back and forth along her waist.

But her position was awkward, and she had to bring herself back to the front seat. On her way, she put a kiss on James's cheek, then his mouth as he drove. He swerved toward the right, trying to get more of her, but corrected quickly. By then the kiss was over.

She took her seat and opened the box of shotgun shells. "Slugs?"

He shouldn't have been surprised she knew what

type of ammo it was. "The shotgun's got nine buckshot in the tube. Slugs after that. I like to hit hard."

"Mmmmmm." She put on a show with a throaty purr. "How hard?"

He chuckled, though his cock took her seriously and thickened. "So hard that I end all pain forever."

"Leaving only pleasure." She made two handfuls of shotgun shells and edged toward him.

"For you." He stopped wishing they could be somewhere private and alone and found himself basking in the desire he felt in the moment. "For you, only pleasure."

She pressed her chest into his arm. He struggled to steer. She whispered into his ear, "Which pockets do you want these in?"

Her voice was so erotic it took him a few seconds to register the question. "Front pockets of the jacket."

She zipped the nearest down, slowly, with a growing grin. He ground in his seat in order to adjust his growing erection. Her hand in his pocket was almost too carnal to handle. She deposited the shells, then lingered there and scratched his belly through the fabric.

"Cheeky bird." He stole a kiss on her ear and nipped the lobe with his teeth.

She faked coy reproach. "I'm just doing what you asked." Then she slithered across his lap to open his other pocket. Their bodies rubbed and surged into a steady rhythm. But they were still on the freeway and not near the safety and open time they needed. She finished her task and returned to her seat. A bemused giggle bubbled from her. "That's so not me."

"You're whatever you want to be." The saucy mood was over, but his body didn't know it yet. He rolled his shoulders and stretched his hands; still his erection was slow to abate. "Probably didn't imagine you'd be a field op either."

"Never." She held up her thick flashlight. "Those fuckers had better watch out."

"Yes, they'd better." He was prepared to take them on with his bare hands if he had to.

She kept the flashlight on her lap. Traffic lightened for a spell, finally allowing them onto the next highway. The high desert roads had fewer cars and fewer streetlamps, sinking the shadows deeper. Planned communities huddled on the side of hills, cut into the rock. Outside the pools of light was the kind of darkness James lived in.

His phone buzzed, and he put his earbud in. Raker came over the line. "We have fresh wheels and are ready to move."

James caught them up on the situation and the vague Quartz Hill location. Raker consulted with Art and they estimated at least two hours of travel time to catch up.

"We'll bunker and wait for you if we can," James told his teammate. "But we're going in with no map, no friendlies, no intel. All we have are bad intentions."

"Sounds ideal. Keep us posted." Raker signed off.

James hung up and informed April, "Raker and Art are two hours out." Her face was drawn, worried. "I told them we'd wait it out—"

"I heard that part." She held up her personal phone. "I just got another email from the hackers. Could they know we're this close?"

"Not possible." His readiness for action ramped up,

and he accounted for all the weapons that were close at hand. "What did they say?"

She read, shaken, "You had a chance to quit and now you're going to die."

"That's it?"

"That's it." She shrank too small.

He scoffed, "It's easy for those worms to type their threats, but they have to hire someone to protect them. The bastards are scared. This is the only way they know how to attack." She searched the night around them, more scared than resolved. He tried to bolster her morale. "If they knew where we were, they'd list some specifics to rattle us. The kind of car we're driving. Our clothes. This…" He tapped her phone. "This is no threat. This is desperation and fear."

She reread it silently, jaw set. "I'm just…so tired of them."

"They've already lost."

The highway stretched through unpopulated black hills, then leveled to a series of small cities that glittered through a narrow valley. April navigated them toward Quartz Hill. Off the main road, then to the west. Suburban developments ran right up to the edge of the high desert. He couldn't tell if man was encroaching on nature, or if the dust and dirt were going to take over the town by dawn.

Streetlights shined down on empty streets. Whole blocks of houses were half-built, and the structures that were completed seemed unoccupied. Heavy equipment and stacks of lumber dotted the landscape. More traffic moved on the far side of the subdivision they drove through. He glimpsed illuminated signs for restaurants and a grocery store.

"Fuck." April peered out the car windows. "They could be anywhere."

He slowed, taking his time to pick apart the buildings. "They're not going to set up in a construction zone. But the complete houses…?"

"Still too risky." Her fingers tapped on her flashlight. "This area's too unoccupied. They couldn't come and go without someone noticing."

Rolling down the window brought cold, dry air and the smell of raw concrete and framing wood. No food or human waste. He drove them toward the activity in town. Most of the roads to his left ended in cul-de-sacs at the edges of the hills. A half-moon turned the large rocks into burly, stoic ghosts.

He turned out the lights and cruised to a stop two blocks from the street with the shops. Two strip malls bracketed the street. Chain restaurants anchored the middle with parking lots in between.

"Do you have binoculars?" She squinted. "I can't see anything from here."

"Slow night." He described what he could detect from the distance. "A few cars for the restaurants. Foot traffic in and out of the convenience store on the right-side strip mall. One drunk stumbler. Man circling the street on a bicycle, and two women chatting by a parked truck."

She typed on her phone. "Both restaurants are open until nine p.m. tonight. Convenience store is twenty-four hours."

"Women parted, one in the truck and another to a car in a parking lot. Bicycle man finished his laps and departed to the west." Everyone behaved normally and not as if they knew high-end computer hackers and their hired mercenaries had set up shop somewhere nearby. "Women are away to the south and to the west."

"This is it for business on this side of town." She clicked off the screen on her phone and was illuminated only by the moon. "More stuff closer to the highway and south."

"So if you were a hacker, where would you be?" He searched for that one detail to latch on to.

"Where it's dark." She sat up with growing intensity. "Where it's real dark." She pointed to the far left. "What's in that strip mall?"

"Tobacco shop, bagel shop, check cashing. All closed."

"Closed for the night or closed for good?" She leaned forward, as if one more foot could bring the street into focus.

"Two shops, for the night." Flyers for local activities were taped to the insides of their windows, and dim lights glowed within. "Check cashing, closed for good." Heavy paper covered those windows. The plastic sign over the door had lost two letters.

"That would work." She gripped the dashboard. "I'm sure there are secure offices. Plenty of power and space for the servers."

He put the car in drive. "They're right at the edge of the desert." A twenty-foot ridge of dirt and rock rose to the east of the mall. "Minimal profile. Easy in and out." They rolled to the next intersection and he made a right, away from the mall. "Good mark." He put his fist out. She bumped it.

"Are we going to wait?" She stretched her neck in an attempt to keep the target in view.

"We're going to scout." He kept driving them farther

away. "Whatever business they're doing, it's through the back, so we need to take a look." Only one car passed them on the suburban streets.

A woman walking her dog waved vaguely at James and April.

"Small community," April remarked. "If we're here, they're assuming they should know us."

"Strangers will stand out," he mused. "Maybe the hackers are locals." He steered the car through a right turn, went two blocks, then made another right to approach the street with the check cashing store. They came from below and hoped to have open territory, but found yet another subdivision of identical homes. An alley led between the cinderblock-walled backyards of these houses and back sides of the shops and restaurants on the street.

He drove past the opening on the far side from the check cashing store. The usual assortment of trash cans and spent restaurant containers lined the business side of the alley and obscured his view of the target. There were two cars and a group of men, at least six who looked to be busy with activity. James was past the alley and couldn't get a complete headcount. But he knew one of them from the hunch of his shoulders. "Hathaway."

April spun in her seat, but the alley was too far behind them. Her voice tightened. "It looked like they were packing up."

James wanted to jam on the accelerator and ram into Hathaway. He needed a tactic. He needed to end this. He needed to keep April safe. He drew his pistol and handed it to her.

CHAPTER TWENTY-ONE

THE GUN WAS as heavy as a curse in her hands. She kept her finger from the trigger and pointed it at the floorboard. Dread pounded through her. "I don't know if I can use this." She knew all the technical aspects of firing the weapon, but only at paper targets.

"It's for protection." James's face was set, eyes determined. He tugged the magazines from his holster and gave them to her. "You're going to be at a distance. I'm making the assault." He continued driving them through the streets until they were back on the edge of the development. The car came to a stop in the same place they'd surveyed the shops from.

James brought himself close to her and pointed to the far left. Their intimate space was betrayed by the fear and danger. "You see that ridge?"

She followed his look to the bare desert landscape at the edge of the development. "I see it."

"I want you to get out of the car here." He indicated all the moves and directions with his hand. "Hit the terrain at the end of this street, then follow it up to that ridge, staying on the backside until you're above the alley. Do you understand?"

She nodded. "I have the high ground."

"Exactly." He smiled, but her nerves continued to hum. "Give me your burner phone."

She tugged it from a coat pocket and handed it over.

He opened the dialer and punched in a number, but didn't hit connect. "That's Automatik," she assumed.

"Correct." He returned the phone. "I'll catch them up now. Use that in an emergency."

"This feels like an emergency." The phone jumped in her hands, and she had difficulty putting it back in her pocket.

How did he stay so calm? "This is my trade, has been for many years and many missions." He took her in, gaze deepening. "But I have a damn good reason for doing it tonight." His fingers stroked her cheek. She reached out and clutched his arm. They came together in a kiss. She tried to absorb all of him, hold on to him. Keep him safe. His passion was undiminished. When they parted, that fierce determination was in his eyes. "We finish them tonight, and we leave here together."

She wasn't ready to let him go. All the terrible possibilities spun through her head. Loss had nearly broken her before. She didn't think she could recover from it again. She kissed him, felt his life, his power, and convinced herself he'd always be that way. "Together."

"Yes," he promised.

After a trembling breath, she opened the door. The magazines fit in her pockets, but the gun was too big. She held it out to him. "You'll need it."

He declined, gazing with malice toward the check cashing store. "I'll get another one." A predatory energy radiated from him. She'd felt that transformation before, when they'd been attacked outside the school. It was a little frightening. She fed off it and tried to let it inhabit her as well.

She had a gun, ammunition, a flashlight like a club. Her orders were clear. Finally. They weren't running.

They were chasing. She left the car and hurried behind it, stuffing the flashlight in her back pocket. She skipped across the street to where the desert rose out of the neighborhood. Dust and rocks slipped under her feet. She kept the pistol safe and used her other hand to help scramble up.

At the top of the ridge, she turned. James held his hand up in a wave, then curled it into a fist. Their gazes parted and he drove away. The car slipped into the neighborhood on a winding route. She climbed over the top of the small hill and pressed forward, staying in the shadows and unseen by anyone in town.

To her left, the landscape spread farther into wilderness. She walked the border, armed and preparing for a fight. A few dozen yards into her trek, she stopped and peeked over the rise in the hill. She'd gained elevation but hadn't reached her destination. The check cashing store was still a block away. She searched over the streets but couldn't see James or the car.

Worry would root her feet in place. She forced them to move toward the position James had indicated. She was a member of Automatik. His partner in this mission. She'd insisted on going along. That meant continuing on while trying to grip the gun with a cold, sweaty palm.

Her steps were impossibly loud. They must've been echoing across the entire valley, alerting everyone to her presence. But there were only pebbles grating together under her shoes. Her nerves strung tight, ready to jump with the sound of gunfire. Was that what James was planning? He had the shotgun and two pocketfuls of shells. There were at least six men outside. With what kinds of weapons? And how many men were in-side the closed store?

One foot in front of the other. Keep moving.

She hiked up the steepest part of the incline and lowered herself to crawl up to the peak. The alley be-hind the check cashing store was a half a block away and below her. There were only four men outside now. They had two cars parked in opposite directions in the alley. Another man came and went through the back door of the store. No one else was around in the alley to see their activity. At times a flashlight would burst with light, then dim as someone loaded a cardboard box into the trunk of one of the cars.

The fuckers were moving. Had they taken the servers out yet? If they had, she was sure they'd back them up in the cloud. She had to get the hard drives. She had to gain access to the hackers' cloud server. But she couldn't just run down from the hill, running and screaming and shooting until they all ran away.

Where was James? The men moved freely. Her heart thundered. They could get away. Was one of the cars running? She thought she saw puffs of smoke from the tailpipe. But it was too far for specifics. She took out the burner phone and laid it on the dirt next to her, ready to connect to Automatik. If there was a signal on the edge of town. The screen indicated one small bar. It could flicker out any second.

Her attention was torn from the phone by a car turn-ing into the alley. It approached from the far side. It was James. When he passed the restaurants, the headlights turned off. The shadows were too thick to see him in the driver's seat. He drove straight toward the cars by the check cashing store. And he wasn't slowing down.

The men in the alley saw him coming and planted their feet, as if their presence alone could stop anyone. But James had no intention of stopping.

The men started shouting and at least one drew a pistol as the car sped nearer. She held her breath. James could survive the impact but would be exposed to the mercenaries. The car slammed into both the parked cars, wedging them apart. The sound of crumpling metal and breaking glass reached all the way to her hill, as did the shouts of the men. James's car's tires continued to screech as it ground forward. The men scattered away from the lurching machine. One of them fired two shots, punching holes in the windshield where the driver was.

She choked a scream back. *James. James.*

The tires spun and burned into thick smoke. The men all had their weapons out and flanked the car. More mercenaries rushed out from the back of the shop, one with a submachine gun. She clenched her jaw and wanted to close her eyes. There was no way out of the car. The man in charge waved for the other's attention. Hathaway. He chopped down with his hand, and the mercenaries opened fire. The car was riddled with bullets. The engine howled and sprayed jets of fluid. A small fire broke out under the hood, forcing the men back two steps.

One man braved the flames and crept to the driver's door, gun ready. He cracked it open. She dreaded seeing James's body flop out. But the man shook his head and reached into the car to turn the engine off.

While the mercenaries were drawn to the car, another figure swept into the alley from the side closest to her. It was James. A wave of relief was short-lived. He held his shotgun and sprang into combat.

His first blast took out the man closest to him. The others spun, weapons ready. James fired again, wounding another mercenary who dove behind one of the cars. The others opened fire, forcing James to take cover around the corner of the building. The brick and plaster chipped away near him, but he remained calm enough to reload the shotgun from the shells she'd put in his pockets.

He whipped around the corner and fired a blast that made the other men seek safety. While they scrambled, he advanced to the first man he'd hit, took his pistol and put it in his shoulder holster.

A mercenary popped up from cover and shot twice, making James leap away. Her blood boiled. She couldn't tell if he'd been hit. He recovered and returned fire. The blast licked a long flame out of the shotgun. The man's scream echoed out.

James retreated again. The mercenaries grew more furious with their gunfire. The shots crackled through the night. Someone must've called the police by now. But what the hell were they going to do against this? And James might be a target as well.

She punched the connect button on her burner phone and prayed for a signal. After one ring, a steady woman's voice answered, "How can I help you?"

"This is April Banks, I'm with James Sant—"

"Has the situation escalated?"

"They're shooting," she hissed a breathless whisper. "Around five men."

"Is James alone?"

"Yes." April winced as her heart contracted. He

maintained his cover at the side of the building, but the mercenaries were coming closer behind their on-going assault.

"We'll scramble assets to your position."

"Th…thank you." April left the line open and put the phone down. The woman's question hammered into April. *Is James alone?* He couldn't survive against the onslaught. Whatever plan he had wasn't working.

But he wasn't alone. April clenched her teeth and aimed her pistol down into the crowd of mercenaries. James edged farther back from where the men fired at him. She pulled the trigger, and the gun bucked. The men below didn't react. Had James given her blanks as a decoy? But she'd loaded the magazines herself. The din in the alley must've masked her shot. She had no idea where the bullet had struck.

April steeled herself and fired again, this time in a quick series of shots. She was sure they'd all go wild but hoped they'd distract the mercenaries enough for James to get to safety. Her bullets streaked down. One popped a hole in the hood of a car. Two more skipped off the asphalt.

The men scattered for cover again, only glancing out to look in her direction. She could see a part of Hath-away behind a Dumpster. He made hand gestures to the others and waved forward.

Two mercenaries broke off from the group. James was just starting to advance when the others resumed firing at him. He tightened himself to cover, shotgun raised and ready. The two men aimed their guns and shot at April as they ran toward her hill. She ducked back as the bullets sprayed dirt over her.

Looking to see where the men were would put her in

the line of fire. The barrage continued toward James. More shots rang out and chipped away the rocks at the top of her ridge. She was pinned. Time was running out.

CHAPTER TWENTY-TWO

No. No. No.

Two mercenaries charged April's hill. James seethed. He was forced to cover by the remaining men and had to get to her. It wouldn't be long until Hathaway and the others advanced on him. He'd counted on that, knowing he could use their bravado against them and pick them off one at a time. After blocking one exit of the alley with the car wreck, he'd have funneled them right toward him.

But April fired and drew too much attention. He didn't blame her. From her perspective, he probably looked like an easy target for the mercenaries. Her concern warmed his heart. But his blood still ran cold.

The men were halfway up the hill. James poked his shotgun around the corner and fired twice to slow Hathaway's advance. No screams. He hadn't hit anyone. But he did stanch their barrage.

He drew the first downed man's gun and with the shotgun in the other hand, sprinted away from the building and toward the hill. Bullets chased him. He sprayed gunfire back at the men in the alley with the pistol, barely looking to aim.

Ahead, the mercenaries didn't stop to engage him. They spread out in flanking positions around where James knew April hid. The one closest to him was almost at the top of the hill. James raised the pistol and loosed a series of shots at the man. He was caught in the upper chest and shoulder and stumbled for a step before disappearing over the other side of the hill.

Bullets from the men in the alley smacked around James. Stinging lines cut into his cheek and forehead from flying chips of rock. He powered up the hill with everything his legs could give. If the man he hit was still alive, he was on the same side as April. Fear spurred James on faster.

He crested the hill to see the man on his back, aiming a gun up at him. James fired first, three shots that ended the man. Bullets whizzed past from another direction. The second man on the hill fired down the ridge at James from twenty yards away. His gut clenched; April was caught in the crossfire.

James got one shot off, then his slide locked open. He dropped the empty pistol and raised the shotgun. If the man was hit, he took it well. Return fire streaked past James, who moved forward and lateral to avoid being targeted. He brought the shotgun to his shoulder and blasted at the man. The first shot knocked him backward and the second put him on the ground forever.

"April! April!" James rushed ahead, peering through the darkness. The silence answering him was terrifying. "April!" It didn't matter if the remaining men below heard him. His voice would be the last thing they heard on earth.

"James," April answered tentatively from the thicker shadows farther into the desert.

Relief nearly knocked him to the ground. He hurried toward her voice. "Are you hit? Are you hurt?"

April emerged from behind a boulder, dusty and

scared but also determined and beautiful. "I'm okay. Are you?"

"Aces." His injuries were painless as he looked at her.

She grew fiercer, grabbed his sleeve and shook him. "You could've told me about your fucking car plan."

Her hand remained on him, and he drew life from the contact. "No time." Together they moved to the back side of the ridge. "And what were you doing breaking cover?"

"You needed help." At the time it had seemed to be going according to his tactical concept, but maybe she'd seen things differently from her high vantage.

"Thank you." He rubbed his hand across her tense shoulders.

Footsteps rushed over the street below. Someone else scrabbled on the hill toward them. James held up a finger to April, asking her to wait, then readied his shotgun. He peeked over the ridge and immediately drew gunfire.

After ducking back, he reloaded the shotgun and racked the slide. April remained taut, the pistol in her hand. He motioned for her to watch the left side of their ridge. His recon had revealed one man coming up the right and another firing from below, just at the edge of the street. If his headcount was correct, there were three other mercenaries after these men, including Hathaway.

He whispered to April, "Take your flashlight and shine it over the ridge but keep your hands clear."

She nodded and blew out a ragged breath in preparation. The light turned on and streaked through the rising dust around them. She crawled on the hill to the edge. Holding the flashlight by the butt, she tipped it so just the lens shined over the top of the hill.

Shots burst, and she recoiled. Dirt and rocks around the flashlight flew. James lunged over the ridge and pointed the barrel at the merc on the right. The man's eyes went wide and he tried to swing his pistol toward James, who fired first. The buckshot lifted the man off the ground. He tumbled, dead, down the hill.

The man on the street shot as he retreated. His bullets flew harmless into the night. James took a breath and aimed, taking into account the man's movement. He fired and dropped the merc before he reached the other two men by the back of the check cashing store. Neither stepped out to retrieve their fallen comrade.

James reloaded again. All slugs. Less spread, more range. He zeroed in on a merc by the shop. The man shouted at the closed back door and crouched behind flimsy cardboard boxes. James let his breath out halfway, then pulled the trigger. The shotgun recoiled into his shoulder and the slug cut the air. The man sprawled to the ground, hit in the leg. He yelled at the other merc in the alley, but that man was already dancing on tentative feet.

He bolted past the burning car and up the alley. Hathaway wasn't paying him enough.

"Police." April had crawled up next to James and pointed to a string of lit-up patrol cars rushing toward the scene from about a mile away.

"They'll set up a perimeter." He gathered himself. "We still have time to work."

Below, the wounded man argued in strained screams with someone inside. James assumed it was Hathaway behind the door. The leader of this platoon of monsters wasn't accounted for anyway. Whatever the conflict was about, the man with the shotgun slug through his leg wasn't getting what he wanted. He brought his submachine gun up and fired a blast into the door. Silence. The door opened a crack, but the conversation was too low to hear. Two shots rang out from the door, and the wounded man slumped, dead.

April gasped and put her hand over her mouth.

He stood close to her and felt her trembling. "You're holding up," he said, trying to convince her.

"Not much." Her gaze bounced from point to point, sometimes landing on the bodies of the men near them, then flitting away.

"I know it doesn't feel like it." He brought himself in front of her and captured her focus. "But you are." He soothed as much as he could with his voice while his own pressure clock threatened to burst. The police were coming. Hathaway was inside. The hackers must be in there. "You gave me the distraction I needed and hid yourself perfectly from the counter attack." She breathed more freely. He smiled at her. "You're smarter than all of them." He guided April higher on the ridge.

He couldn't leave her on the hill alone now. There was one merc on the loose, probably running away, but he couldn't count on that completely. And the police might sweep her up as they set the edge of the conflict. He climbed over the peak and put his hand out for her to follow. "We're going to end this together."

BODIES LAY ON the hill and at the bottom of it. Death made the men inert in the alley. And the fight wasn't over. But she was still alive. Not completely by luck, but mostly thanks to James and his skill. The safest place in this was with him.

April gathered up her flashlight and the burner phone. She turned the flashlight off and took his hand. The touch of his skin startled her. It had seemed like any pleasure she'd known had been replaced by fear and fire, but the small contact reminded her of her humanity. She screwed her focus down, determined to get through this and not let go of the new life she'd just started to build. James helped her over the ridge, then released her to motion their path. She slipped in the loose dirt, caught her footing and trailed behind him.

He stalked forward, shotgun ready at his hip. Once they hit the street, he indicated that she should go to the corner of the building, the same place he'd been sheltering while the men fired at him. She took up her position next to the brick and plaster that had been chewed up by the bullets.

Police sirens grew closer, driving the urgency. James moved past her and to the bullet-riddled back door of the shop. He gave her a nod, she nodded back and raised the pistol, ready, but shaking in her hand.

James coiled, then released a kick into the door. He jumped back just as a burst of fire came from within. He stuck his shotgun through the opening and shot back twice. The blasts rocked the building. April jumped, startled.

She regained her composure and saw Hathaway lunge out of the doorway and grab the barrel of James's shotgun. James fired it, but Hathaway sidestepped. The two men struggled over the gun in the doorway, both landing knees and elbows into the other's body.

April rushed toward them, pistol outstretched. But

the men twisted and turned. She couldn't risk hitting James. "Stop!" she shouted. "Stop!"

She came too close. Hathaway held James off and kicked her in the stomach. Pain edged her vision in white as the wind was knocked from her. She started to fall backward but was stopped when Hathaway grabbed her wrist. He twisted the pistol from her hand and turned it toward James.

Her body locked in agony and she fell to her knees. She couldn't help James. His face went deadly calm. In a swift move, he turned his shoulders and wrenched the shotgun from Hathaway's grip. The weapon twisted from James's hands as well and skittered under one of the cars in the alley.

Hathaway fired the pistol. She tried to scream but had no air. Freezing blood jolted up her spine. James ducked the shot and locked up again with Hathaway, both of them struggling for control of the gun. They banged against the doorframe and shattered door. James bared his teeth and spoke, but her ears rang too loud.

His voice reached her from a great distance. "The hacker."

She tried to stand, but only gasped. James's eyes directed her into the store before he was consumed again with the struggle against Hathaway. It took all her effort to make a fist. She put her knuckles on the ground and willed her arm to push her up. Breath choked into her lungs. She brought a leg under her and stood. Flitting white streaks danced before her eyes. She stumbled forward, gaining strength with every step.

James saw her coming and spun Hathaway's back into the wall, then shoved him into the store. She chased after them and had to get her bearings in the new space. Waist-high walls and boxes made a maze out of the back area. James and Hathaway crashed into one of these dividers, cracking the wood. James locked up Hathaway's arm and pried the pistol from his grip, but it tumbled away from both of them and disappeared into the deep shadows of the room.

Hathaway drew a knife with his free hand. James sprung away, pulling his own blade. The men circled. James took a sliver of a second to direct her with his eyes. An enclosed office on the far wall had high windows that glowed with electric light within.

She bolted for the room. The door was locked. As she rattled the knob, she heard movement inside. Typing on a keyboard. She reared back and kicked the door. Again and again. It was hollow and started to split. She released all her fury until the wood gave way. Laminate cracked away from one hinge, she stepped back and lowered her shoulder into the door.

The wood shattered away, and she stumbled into the cramped office. One man stood next to a desk jammed in a corner. She'd imagined a strung-out cyber junkie with greasy hair. Or a team of evil-looking men in matching vests. But the hacker was just a white man in his thirties with a tidy haircut and a down jacket over his button-down shirt. An IT man.

His look of confusion was probably the same as hers. The hacker snapped out of it quickly and turned back to the computer terminal on the desk. April vaguely registered the mass of cables from the computer to the two server towers on the floor as she lunged for the man.

He threw an arm out and caught her in the top of her chest with his elbow. She turned away from the blow, lessening the impact, and pulled the flashlight from her back pocket. It swung out, heavy, into the man's side. If only he'd shattered like the door. The man winced and grunted, but still reached for his keyboard. She raised the flashlight and crashed it into the backs of his hands. He screamed and drew his arms tight to his chest. Finally, the man couldn't hurt her. She hit him in the jaw with the flashlight and sent him to the floor.

Adrenaline pumped so hard through her it was nearly impossible to steady her fingers on the keyboard. On the screen was the man's cloud server. The window revealed file after file with her website name and coded numbers. Within a few keystrokes, she erased all of the data.

The hacker groaned on the ground, rolling with his crushed hands crossed in front of him.

She spat, "You never broke me." He mumbled a response through bloody teeth.

Outside of the office, bodies slammed together and crashed into the partition walls. She rushed out to see James and Hathaway locked in a deadly combat. They swiped with the knives, punched and kicked at any opening. Blood trickled from the corner of James's scowling mouth.

The pain in her own body cut deep. Her stomach and chest throbbed, as if she could feel his injuries as well. The fight was too furious for her to intervene.

James dodged a knife attack but was rocked by a punch just below his throat. He slashed back and almost caught Hathaway. The mercenary tried to kick James, but James swiped the blow away with one arm and stabbed forward with the other. What looked like the killing strike missed as Hathaway curled from the steel. James doubled his attack while the other man was off balance. They both careened off a partition wall. The room shook and dust sifted from the unstable ceiling. A balance shifted. Hathaway grew more desperate with a wide attack, but James remained deadly calm. He sidestepped and wrapped up the mercenary's arm with his own. Swift and brutal, James wrenched to the side and broke Hathaway's elbow backward. The mercenary's face tightened, but he didn't make a sound. James buried his knife in the man's ribs and pushed harder and harder until Hathaway hissed a curse with a strained breath.

James stepped back, letting Hathaway's body fall away from him. Life drained from the broken mercenary. James stared at him with grim finality. He leaned down, wiped the blood from his knife on the man's sleeve, then walked away from him.

She hurried to James. He sheathed his knife and wrapped her in his arms. They held each other. He was real and whole and alive. But the tension hadn't been completely drained from him. He looked to the office. "The hacker?"

They went there together. The man had propped himself against a wall and looked on with fear as they entered. She immediately went to the computer terminal as James crouched down over the hacker.

She opened the server windows and scanned over the pieces of her site. For the first time since the hack, she logged in using her encryption and looked over the data. He hadn't gotten through. The identities and financial information of the women from the forum were safe. She erased everything from his server, then did a deep search for any other fragments of her work. She located some in hidden files and deleted them. Nothing remained.

James turned to her. "Secure?"

"He didn't get anything." She yanked the cables from the servers and dragged them away from the wall. The hard drives would need to be completely destroyed.

James balled a fist into the hacker's shirt. "The man you hired to protect you is dead. The man you hired to kill her is dead."

The hacker whimpered as James pulled him to his feet. The man stumbled along with James out of the office. April followed with the servers. James dragged the hacker next to the inert body of Hathaway and let him fall to the ground there.

He took one of the servers from April as they left the store. The silent alley was pierced with searchlights and the flashing red and blue of police cars. She couldn't see them but knew they enclosed the area. "How the fuck are we going to explain this?"

James put his earbud in calmly. "We're not going to explain anything." He tipped his head toward the opening of the alley and put his free arm around her waist. She leaned into him, and he supported himself on her. He spoke into his mic, "Affirmative. Evac is desirable."

They walked to the end of the alley. Police cars were parked at angles a block and a half away in both directions. There was no way out. Her body had just started to come down from the rush of terror. She tried to convince it to gear up again for another fight.

An authoritative voice commanded through a loudspeaker in the distance, "Drop what you're holding, put your hands on your head and get to your knees."

April looked to James. He winked and smiled with a secret. "We're not going to drive out of here," she said. The street was blocked and the alley crammed with wrecked cars.

"No, luv, we're not." She couldn't read the cryptic glint in his eye.

The police tried again. "You're surrounded. Drop what you're holding, put your hands…" The directive was drowned out by a deep thumping that quaked the air. A black mass blotted the dim stars in the sky. Swirling wind spun dust and debris up from the alley and street and desert. A black helicopter descended from the night and hovered at the top of the hill opposite the alley.

James urged April forward. "Dust off."

"What?" Her feet wouldn't move.

"That's our ride." He indicated their path up the hill and secured the other server in his grip. "Quick, before the coppers see too much."

She decided that an unmarked helicopter waiting for them wasn't any more unreal than everything else that had happened in the past few days. Side by side with James, she hurried across the street, carrying a server. He had the other one and led the way up the hill. The motor thundered, and the blowing dust chafed her skin. Her legs burned after all the stress and strain of the night, but her muscles held out long enough to get her to the peak.

James tossed his server into the helicopter then jumped into the large side door. He grabbed her server and helped her in. As soon as they were inside, it started to lift. James hurried her to a side chair in the bay and strapped her in before doing the same for himself.

Police searchlights chased them but couldn't catch up. The helicopter turned and ascended. The landscape spun below her and grew smaller. April lost her sense of equilibrium. The craft nosed down and sped beyond the lights of civilization and toward an endless black landscape.

James shouted next to her, "We rendezvous with more friendlies at Edwards."

She had a vague idea that the Air Force base was in Southern California. "Who cleans up?" Her voice strained. All her energy flagged.

"We'll point the FBI at the hacker. He'll go down." He placed his hand on her thigh. "And we were never here."

"Invisible." The mission was over. It had meant everything. It had driven her and James together. Had motivated her to stand and battle. She'd found new life where it had been hidden. But now?

James brought his mouth to her ear. "You'll never be invisible to me."

The knots across her body loosened. She wasn't judged. She was free to chase after and hold the life she wanted. Her hand found his. They'd survived. She turned and kissed him, tasting blood and his sweat and his commitment.

EPILOGUE

APRIL HELPED PUSH the tables together in the middle of Hayley and Art's restaurant. After hours, and *Da/Sí* was reserved for exclusive diners. The door was locked and the lights low, darkening the lustrous wood décor. James swiveled another table into place on the other end of the row, creating enough space for everyone.

Raker brought two chairs to the long table, followed by his wife, Liv, an African-American woman, who curtsied polite thanks to him. He tipped an invisible hat and pulled out her chair.

Art also collected chairs, aided by other members of Automatik April hadn't gotten to know as well. But tonight was a good venue to talk to Ben Jackson and Mary Kuri, who spent most of the time so far sassing each other. Ben's former SEAL teammate Harper was in the mix, too, not letting a slight limp keep him from giving Ben hell about moving to San Francisco with Mary. The woman was reserved, but not cold, and April saw her affection for Ben.

Hayley stepped out of the kitchen in her chef's coat and asked, "Drinks?"

Art tapped James on the shoulder. "Beer and wine." The two of them moved to the back of the restaurant, disappearing with Hayley into the kitchen.

Raker and Liv sat next to each other and talked

close. The others all knew each other well. April felt
adrift and considered taking out her phone to feel busy.

But Ben came over to her with a genial smile. "If I'd
known you were relocating to San Diego with Sant, I
could've set you up with my old apartment."

Mary stood at his shoulder, shaking her head slowly.
"No one wants to pull your old mirrors off the ceiling."

April shrugged. "Maybe we would've left them up."

This garnered a genuine smile from Mary. Ben nodded approval. "I knew you were good people."

"Drinks," James announced with his return. He and
Art carried bottles of wine and ice-filled buckets of
beer. The people collected around them as they went
down on the table.

Raker opened a bottle of white wine and poured a
glass for Liv. He waved the bottle at April. She took
an empty glass from the table, and he filled it. While
April was at her shoulder, Liv spoke in a low tone, "I
know we're not here for shop talk, but I wanted you to
know that the FBI warrants on Tomas Miller's computers were fruitful. They're piling identity theft and
cyber fraud charges on him."

It had taken a week after Quartz Hill for her to learn
the hacker's name. That time had been a whirlwind of
travel and debriefings with Automatik. James hadn't
left her side the whole time. But Liv hadn't been in on
any of those meetings. "I didn't know you were…"

Liv smiled. "I'm still active duty in the army."

Raker tapped his temple. "Intelligence."

"Ah." April puzzled pieces together. Automatik
worked with the military for certain resources. That
was how they'd been able to get a helicopter from Edwards Air Force Base so quickly. Liv must be another

one of the ties. "Thanks for the update." She clinked Liv's glass.

The woman toasted her back, "Here's hoping he rots." They both drank. "I know his handwriting will never be the same."

April shook less when she thought about that night. James had talked to her about his experiences in combat, and that helped to normalize things. Establishing a new house in a new city with him had softened some of the memories as well. Her website was back up, the community there thriving and she was growing in new light as well. And she'd entered into a new community of close-knit friends and partners. Soldiers who trusted each other with their lives and shared the ethic of Automatik.

James came over to her with a beer in his hand. He put his arm around her waist. Their bodies locked together. Her house in El Paso was in escrow, and she didn't trust the deal would go through completely until all the signatures were in place. Their new home wasn't completely furnished after two months. But the disarray didn't grind her nerves the way it used to. She learned to ride the waves of life, sometimes steering, sometimes letting the currents take her.

"What're we toasting?" James asked.

Liv held up her glass. "April's flashlight."

"I'll drink to that." James clinked glasses with April, Liv and Raker.

The rest of the group collected around them, Ben inquiring, "What's the toast?"

James's gaze enveloped April in admiration. "To the newest Automatik operator."

A flush crept across April's chest. They all tapped

glasses and drank. She was in the network now, part of the cyber security team. James leaned down and kissed her temple. The heat rose higher on her face. He tapped her glass with his bottle. "To my cheeky bird."

"Food," Hayley announced from the back. Art moved to her and helped carry trays with bowls of salads and steaming pastas. Plates were passed, and everyone piled on the delicious-smelling dinner.

April sat next to James and took in the group. Some quiet and observing, others lively. She belonged at the table with them. The group thrived on challenges. They overcame. So did she. She leaned her shoulder into James. He brushed his knuckles on her thigh. Her blush deepened to a warm glow. The next second, and the one after that, were unknown. But that didn't chase her into the darkness. She couldn't wait to find out.

* * * * *

AUTHOR'S NOTE

THE WEBSITE FOUNDAFTER.COM is fictitious; however, if you visit it, I've listed links to other real websites that support widows and families of service people. Neither I nor my publisher have direct associations with these sites, and the list does not represent an endorsement or advertisement.

ABOUT THE AUTHOR

NICO ROSSO DISCOVERED the romance genre through his wife, romance author Zoe Archer (aka Eva Leigh). He's published a wide range of romance stories, including some with demon rock stars, a sci-fi space opera, steampunk Westerns and now romantic suspense with the series Black Ops: Automatik. When he isn't at his desk, he can be found in the workshop, building furniture and completing other projects for his new home with Zoe in central California. Check out his website at nicorosso.com, and find him on Twitter at Twitter.com/nico_rosso and Facebook at Facebook. com/nicorossoauthor.